ROBERT
PORTER

TEACHER, SON, FRIEND

THE GIRL AND THE 7 DEADLY SINS

A.J. RIVERS

The Girl and the 7 Deadly Sins
Copyright © 2022 by A.J. Rivers

PROLOGUE

Years ago…

S HE KNEW HE WAS THERE.
It was obvious by the way she moved. The tiny twitches of her head and the wiggle of her fingers beside her thigh.

She was trying not to show it. She kept her chin held high and her shoulders square to make herself look confident, like a throwback to some self-defense lecture or class from years past. Some twisted mirror of her own voice droned through her mind, offering the same old fairly useless wisdom: be vigilant and aware, always be on alert, but never look afraid.

Looking afraid created vulnerability. That was the message. She had to remain steady and move straight ahead without looking around. She never glanced over her shoulder, even when she heard the sounds of the footsteps behind her. Even if he got close enough for her to sense his breath changing the air. Even if he whispered her name just to see if she would bristle. If she kept her eyes ahead and didn't react to anything, she would be protected.

Never show hesitation. Never show distraction. Never show worry. Never show fear.

That fed the danger. It was like offering herself up to it.

She knew he was there. But she wasn't going to react. There was a level of control there. She was holding everything in and refusing to pick up her pace or say anything.

He didn't know if she really believed that old seminar and its lessons that told her to look big and imposing. Like they were teaching her to ward off a bear. Or unmoved and aloof as if playing hard to get.

She did believe in control. He knew that. She wanted to maintain it, over herself and over him. She didn't know exactly what he was after, but refusing to react to his presence meant she could skim off some of the effect. If he craved her fear, he wasn't going to get it. If he craved her panic, she wasn't going to offer it. If he craved a chase, it wasn't going to happen.

It was arrogance.

It was manipulation.

It was *her*.

None of it mattered to him. This wasn't a game. He wasn't hunting her or trying to instill terror he could use like a drug to build himself up. He didn't need any of that. It wasn't why he was there.

What he wanted wasn't actually about her. Not really. But it wasn't ever truly, was it?

That was what the experts always said, those big names with alphabet soup scattered after them and fancy titles to introduce themselves with. They held their heads and tilted their glasses in a way that said they smelled of ink and old paper, of dust and disinfectant—not of the real world. They believed they were shaping the future by grabbing up handfuls of the past and throwing it on their stones.

It was easier that way. Everything was already there for them. All the answers laid out in advance for them to fill in the blanks. They just had to take what had become soft and hazy and give it new shape. The hard corners and stiff planes of reality had become bendable after no longer existing in enough living minds. Then they claimed that new shape was the one reality had always held and there weren't enough voices left to combat it.

They would say it wasn't about her. They'd pretend to see his mind like a series of circuits and lights, to be able to watch the pattern of them flickering and glowing. They knew his thoughts; they could comfortably and neatly arrange them into compartments. Like little waiting room doors, behind which were all the same thoughts, thought by different people, all meaning the same thing even if they said they didn't. Behind those doors were the most dangerous thoughts. The ones that were tucked away without question, where they could hide away in secrecy.

When the experts said it wasn't about her, they would almost be right. But not in the way they wanted to believe they were. Because it was about her. It was her face every time he closed his eyes. It was her face he looked for when he disappeared in the crowds so she didn't even notice he was there. It was her patterns he learned and her schedule he kept. It was her he had followed many times before, gradually getting closer as he tested just how much space he could close between them before she noticed the shift in her surroundings and sensed he was there.

But he hadn't *chosen* her. He hadn't selected her from all the faces he saw on a regular basis or out of convenience. He could easily fall into those same footprints and no one would know, but that wasn't why. He knew her name, her voice, the smell of her favorite mints on her breath, and the cold feeling of her hands. He hadn't chosen this for her. She had.

He didn't know if she'd noticed his message.

The spiral. He'd meticulously painted it the night before, making sure it had exactly nine rotations. All according to his plan.

It wasn't a warning, though it would probably be called that. A warning meant something could be changed before the fateful moment. This was a decision.

She knew he was there.

She was becoming more aware as she moved away from the open space and past the empty attendant booth. As she stepped off the sidewalk into the parking garage, she glanced in either direction. Maybe trying to decide if she was going to follow the same way she always did. Maybe hoping someone else was there.

The elevator was only a few yards away. She never used it. She parked in the exact same spot every day. Second floor. Fourth row. Eighth spot. She always walked. Never the elevator. Never the stairs encased in the dark concrete tubes in the corners of the deck.

She always walked around the edge, following the narrow sidewalk that passed in front of the parked cars and kept her away from the ones spiraling through, looking for a spot to park or leaving at the end of the day.

Today was different. Her steps didn't falter as she moved into the direct center of the driveway, so precise that the toe of her boot covered the very tip of the directional arrow painted on the black surface. She didn't turn back, but she didn't move away from the center, away from the cars and the sidewalks and the doors to the dark stairwells. She stayed out in the open.

He kept watching her as she made her way toward the first curve that would lead her from the main access point to the next level. She didn't notice when he sank back and moved into the shadow of the cars. She was too firm in her awareness, in her vigilance, to know when what she was aware of changed.

She thought he was right behind her. She'd primed herself for it. She'd latched onto the feeling of him following her and was doing what she thought she needed to do to handle it. She thought she was focused, but she'd lost track. She was distracted by her own concentration and didn't realize he hadn't fallen into step behind her.

He didn't know whether she'd heard the door. He couldn't see her once he was past it. But the thick walls kept his footsteps muffled. She wouldn't know he was taking the more direct route to the second floor.

He got there before she did. Long legs made it easy to cover several steps at once, so he was able to slip out of the door before she came around the corner. The parking deck was curved tightly in on itself to fit more floors in the tall building without needing as much space. Cars wound around the open core to get to the next floor, then went down a ramp from the top floor that came all the way down to the road.

The first time he'd seen this ramp he was small enough for it to look like a mountain. He'd seen a thousand near-identical parking garages over the years, of course, but this one stood brightly out in his memory. 14th and Barton. All that had come to mind as a child was teetering up at the top with his sled and how it would feel to let it tip and the rush of flying down the snow. He hadn't thought about the stone retaining wall at the bottom or the street it fed into. There hadn't been room in his brain for those kinds of thoughts then.

Now there wasn't room for anything but her.

He saw her shadow before her feet.

She knew he was there.

But she thought he was behind her. She wasn't ready for him to jump out of the shadows and bury his knee in the middle of her back. It dropped her to the concrete and scattered the items in her bag. Makeup, coins, a wallet, lip balm. A canister of pepper spray that should have been in her hand. The bag landed heavily, so he knew she hadn't left her gun behind. She just hadn't reached for it fast enough.

He'd seen her with it a couple of times in his observations. He'd started noticing it years before. There was a certain popularity around guns now. It was like everyone had decided they needed one. Some because they were afraid. Some because others were. Some because they just wanted to feel the weight of the weapon tugging on their belt or their bag. It comforted them, even if they never actually intended on using it.

She was different. She had one for a purpose.

He needed to wrest that purpose from her.

Her face hit the ground roughly and seemed to shock her into action. Everything she constructed around herself as she walked away from him dissolved and she went into action. Her body bucked up, forcing him up and away from her enough so she rolled over onto her back. Rather than leaving herself vulnerable, she bent her knee to keep space between them and used the other leg to kick him in the side of the head.

He tumbled to the side, dazed by the impact, but he recovered before she could scramble to her bag. He grabbed her by the back of her shirt, stopping her momentum and sending her back to the ground. This time, he held her in place as he reached into his pocket for the knife.

Somewhere above them, he heard voices. Someone must have gone into the elevator and ridden up to a higher floor.

She knew they were there.

He reached for her mouth to cover it, but the scream had already gotten out. Maybe less of a fearful scream than a roar of rage. But that was what made her unique.

He shifted his weight to look behind him at the entrance to the stairs, and in that second, he lost control. One hand grabbed the side of his face and forced it hard so his head turned until it felt like it couldn't turn further. The rest of his body went with it; she pressed up and to the side to toss him to the ground. As she tried to get to her feet, he managed to swing the knife and slice across the back of her leg.

It dropped her and another scream bounced from the walls. The others must have heard it. His time was counted down by the footsteps pounding on the cement toward them. He launched forward and tackled her backward to pin her down, his leg pressing her wounded calf into the cement and stopping her from moving.

"Hey!" someone shouted.

He didn't look up to see if they were close enough to realize what was happening. He lifted his knife and she swiped at him, her fingernails cutting into the skin at the side of his neck. Her other hand grasped at his shirt and he knew rather than trying to get away, this time she was trying to hold him in place. The others would be coming soon and she wanted to keep him there so they could call the police.

He got to his feet and she sat up, grabbing at him harder so her fingers ripped away the pocket on the front of his shirt. There was no missing the other people now. They'd run down from the upper floor and were coming toward them. He couldn't stop to get the shredded pocket or the small paper tag that had fallen out of it. All he could do was run.

The two women who came down did exactly what he would expect them to do. They stopped. As soon as they saw the blood spreading across the pavement, they didn't think about chasing him anymore.

She tried to tell them to go after him. She told them to call the police, to chase him, but they wanted to stop her bleeding and stay by her side. By the time one of them thought enough to follow after him, he was up the dark stairs. He heard the door slam beneath him but didn't stop.

He paused only for a second at the top of the ramp. He could almost see the snow.

His feet nearly went out from under him as he approached the bottom, but he bounced himself from the retaining wall, redirected his momentum, and continued on. When he finally stopped, he touched his hand to his chest and felt where the pocket had been. They'd find it.

He'd have to take some time before he tried again.

CHAPTER ONE

Now

"WHAT DID HE DO TO HER? WHAT DID THAT PSYCHO DO TO MARIE?"

I reach up both hands to try to calm Sam. It's a useless gesture, but it's one of those many compulsory human gestures that come to mind in situations like this. My husband is pacing back and forth across the living room like an angry bear, filling up the space with his rabid energy. I can see the fury in his eyes and feel it radiating off him.

"Sam, take a breath," I warn him.

"A breath? You're seriously telling me to take a breath?"

"You're getting really worked up. I just want you to calm down," I say.

"Of course, I'm getting worked up," he counters. "Did you see this?"

He shoves the picture toward me and I look at it for the thousandth time. I don't know what I'd been expecting inside the ornament Jonah had left for me on Christmas, but it hadn't been the picture of his cousin.

"I did," I say. "I saw it. And I read the note. I know this looks really bad."

"It looks really bad?" Sam sputters incredulously. "My cousin went missing and we found her decomposed corpse in a drug warehouse and haven't been able to figure out anything that happened to her because none of it makes any sense. The drug dealer who she was supposedly getting her stash from or selling for got murdered in prison, her apartment got broken into, but none of that seems to have had anything to do with it.

"The police aren't doing anything about it because they say she was nothing but a druggie who overdosed, even though both of us know for damn sure that isn't what actually happened. Then lo and behold, your psychopath cult leader of an uncle who is known to have murdered countless people hides a picture of her in an ornament along with a note telling us to find the truth, and all you can say is it looks really bad?"

"Why are you treating me like this is my fault? Like I'm the enemy here? I didn't do anything wrong, Sam," I protest.

"I just don't understand why you are protecting him."

"I'm not protecting him. I'm trying to think through this logically. And the reality is, neither one of us know why that picture is in the ornament or what he means by it."

"It's in there because he's playing another one of his sick games," Sam mutters. "He did something to Marie, and now he wants to act like a puppet master, dancing around watching you try to figure it out. This is all fun for him. Like it's been ever since you realized he existed."

"Sam, listen to me. It doesn't make any sense for Jonah to have done something to Marie."

"And it made total sense for him to kill all those other people?" he asks.

I shrug slightly. "In his way, yes."

Sam scoffs, starting to pace in the other direction again. "I'm so glad you've started seeing things his way. I'm sure he'll be so proud."

I bristle, my spine tightening and my jaw hardening. I fight to keep the anger down, reminding myself he is going through a difficult time. Seeing that picture of his cousin was a major shock for him. It's been sitting in our house for weeks now. My uncle left it in the front yard among our Christmas decorations, but we didn't find it until early February when we finally got around to breaking down the display.

When I first found the oversized ornament, I thought it was nothing more than a strange bauble, something he wanted me to look at and think of him. He may have come to terms with the fact that he isn't my father, or at least is willing to say that, but that doesn't mean he's rid himself of the delusion that we are a happy family. He dreams of one day playing an important role in my life, of celebrating holidays together, of reuniting with his son: my cousin Dean.

It will never happen. There's a reason I blocked out his very existence when I was a little girl and didn't even remember he existed or that my father had a twin brother until I was a full-grown adult.

When I realized the ornament actually opened, I discovered an assortment of pictures of Salvador Marini, a man whose death I've been investigating—an investigation that is unfortunately inextricable from Jonah. Marini was responsible for the death of someone Jonah cared about, a murder Jonah himself was blamed for. It was up to me to clear his name and make sure the right person was brought to justice.

Only that justice ended up coming in the form of a heart attack the morning he was scheduled to turn himself over to the authorities for Serena's murder. There are strong indications it wasn't a natural death, and Jonah has been just as forceful in getting me to solve this crime as he was in Serena's death.

But it's the pictures of Sam's cousin that have thrown both of us off. Neither of us expected to find the secondary compartment within the ornament that contained the picture of her and the cryptic note we still can't figure out.

Find the Cleaners, find the truth.

Sam is convinced it means this is another one of Jonah's games. He believes Jonah murdered Marie and is trailing me along. I can't make myself believe the same thing.

"I'm going to give you a pass on that because I know you're worked up right now," I say.

"You don't need to," Sam says.

I stand up and step closer to my husband. My eyes meet his now, no longer with the tender compassion I was trying to show him when he first got upset. He needs to get his head on straight. I'm dealing with enough right now. I'm not going to add his bullshit to it.

"There would be no point in Jonah doing anything to Marie. None. She was a non-entity to him. She was barely a part of my life, Sam. Just because she was the cousin of my husband doesn't mean she was consequential enough to me for him to concoct some elaborate scheme. Frankly, there are dozens of people right here in Sherwood that would have been better candidates. There would be no purpose. Every one of his murders had some meaning. There was a point.

"He asked about Marie and expressed his condolences as soon as he heard she was missing. Then he went completely silent about it. Didn't ask me about it again. Didn't send any clues or try to get me to figure anything out. Not until now. Why the hell would he do that if he was trying to play with me? The fun of that for him is watching the puzzle."

"You went to Michigan with me to figure it out," Sam points out.

"And he said nothing. He didn't send any notes. He didn't give any clues or hints. He did nothing that would suggest he was getting any-thing out of me being a part of it. And what do you think he did? Get in touch with the police and get them to drag their feet, then pick a drug dealer he has no reason to know anything about, make it seem like he had something to do with it, infiltrate a jail unnoticed to have him murdered, and then still not say anything? That's absurd. Jonah would get nothing out of her disappearance or her death. He obviously knows something or he wouldn't have included her in here. He must have picked up something along the way, but he didn't hurt her."

Sam shakes his head at me, his eyes dark and his arms crossed over his chest. "You've gotten soft toward him."

That's all I can take of this. I take a step back and look at him for a second, just to make sure I'm actually looking at the man I think I am. It's my turn to shake my head.

"I can't be near you right now."

I walk around him toward the door, snatching up my keys and phone as I go.

"What's that supposed to mean?" he asks.

I let the slamming of the door behind me answer his question.

CHAPTER TWO

HALF AN HOUR LATER I'M SITTING AT MY FAVORITE BOOTH AT Pearl's Diner, bent over my plate as I scroll through emails on my phone, almost waiting for it to ring.

"Biscuits and gravy."

Sam's voice is much calmer now, but I don't bother to look at him until he slides into the bench across the table from me. I finish the bite I just took and set my fork down on the edge of my plate.

"Call me predictable," I mutter.

"Yes," he says with a nod, obviously trying to inject some levity into his voice, but I'm not giving in to it. "If you don't feel like baking cinnamon rolls, biscuits and gravy are your go-to food if you're angry. Or sad. Or happy. Or it's a Tuesday."

"And yet it still took you this long to find me here," I point out. I'm still looking at my phone. I barely want to acknowledge Sam right now, much less stop doing what I was doing just to pay attention to him.

"I knew you were coming here the second you stormed out of the house," he says. "I just figured I would give you a little bit of time to cool off before I came and found you." He pauses for a second, waiting for me to respond. When I don't, he reaches over and rests his hand on the top of my phone. "You want to put that down?"

I sigh and toss my phone to the table beside my plate. Dropping back against the bench, I stare across the table at him. We sit there in stony silence for a few seconds before I throw my hands up.

"Why are you here, Sam? What was the point of you coming to find me? So you can continue to insult me and imply I've somehow tapped into a primal part of my brain that will inevitably align me with Jonah? Because I've heard that performance, and I really don't need a repeat. I left and came here so I could be by myself for a while."

"And that's why I came to find you. You can't just walk away, Emma. You can be mad. You can disagree with me. You can be pissed off and think I'm the biggest jerk on the face of the planet. But you can't walk away. It's not my favorite thing in the world to think about, but let me remind you that you did that once before and it cost us seven years together. You can say whatever it is you want to say to me. We can have it out as much as you want to. But we do it at home, or we go somewhere together. It can't be that easy for you to just walk away from me," he says.

Sam's words hit me hard. Just like he hates to bring it up, I hate to think about the breakup when I was in college that tore us apart. Sam has been my everything since I was a little girl. He was one of the very few things I could count on that was consistent and reliable even when everything else in my life felt like nothing but upheaval.

No matter where I went in the world. No matter how far my parents took me, or how many times I had to bounce around and try to find my grip in a new reality, I knew back in Sherwood, Sam was there. That at some point, we would go back there. We would spend time with my grandparents, and I would get to see him.

I fell in love with him then and I knew he was going to be my future. I believed that with everything, which is exactly why I had to leave him behind when I made the final decision to join the FBI. At that point, I didn't believe there was enough of me to dedicate to both, and if I had to choose, it would be Sam. But I owed it to my mother and my father to give my life to combating crime.

When I walked away from him then, it was with the intention of never seeing him, or Sherwood, again. I wasn't ever going to go back there or try to be a part of that life again. It was too hard. But he found me. He drew me back. It is the best thing that ever happened to me.

"I'm sorry," I say. "You're right. I shouldn't have left like that. But you really did piss me off."

He nods. "I know. I shouldn't have said that."

"I can understand why you did," I admit. "I think if anyone else was looking into this and didn't know everything that has happened with Jonah, they would think the same thing. He shouldn't still exist in my life."

"He makes it impossible for him not to," Sam says.

"It's not impossible," I clarify. "He's going to be gone. I won't live the rest of my life waiting for the next game, figuring out the next crime, trying to decide if there's actually something wrong or if he is just trying to keep me close. It's not something I can do."

"You are the only person in this world who could have survived it for this long," he says. "Anyone else would have given up."

"I can't," I say. "Not until all these loose ends are tied up. He deserves to be back in his cage until the end of the known universe, and one day, one day very soon, I'm going to make sure that happens. But I have to think about the other people who are involved in everything he's done. They deserve to be recognized."

"I know," Sam says.

My breath slides out of my lungs as I lean forward on the edge of the table and poke at my biscuits and gravy with the fork.

"I'm sorry for what I said about Marie. She isn't inconsequential," I say. "That was wrong of me. She's your family. She didn't deserve me talking about her that way."

"Thank you," Sam whispers, and he reaches out a hand. I accept the peace offering and rub over his hand with my thumb. We sit there for a minute in silence, allowing ourselves to get back, the way we always do.

Sam breaks the hold and rubs his chin with his hand as if deep in thought.

"But you were right. She is," he says. "Not to me. And not to you. But to most people, she's just a woman from Michigan. There aren't really any stakes with her disappearance or her death, and that's what is making me so angry. You were right when you said there would be no reason Jonah would want to hurt her. It wouldn't do anything for him."

"There still has to be a reason he sent that picture along with the ones of Marini. That's not accidental. If he wanted both of those things to be separate, he would've made them separate. It's not like efficiency is all that valuable to him. He put both sets of pictures in the same ornament to show that they are connected in some way. But I honestly think he separated them into the two compartments to show that they are separate."

"So, how do you think they're connected?" Sam asks, taking the fork out of my hand and spearing some of my biscuits and gravy off the plate.

"Are you stealing my food?" I sputter.

"We're married. It's mutual food," he winks. "Besides, you always tell me you eat too much when you're upset."

I snatch my fork back. "Get your own fork." I eat a couple of bites while he gestures to the waitress. She smiles as she brings it to him. "I think we can eliminate the idea that Marie was one of Salvador's Emperor victims."

"Why?" Sam asks.

"He killed those women in different states, but the states are all along the Eastern Seaboard. There aren't any far-flung ones as far as we've been able to find, and we've been searching through a never-ending mountain of cold case murders that even vaguely match up with those murders. Marie was too far away. And nothing about her death matches up. None of the other victims had coverups. They all corresponded to something. It would be much too convenient for her to have been killed by the same serial killer I'm already investigating," I explain.

"That's true. I guess I just sometimes wish things could be that convenient."

"I know," I nod. "Me too. But we're going to figure this out. We just have to dismantle it piece by piece."

"What do you think about the Cleaners?" he asks. "Find the Cleaners, find the truth. What does that mean?"

"Jonah loves his riddles. But this time I don't think there's anything mysterious about his meaning. I think he really is saying if we find these Cleaners, we'll find out what happened. Maybe to both Marie and Marini."

"I guess it couldn't be the similarity in their names?" Sam offers.

I give him a withering look but chuckle. "No. I don't think that factors in here."

"So, Cleaners. You don't think he could possibly be talking literally. Cleaners as in housekeepers? Dry cleaners?" he asks. "But you already talked to pretty much all of his staff, right? The ones that would speak to you, anyway?"

"Still working on a few. I'm not so sure it'll be of much use though."

"Cleaners…" he muses. "It wouldn't be that literal, would it?"

"See, I want to laugh, but I have so little else to go on that I really don't have that luxury. If Xavier were here, he'd—well, first he would restart his conversation about how biscuits and gravy are the most problematic of diner foods because of their inability to establish themselves within the constraints of a single meal by merit of their unusual carbohydrate, dairy, meat accent construction, but in being problematic and incongruous are truly the breakfast-brunch-lunch-dinner food of the modern era."

"Yes, he would."

"Yes. But then he would point out the capital 'C.'"

"The capital 'C?'" Sam asks.

"On the note. Cleaners is capitalized. That's intentional. It's an entity. Not a descriptor," I explain. "I don't think he means a housekeeper."

He nods and eats another massive bite of rich, savory ambiguous food. "You're still going to go talk to the housekeeper, though, aren't you?"

I sigh. "You know I am."

CHAPTER THREE

L OUISE DOESN'T LOOK PARTICULARLY THRILLED TO SEE ME WHEN she opens the door the next day. I give a tight wave and show her my phone as if it's going to act as my evidence as I plead my case to her.

"Already spoke with the Stevensons," I tell her.

"I know," she says. "My new employers are very understanding considering I'm apparently in the midst of a suspicious death investigation, but I would still appreciate it if you would speak with me outside of business hours. I have work to do."

"I understand. And I'm sorry for interrupting. That's why I called ahead. I wanted to make sure it was alright for me to come here and speak with you. It'll only be a quick conversation and I wanted to make sure they understood I was the one pushing it, not you," I say.

"I'm capable of communicating that myself," she says. "You didn't need to go over my head. Mr. Marini might have wanted to think of us as his possessions, but we weren't. And I don't belong to the Stevensons, either."

She's obviously on edge, still angry and hurt by everything she went through with Salvador Marini. I don't even know the extent of it. She's one of very few of his former staff who has even been willing to speak to me about him, and she made it clear she didn't want to do it again. She, along with everyone else who worked for him, just wanted to put him as far behind her as she possibly could and not ever think about him again.

I realize my mistake, but I don't think it would do any good to try to talk my way out of it. All I can do is nod.

"Of course," I say. "I'm sorry. You've already been so helpful, and I just have a few more questions. The investigation into his death is extremely complicated. There are details I haven't shared, that I can't share right now, but please know this is about more than just a man dying on his foyer floor."

The details of Marini's serial killing ways haven't been made public yet. It's been a fight to keep them confidential, but I think it's critical for the integrity of the case to not start pouring out the entire sordid tale just yet. There's still so much left to be understood and untangled. The entire truth hasn't been uncovered.

What I know for an absolute fact is that he is responsible for the deaths of dozens of women offered to him by Serena as sex toys and playthings. He would have her pose as a goddess and lure them into his circle. The men weren't much luckier: they would be drugged, tortured, and forced to participate in modern-day gladiator fights to the death in vast underground facilities. Eric's undercover participation in one of the deathmatches helped us find a lead, but I know there's still so much more we don't know.

Marini's death rendered the investigation essentially closed, but I'm not willing to let it go. There might no longer be an Emperor to prosecute, but he had minions. He had slaves who would do as he commanded. I need to find them and know everything they do. I need to know the names of the people he brutalized and be able to give them back to their families. I need to find the dens and arenas he used to torture and kill and make sure they are destroyed. I need to know how he did what he did so that it can't ever happen again.

The further I dig, though, the more aware I am that it's all going to come out sooner or later. In order to get to the truth, I have to tell the truth. But now is not that time.

"Come in," she finally says. "I'm sorry to be so short with you. I know you aren't trying to protect him."

It's the second time in as many days that I've been accused of trying to protect one of the most horrific men I've ever encountered. It makes my teeth grind and the muscles along the sides of my neck tighten painfully. But I have to swallow it down and push it aside. Sometimes it's hard to see what's actually being done. Sometimes I just have to understand that and move forward.

"I'm not," I tell her as firmly as I can without sounding aggressive. "This is not about him. And anything you can tell me, any help you can give me, could make a huge difference in some very important investigations."

Louise nods as she leads me into the kitchen. "Can I make you a cup of tea?" I nod and she fills a kettle to put on the stove. "How else can I help?"

"His dry cleaning," I say.

She gives me a questioning look. "His dry cleaning?"

"Yes. I know this sounds incredibly dumb. It actually sounds even dumber coming out of my mouth than it did in my head. But I need you to trust me and just go with it. Did he have any dry cleaning out at the time he died?"

She's still looking at me like she thinks I might be joking. I can't really blame her. As far as she knows, she doesn't have to work for the devil incarnate anymore because of the blessed combination of a looming prison sentence and a fatal heart attack. None of the few members of his former staff I've spoken to have given any indication they thought anything else about his death. No suspicion. No questions. Just celebration.

And now here I am, stirring things up in the most confounding ways I can.

"Um," she starts, rebounding from the stunned moment of silence. "I can't be completely sure." Something crosses her face as the kettle whistles and she goes back across the kitchen to take it off the heat. "Actually, yes, I can. The day he died, I went back to the house. The police wanted me to do a general walk-through to make sure nothing was out of place. They were taking pictures of the different rooms. I guess to establish what it looked like at the time of death."

I nod. "That's pretty standard. Especially considering the strange circumstances. He was surrendering himself that day, so there would be some initial suspicion of potential suicide. And until next of kin or another beneficiary could be identified, the house would need to be secured and documented for security and transparency purposes."

"I guess that makes sense. When we were going through his bedroom, they had me open the closet and I noticed a new set of dry-cleaning hanging in there. It was still in the bag, but there was no receipt."

"Is that unusual?" I ask.

"For his dry cleaning to be in the closet? Or for there to be no receipt?" Louise asks.

"Any of it."

"Generally, I would take his dry cleaning out of the bag before hanging in the closet after it was delivered, but the items that had just been cleaned were out of season. They were clean so they could be put into storage, so maybe he could've put them in the bag. I suppose since he knew he wasn't going to be wearing them the next year, that could also have contributed to him not really needing to care how they were hung," she explains.

"He had his dry cleaning delivered to the house regularly?" I ask.

"Yes. Same day and time every week. He liked things on his schedule."

She suddenly looks confused.

"What is it?"

"I don't know. Maybe nothing. It's just… I don't understand how the clothes were hanging in the closet. I didn't think about it before, but they would have been delivered after the time that he supposedly died. I know they don't have an exact time of death, but there's a range, and if the dry cleaners delivered at the same time they always did, which they never faltered on, he would have been dead or certainly in the process of dying when they were delivered."

"And chances are he wouldn't have opened the door, accepted his clothes, brought them up to his bedroom, and hung them in the closet," I note.

"I would think that would probably be low on his priority list at that particular moment," Louisa agrees. "It's strange enough that he would do it even if he was in good health. I honestly can't imagine that man ever doing something as independent as carrying clothes upstairs and hanging them in his closet. That's the kind of thing he would only ever have us do. But I guess since he'd fired all of us leading up to his self-surrender, he didn't have anyone to do it for him."

"He must have," I say. "If the timeline is accurate, someone else had to be there. Somebody accepted the delivery from the dry cleaners, and someone brought the clothes upstairs. And took the receipt. But why would they do that?"

"To conceal the time of delivery?" Louise offers. "They always write it as soon as they pull into the driveway, so it's always accurate."

"If whoever was here didn't know Marini had such a firm schedule of delivery, they might not realize people would know what time it came anyway," I point out.

She shrugs and hands me a cup of tea. I hold it between my hands, absorbing the warmth as I try to work these new details through my mind.

Just who are the Cleaners?

CHAPTER FOUR

"I 'VE ALREADY CONFIRMED IT WITH THE DRY CLEANERS," I SAY. "The driver who made the delivery said it was brought to Marini's house at the exact same time it was every week. He apparently hadn't thought about not having his cleaning delivered on the day he was supposed to go to prison."

"Who took it from the driver?" Eric asks. His voice comes to me from my phone where I have it mounted on the dashboard as I drive away from the dry cleaner to head back toward Dean's house. "Do they have someone sign for it when they drop it off?"

"No, unfortunately. And he wasn't able to give a very clear description. Apparently, he knocked on the door expecting Louise or one of the other staff, but someone called through the door to just leave it. He said he tried to convince whomever it was to open the door and take it, but he wouldn't, so he hung the hangers on the door knocker and left."

"But it was definitely a man?" Eric asks.

"The driver said 'he.' So I'm assuming it was either a man or a woman with a really deep voice. It was on the other side of a door, and clearly whoever it was didn't want to be seen, so I wouldn't put it past someone to alter their voice. What really matters is this at least gets us a little bit closer to proving that Salvador Marini was not alone the morning he died. If not proves it outright."

"That's great. And hopefully, pretty soon we'll have some more information about his fitness tracker," Eric adds.

"I wanted to ask you about that. It wasn't found?"

"No. it's still missing. But I'm working on getting us access to the cloud storage of the data. Trackers like that don't just keep the details on the device themselves. They're uploaded to a cloud-based program that allows users to check on their progress, see graphs, set goals for themselves, all sorts of fantastic fitness data porn," he tells me.

"Please don't say that again," I groan.

Eric laughs. "The point is, the tracker could have valuable information on it, just like you thought. But we don't have to have the tracker itself to get it. Hopefully, we'll be able to access his storage and find out everything it has to tell us."

"Like his exact time of death," I say.

Eric makes an acknowledging sound. "As long as he was wearing it that morning, the data would pinpoint the moment when his heart stopped beating."

"Maybe that's why it's missing," I offer. "Someone doesn't want anyone to know when he actually died."

"It's entirely possible," Eric says. "The challenge is figuring out how to access it. It's not as simple as getting to cloud storage off of, say, a computer or a tablet. With those, you can usually just use an email address to get into those accounts from any device."

"I do have a passing familiarity with the concept," I say with just a note of bitterness in my voice. I might not be the most with it when it comes to technology, but I haven't been left completely unplugged.

"Just making sure. Anyway, with the fitness tracker, it's not just in a normal cloud. It's only saved within the app. That program is saved only on his phone, so that's the way it's accessible," Eric explains.

"So, can't you just break the security on his phone and get to the app?" I ask. "I've seen you do some wizardry, including a lot of very creative things with phones. I wouldn't think being able to get into a simple app would pose that much of a challenge to you."

"It is if there's no phone to break into," he says.

"Ah. Well, yes, I can see where that might act as a barrier. Wait. You don't have his phone?" I ask. "Did the police not turn it over to you when the Bureau took over the investigation?"

"His phone was never found," Eric says. "So they didn't have it to transfer custody."

"I thought there was a phone found near his body. They thought he might have been trying to call for emergency medical services," I say.

"There was *a* phone, but it wasn't his. Or at least it wasn't his for long. It couldn't have been a burner because it did have some of his information on it. It's possible it was purchased very soon before his death and just hadn't been fully set up," Eric tells me. "But either way, it had a few shell apps and programs on it, but not everything he would have had."

"Like his fitness tracking program," I say.

"Exactly. Some of his activities suggest that he had several different apps on his phone that weren't found on the one near him. And that phone is nowhere to be found."

"A dummy phone," I say. I let out a breath. "That sounds familiar."

It's far from the first time I've encountered phones being used fraudulently or being replaced by others, but I'm not thinking deep into the past chronicles of my cases. I'm thinking far more recently, to when Sam searched Marie's apartment before we knew she was dead. He found a replacement phone there as well. An old-style flip phone containing the contact information for a drug dealer who swore he had never met Marie, and then was found dead shortly after.

"The question is, why would he bother with a new phone? This man was getting ready to take the long walk through the prison doors never to be seen again. It wasn't like he thought he had a chance of getting out on bail, or that he was going to only serve a short time and wanted to be able to stay in touch with a significant other. Even if that was allowed." I sigh. "Though, according to Xavier, the phone communication opportunities inside his prison are alive and well. Just one of the many delightful shortcomings of the facility I'm becoming aware of only now."

"Emma, you can't have possibly thought the prison was perfect," Eric replies. "That it was going to be an impenetrable steel box where nothing could ever go wrong."

"I can hope," I say. "And I did. I hoped when they finally got Jonah sentenced and put away, it was going to be in a place that could hold him and had guards doing their jobs."

"They are doing their jobs," Eric counters. "But they can't be everywhere all the time. You know that as well as I do. They do what they can to control the men in their custody, but they can't always stop them. Short of leaving them in their cells twenty-four hours a day without any contact with the outside world or even the people and staff in the building with them, it isn't realistic to think they can have total compliance with all of the regulations. You know that."

I do. As much as my drive has been to dedicate my life to fighting against crime, I've also seen the corruption that can exist within the same institutions and the pain it can cause. It's been a struggle; I'll be the first to admit I haven't always been able to see the good in people. Sometimes I have doubts as to whether it even does exist. But I've learned to see beneath the surface. Redemption does exist.

Maybe not for all people. I haven't gotten to the point yet where I can believe that every person on this planet has something good to offer. Maybe I never will. But that doesn't mean I don't believe in rehabilitation. In giving chances when they are possible. In continuing to fight for those who are vulnerable, who have been victimized, or who are facing darkness, even when they are the ones who are behind bars.

"I know," I say. "But it still makes me question why he got a new phone and where the other one went. He wasn't married. Thank the Lord for small favors on that front. He didn't have children. His sister made it clear they weren't close. What was he trying to do?"

"Or what was someone else trying to do?" Eric adds. "The fitness tracker and the phone are missing. You just proved someone else was in the house. I think whoever was there that morning is the one who has those things."

"Alright. I need you to get in touch with the phone company. They have records. Even if we can't get access to the phone itself, they can give us information from it. I need everything you can get about it," I tell him.

Eric laughs. "Have you forgotten I'm the boss around here?"

"Interim," I point out.

"Wouldn't matter even if I wasn't, would it?" he chuckles.

"Probably not."

"Why should it? You've never been great at doing what the boss tells you anyway."

"True. Alright. I just got to Dean's house. I've got to fill him in and see what he thinks," I say.

"Wait, I never got to the whole reason I called you," he says. "You jumped into talking about Salvador Marini."

"Oh. Sorry," I say. "Why did you call?"

"Have you read the article I sent you?"

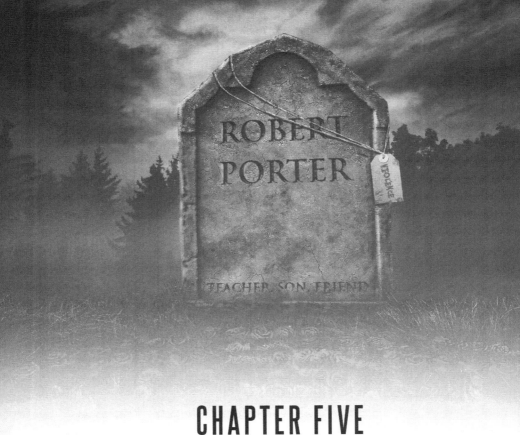

CHAPTER FIVE

'VE READ THROUGH THE ARTICLE THAT WAS IN MY EMAIL FROM Eric at least ten times and I still can't believe what I'm seeing.

"Is this for real?" Dean asks.

"It is," Sam chimes in from the video chat I have pulled up on my phone. I forwarded him the email so he could read it and now have him propped up on the table so he can be a part of the conversation. "I searched around some and found more articles and references to forums."

"What forums?" Dean asks.

"Whatever kind of forums an underground government conspiracy group uses to declare an FBI agent Public Enemy Number One," I mutter.

"Honestly, that doesn't really narrow it down," Dean notes. "There are some whackjobs out there and they all have internet access."

Sam glares at him. "Not helpful."

"Babe, it's fine," I say, somewhere between being aggravated and laughing at the whole situation. This hasn't happened before, so I'm not entirely sure how I'm supposed to feel about it.

"It's not fine," Sam insists. "Didn't you read the article? These people are blaming Emma personally for the things they think are going wrong with the country. They're calling her a murderer and a traitor. It says they believe all the criminals she has brought down and the crimes she's solved haven't actually been real. They've all been a smokescreen to cover up the things she's doing."

"Exactly," I say. "It's completely ridiculous. What, they call themselves the Seers? Like they alone are the ones who know anything? Give me a break."

"No one actually believes this kind of thing," Dean remarks.

"Well," I say. "I don't know if I would go that far. The Bureau has investigated a lot of these kinds of groups. In fact, we're kind of always investigating these kinds of groups. They are all over the place. Fortunately, most of them are fairly small and don't really get a lot of traction. They make a bunch of noise and can get obnoxious and get in the way, but they don't actually cause real trouble."

"Not this one," Sam says. "The Seers? They've become a pretty big deal the last couple of years. And they have caused trouble."

"They aren't on my radar yet. This is the kind of thing I investigate with the Bureau. Serial killers, cults, organized crime. It's what I do. And this group isn't even a blip."

"Maybe they should be," Dean muses.

"What do you mean?" I ask.

He looks far more serious now and I notice he's holding his phone, scrolling through something on the screen.

"I just did a little bit of research and even just a quick search comes up with a lot about these people. They've been around for a while, but really deep underground. Recently they've picked up a lot of speed and a lot more members. They're good at hiding what they are doing and the identities of their members, so that might be why you haven't heard of an investigation," Dean says. "It's not really an organization in the way you'd think of a cult or a crime ring. Anybody who wants to call themselves a Seer can engage in discourse with them."

"What have they done?" I ask.

I'm trying to understand who these people are, and what's coming to mind are the organized crime groups I've waded knee-deep through over the past several years. The Society for the Betterment of the Future. Leviathan. The Order of Prometheus. The Dragon's organization. But this is different. This isn't a cult or an organized crime ring. This is a group of people posturing themselves as an intellectual group, a philosophical meeting of the minds tasked with solving the ills of the nation and protecting its people.

In a way, it sounds noble. But these kinds of intentions rarely actually come with the level of intelligence they want to have or a clear grasp on reality. That's a dangerous combination.

"They don't take credit for anything," Dean tells me. "According to what I can find about them, they claim to only offer information. They say, well, that they're the ones who can see the truth. They share it freely and openly, and what people choose to do with it is up to them."

"I bought the gun, loaded it, taught her how to shoot it, aimed it for her, and told her to squeeze the trigger, but I'm not responsible for the murder, Your Honor," I say sarcastically under my breath.

"Something like that," Dean nods. "I mean, like with any group, there have been individual members that have been linked to some criminal activity, but that's hard to prove when there's not much of a discernable structure and it's all very vague online chatter. There was one break-in that seemed like it had some sort of loose connection to a person the group had been targeting, but what makes them so slippery is they think like a mob but don't move like one."

"If these truth-seers are so deep underground that they aren't even on the Bureau's list, how is it you're finding all this information?" I ask.

"The Bureau looks where it wants to look, when it wants to look there," Dean shrugs. I cock my eyebrow at him. "I have my ways."

I don't like to pry when he says things like that. It would be like asking a magician to show me how he cuts the girl in half, or peeking behind the curtain and seeing the strange little man on the stool with the fog machine. That and if I knew about some of his techniques, I would probably feel the moral and professional obligation to report him, and I really don't want to do that. He's family.

"Let me use your phone," I say, reaching for it.

Dean hands it to me and I call Eric. I don't want to end my video call with Sam before he can get some reassurance I'm going to be alright. He's back in Sherwood fulfilling his duties as sheriff, but the sprawling nature of the cases I've been working means I've been bouncing around a lot lately.

It's wearing on us, but I do everything I can to keep him up to date on what's going on and make him feel secure that I'm going to be alright. I do my best not to always leave him scared. It's not something I can promise, and he would never ask me to because he knows it's not something I always have control over, but I try. I'm more than aware that marriage to me should have come with some sort of parental advisory, but at least I can soften it by keeping him informed.

"Hey there, Most Wanted," Eric answers when he picks up. How he figured out it was me calling from Dean's phone, I have no idea.

"You're on speakerphone," I say.

"Not helpful, Eric," Sam grumbles.

Apparently, no one is helping today.

"Oh, hi," Eric says.

"Dean's here, too," I inform him.

"Hey, Eric."

"Hey, Dean." There's an awkward pause. "I don't know where to go from here."

"Sam is worried," I explain. "He thinks this conspiracy thing is dangerous for me."

"It is," he replies without hesitation.

"Wow. You really aren't helpful."

"I mean, it's not imminent. They haven't put out threats against you or a hit on you or anything," Eric says.

"How comforting."

"Are those options?" Sam asks. "Is that something these people do?"

"They make suggestions," Eric says. "It's not like the kinds of hits we've all seen. They don't hand their members pictures of their targets and say, 'go get 'em.'"

"No, they just post pictures of them all over the internet and brand them the root cause of the downfall of decent society and all humanity as we know it," Sam mutters.

"Something like that," Eric acknowledges.

"It seems like you know a lot about these Seers," I say. "I didn't think the Bureau was even considering them."

"There are investigations you don't know about, Emma," he says. "Granted, not many, but there are. This one isn't so much an investigation as it is a bit of supervision. Just watching. Seeing what they are up to."

"What they are up to is threatening my wife," Sam presses. "You can't do anything about that?"

"You know that free country Emma is supposedly threatening the future existence of with all her murder and illicit sex?" Eric asks. "That country says we can't arrest someone just for putting a person's picture up."

"The things they're saying about her are libel," Dean points out. "They could compromise her reputation, and being so public could damage her integrity as an agent."

"Those pictures are far from what put Emma in the public eye," Eric points out. "She's already plenty well known. As for her integrity and her safety, we're working on finding out who originated this and resolving it. For right now, I don't think there's any reason to panic. These people find mundane things to be angry about all the time. It eventually dies down. And if it doesn't, we handle it."

"And think of it this way," I add. "I've never been branded a super villain before."

"That's right," Eric says. "I think your Bingo board is officially full."

"I'm glad this whole thing is so amusing to all of you," Sam grumbles.

"Sam, I promise we're keeping an eye on it," Eric assures him.

"I hope so," Sam says. "I've got to go. I have a call."

"I love you," I say. "I'll call you when I'm on my way home."

"I love you."

He hangs up.

"Should I be taking this more seriously?" I ask Eric. "Right now it feels more annoying than it does frightening."

"Keep it that way," he tells me. "If there's a threat, we'll figure it out. For right this second, you're just the crazies' deluded shiny thing of the day."

"Okay. Thank you, Eric."

"I'll get right on those phone records."

I laugh. "Goodbye, Eric. Tell Bellamy I love her and kiss Bebe for me."

Almost as soon as I hang up, my phone rings again. I don't recognize the number, but I pick it up. I already know who it is.

"Hello, Emma."

Pulling up a notepad on my computer, I type to Dean.

Jonah.

CHAPTER SIX

DEAN'S EYES NARROW WHEN HE SEES THE NAME TYPED ON MY computer screen.

"Did you reach out to him?" he whispers.

I shake my head. It's always disruptive to hear from Jonah this way. It means something is wrong.

For the last year since he escaped from prison, we've had a method for keeping in touch. That's not something I ever would have thought I would have, or would even contemplate, but these aren't normal circumstances. I'm not trying to guard him or keep him from being captured. Quite the contrary—I am always trying to figure out where he is so I can end his farewell tour.

Communicating with my uncle has been about keeping him on a hook so he doesn't completely disappear into the ether as he has been known to do before. But he also provides insight and details into cases I'm investigating so I can navigate my way through them. I shudder at even the thought that he's helping me, but that is the reality. It is also the reality that the cases he's been contributing to are ones he has dropped at my feet.

I've made it clear to him that I don't want to pretend we're close or that these phone calls are about catching up and maintaining our relationship. If we're talking, I want it to be because something important is happening. He has been far better at respecting that than I would have thought. Of course, that means rather than just calling at Christmas, he crept up on my porch and left me a card, then hid a giant lawn decoration right outside my living room window.

He can simply call when he needs to tell me something or wants to ask a question about an investigation, but I can't do the same in return. For obvious reasons, I don't have his direct contact information. If I call the number he used to call me, it always comes back as disconnected or nonexistent, even just seconds after we've hung up. I don't know how he does it.

If I ever want to contact him, I have to send him a message through blog post comments and wait for him to call. That didn't happen this time. It's an unprovoked call, which gives me a knot in the pit of my stomach.

"What do you know about Marie?" I ask.

"Right off the bat, Emma? You're just going to start hurling questions at me?" he starts.

"I have absolutely no other reason to speak with you, Jonah. I want to know what kind of disturbed game you're playing with those pictures, and what you know about Marie," I fire back.

"The note was clear enough," Jonah says.

"The Cleaners?" I ask. "You think that was clear enough?"

"It's all I can tell you. You know that."

This is one of the many reasons my blood pressure rises so much the second I hear his voice or even think about talking to him. He's disgustingly calm and slippery, and there's always a vagueness to what he's saying that can make it hard to slosh through and find the actual meaning.

This time, though, I do know what he's getting at. It's the same thing he told me when he got in touch with me months after his escape from prison. He was being accused of the murder of a young woman found frozen to the ground in a field the year before. She had no identity for nearly a year after she was killed, and when the police started piecing it together, they realized she had connections to Jonah.

He called me to ask for my help clearing his name. He wanted it proven he didn't kill Serena and to find out who did. He had his suspicions, but he wouldn't tell me. He would guide me along and give me nudges, but the final digging and solving had to be on me. If I relied too much on what he was telling me, or he just laid it all out for me and I told the police, there would be no actual case. I needed to figure it out for myself so there was enough real, concrete evidence that could be used for an arrest or brought to trial.

I thought Serena's death was all he'd saddle me with. I was willing to do it not because I wanted him to look better or to salvage his reputation. I did it because she deserved to have her story told. But it wasn't over when I thought it was. It never seems to end.

"Did you do something to her?" I ask.

"Now, Emma, you should know better than that," he counters.

"Stop it," I say sharply. "Stop talking to me like I'm a little girl who's telling you I'm afraid of the dark. I want to know why you put her picture in that ornament and what you know about her disappearance."

There's a pause as he takes a breath.

"You already know more than you realize, Emma. Marie was a good girl. I remember Sam's father talking about her when we were all younger," he says.

It's surreal hearing him talk that way. Though I know in the logical part of my brain he did once have a place in the family, including being raised by my beloved grandparents and spending time with my father and mother, I have no memories of him other than the night my father thought he was killed. I was very young the night a horrific car crash should have taken his life but didn't.

Everyone thought he was dead, and so they immediately started crafting a reality for me that he had never existed. That my father was an only child. That I had no uncle. Everything about his life was hidden in the attic, sealed in a secret room. It must have broken their hearts not only to lose a son but to have to bury his whole existence away.

I know that he was once part of my life, but it's surreal to think about. It's strange to think about him being visible enough to have spoken to Sam's father about their extended family. None of them ever mentioned an uncle to me. It could have been that my grandmother went around to friends and asked them to respect what they were going to do, which was to never mention him again. To keep up the charade that Jonah had never been.

"But I'm not calling to talk about Marie."

"I want to talk about Marie. We found her, you know. We found her body," I say.

"I know," Jonah acknowledges. "I know you did. And my deepest sympathies for that. But I'm calling about the conspiracy involving you."

I should have known he would have heard about it, but I wasn't expecting him to make a special call about it.

"Yes," I say. "There's a group who has decided I'm dangerous. The Seekers or whatever."

I try to sound dismissive about it. Like it doesn't really matter. I don't want to hear his opinion. I don't want him to feel like I'm trying to confide in him or that I'm looking for him to make me feel better. He's taken enough liberties. I'm not going to offer anything up to him.

"The Seers," he corrects me. "I know."

There's a hardness in his voice, something that says he's taking this very seriously. Or that he doesn't like me questioning what he knows. Possibly both. That's one of the strange dichotomies that embodies Jonah. On one hand, he wants so much for me to not think of him negatively. He doesn't want me to focus on the evil he's capable of. He doesn't want to remind me of the pain and horror he has committed. He doesn't want me to blame him for the deaths and destruction in an accusatory or judgmental way. He wants to be seen as good and beneficial, capable of improving my life, and deserving of a place in it.

On the other hand, his feathers get ruffled if there's even the slightest hint he doesn't know about all the inner workings of the criminal world. He wants to bear witness to every cog, every gear, every operational decision. There are other groups. There are other organized crime syndicates. There are gangs and cartels and cults. Jonah acknowledges them. He's even worked with them. But the thought that any could be in operation and thriving without his input or intimate knowledge is something he won't accept.

To him, he is at the top of the hierarchy. He wants to know about everything and perhaps feel like he has contributed in some way. Me telling him about the organization means I don't believe he knows everything. It cuts down what he thinks of himself: a towering, almost omnipotent being that can control anything and everything he wants. He can't fathom a reality where someone is capable of orchestrating terror and controlling minds without him not only knowing about it but having some hand in making it happen.

"It doesn't matter," I say. "The group barely registers as existing."

"You don't know that," he says.

"And you do?" I ask.

The suspicion is instinctual for me. I've learned not to take anything I hear at face value, especially from my uncle. The man is an expert at hiding his true motives.

"I know enough."

"What the hell does that mean?"

"It means if they are putting you up as one of their targets, they're something we should be paying attention to," he says.

"There is no 'we,' Jonah," I say. "If I need to pay attention to something, I will. But I don't need you telling me. This isn't the first time I've been named a target by an unhinged mob. You of all people should know that."

"These aren't just random crazy people," he insists. "They have an agenda. And a message. And that makes them even crazier."

I can't help but let out an incredulous scoff. "You can't be serious. You're going to sit there and call people crazy like it's a judgment? You think you have room to make assessments of anyone?"

"You need to be careful. You need to pay attention to your surroundings and notice if there's anyone being unusual around you."

"You clearly aren't aware of the people I tend to keep company with," I fire back at him.

"This isn't a joke, Emma," he snaps. "These people could be coming for you, and you have important things you need to be doing. You can't be distracted by these people."

The anger in his voice makes my jaw tighten and his selfishness makes a flash of angry heat sting across my cheeks.

"Fuck you, Jonah," I growl. "I'm done. I'm done with all of this. You act like you care that my face is being splashed over the internet for the addle-brained conspiracy whores to stick up over their dartboards and play a few rounds to decide how they're going to wipe me out, but you don't give a shit. All that matters to you is that I keep doing the grunt work for you to help you find a girl you apparently misplaced, but won't tell me how or why, and tormenting my husband while he tries to deal with the death of his cousin. And I'm finished. I'm not going to be your pawn anymore. I've played your game. It's over now. Don't call me anymore."

I slam my finger on the "end call" button and realize I'm out of breath, my chest heaving. I didn't realize how angry I really was until it all started spilling out. Dean stares at me for a few seconds before he speaks.

"Addle-brained conspiracy whores?"

"Did I say that?" I ask.

He nods slowly. "You did. I'm a little bit impressed. And a little bit concerned. It goes back and forth on which one is on top."

I run my fingers back through my hair and let out a sigh.

"I just can't deal with him anymore, Dean. I can't give over more of my life to him. I want him gone."

"Haven't you always?"

"It's different now. Yes, I've wanted him out of my life since the second I found out he exists. But there's always been that part of me…"

My voice trails off as I realize I don't really know how that sentence ends. I can feel the knot of the feeling in the back of my chest, lodged in my spine, pressing against my heart and lungs. It's hard to put into words what it is, but if there's anyone in this world who can understand it, it's Dean.

"You want to find some reason for everything," Dean says. "You want to make up for it. You feel responsible for keeping him under control, and you want to be the one who stops him."

I nod. "But I can't anymore. I can't let him take my attention away from other cases and other things in my life so that I can feel like I have him on a leash. What's really happening is he has me on one, and I can't let him."

"What about the cases you've been working on for him?" Dean asks.

I shake my head. "Those aren't my responsibility. If he wants to know what happened, he can figure it out for himself. He already knows a lot more than he's telling me, he just won't go to the police or provide any information about it because he doesn't want to get caught. He wants to be the one in control.

"Either he's going to care enough to say something so it can be properly investigated, or he's going to let it go. Either way, I'm not his personal investigator. It's not my job to run around trying to figure things out for him. And as for stopping him, it's going to happen. One of these days, he's going to make a mistake. And when he does, he'll end up right where he belongs."

ROBERT
PORTER

TEACHER SON FRIEND

CHAPTER SEVEN

WHEN I GET HOME LATER THAT NIGHT, THE HOUSE SMELLS LIKE garlic and onions, and I can hear Sam in the kitchen singing to himself as he cooks. He always sings when he makes pasta. I'm not sure if it's because he's occupying his mind during the long process, or if he's giving himself background music because he's imagining himself in a movie, but either way, it always makes me happy to hear the sound. And not just because it means pasta for supper and my husband happens to make the world's best pasta sauce. Or at least, Sherwood, Virginia's best pasta sauce.

"Hi, honey, I'm home," I call out from the front door.

His head pops around the doorway and he grins. "You love saying that, don't you?"

"I do," I grin, unzipping my boots and taking them off.

I notice some mail stacked on the table beside the couch and glance at it as I walk past but don't pick any of it up. My first stop is a kiss from my husband, then a visit to the stove to taste the sauce. It tastes right at that point where he'll be putting the noodles into the water and the garlic bread in the oven soon. He has this particular meal down to a science. And if I know him as well as I think I do, there's a cheesecake from Pearl's diner sitting in the refrigerator for dessert.

"How's Dean?" he asks as I head back through the house to the stairs.

"Doing okay. I think he's still figuring out life without taking care of Xavier. Just when he gets used to it, Xavier will be back. At least the starters are getting a lot of attention," I say.

"I'm sure they appreciate that. How about the Cold Valley case?"

By this point I'm upstairs, stripping down out of the clothes I wear when I have to be presentable to other people, and jumping into the sweatsuit and thick slipper socks I've been craving since the instant I stepped out to the car for the drive home.

"Right now, he doesn't have a lot to do with it. Technically, the investigation is still ongoing, but Genevieve is cooperating. I don't think she's ever going to fully recover from any of it."

"I don't think it's possible to recover from that," Sam muses. "Even if she could compartmentalize what she did to her family, watching what happened to Sheriff Boyd is enough to break just about anybody."

My last case was quite a doozy. Boyd had a twisted scheme of blackmail and corruption over the entire town. He had a money-laundering scheme based on the mass murder and cover-ups of migrant farmworkers in the town, and when an undercover FBI agent caught onto it, Boyd had him murdered as well. In his bid to become the mayor and flex his power even further, he convinced a teenage girl to fall in love with him and manipulated her into doing his bidding. She burned down her house, inadvertently killed her mother and one of her friends, and then kidnapped another friend. And then her stepfather-slash-lover turned a gun on himself and pulled the trigger right in front of her—and me.

I'll never forget the look of sheer horror on Genevieve's face in that moment. In that moment, she wasn't an arsonist or a kidnapper—she was a seventeen-year-old girl. Don't get me wrong, she'll be going away for a long time for her actions, but my heart breaks for the girl who was so obviously manipulated and abused by practically every man in her life. The men who were supposed to help her become an adult member of society just wanted her as their personal plaything. The whole situation makes me sick.

I go silent as I dress, trying not to let my mind remember that moment. This is far from the first memory of its kind to be in my brain, but I don't like dwelling on any of them. Witnessing the last moments of a person's life is usually horrific. When it comes suddenly, it's often worse. And when it's violent and shocking, it's indescribable.

Part of me struggles with feeling responsible for that moment in the sheriff's life. I know in the most logical and clear part of my thoughts that I had nothing to do with it. It didn't matter what I'd discovered about him. It didn't matter that he knew what he was facing when I found all the evidence of his horrific crimes.

I've been in that exact situation before, with more people than I can count. I've stood and looked into the eyes of men and women who knew they were about to be dragged through a trial with their only hope being that they would spend the rest of their lives in prison rather than being executed. For some, the execution would have been preferable.

Either way, they took that walk. They faced the future they had created for themselves.

It wasn't my fault that he took his own life. It was his choice. And there was no way I could have stopped him. Sometimes I find it easy to let that dark part of my mind venture into the open, treacherous expanse. Sometimes I let myself take the fall for what he did or tell myself there was something I could have done to stop him. When it's quiet and I can't stop the images of those last moments from flashing across the backs of my eyes, I wonder if there was something I missed that would have revealed to me what he was doing.

But there wasn't. I didn't expect it and I couldn't have stopped it. Sam knows that. He also knows about the thoughts and the questions. He doesn't ask about them. He doesn't need to.

I go back downstairs and find him pouring the dry pasta into boiling water.

"At some point, I'm probably going to have to go back to Cold Valley and participate in the investigation. Or at least be ready to testify in the trial when it comes," I say.

"I know. But hopefully you can do it on video calls. That would make it a lot easier than doing all that travel."

I agree and head back into the living room to sort through the mail I'd seen sitting on the side table. One envelope particularly interests me. I save it for last, first going through the bills and junk mail. I set aside two pieces that belong to neighbors on the block.

It always amuses me when I find wayward mail like that, or when one of my neighbors shows up on the front porch to hand over something that's rightfully mine. With a town as small as Sherwood, I know for a fact the mail carrier is not only familiar with everybody who lives on the street and what their actual addresses are but is close personal friends with many of them.

I think she does it on purpose. It's her way of making sure all of us interact with each other and keep up our connections. She's one of the many lifetime residents of the town who are less than delighted at what they consider an influx of outsiders coming in over the last couple of years.

It doesn't really seem to matter to them that I wouldn't even need to borrow all of Sam's fingers to count the number of new residents moving in. To them, anyone new is a stranger until otherwise notified. They also represent the downfall of the close-knit community where everybody knew everybody and we all looked out for each other. I think it's a bit of a stretch to think that just because there are a few faces we can't automatically attach to memories from our youths, or connect the dots to generations of family members, that we are all descending into post-apocalyptic anonymity, but they are stubborn people.

At least they aren't aggressive or outrightly rude to the new folks. In fact, they seem just as friendly as anyone else. That's the kicker in small towns. That polite woman bringing you a casserole on your first day in town and asking you to come over for game night with her family to get to know you could just as easily be sizing you up and trying to gauge your potential for corrupting the town.

For some people, the reaction to the newcomers is upsetting and even disturbing. They don't want to think of their fellow Sherwoodians as unwelcoming people. They worry, possibly rightfully so, that it's this attitude that's actually going to diminish the town culture. I could easily feel that way. After all, I've spent more of my life living outside of Sherwood than in. I wasn't born here either. I could be seen as an outsider, too.

Or I could go down the darker route and worry I'm at the brink of some of the horrors I've seen played out with no other justification than hate.

But that would be just as much of a leap. It would drag up feelings I'd rather not encourage. I've decided to stick with being amused. As long as it doesn't turn nasty, I'll let the little faction of loyalists worry about whatever random detail about the newcomers caught their attention that day. I'll chuckle at the gossip I'll inevitably hear in the bakery or during my occasional visit to the hairdresser, knowing full well it'll all pass and a year from now they'll forget they were ever suspicious of their bowling partner or fishing buddy or new girlfriend.

And I'll happily keep going over to my neighbors' houses with their mail and pretending it's all a big mix-up so we can exchange a few pleasantries. If nothing else, it does let me keep up with the people around me, which is something I'm not always the best at. It's not that I don't care or that I don't want to keep in touch. I just get busy and distracted and sometimes don't notice when it's been weeks or even months since I've interacted with the people who live fifteen feet away. I still need to thank them for when they came over and shoveled the snow off my sidewalk this winter when Sam was away just to be friendly.

When I'm finished sorting through the stack, I pick up the final envelope and bring it over to the couch with me. Curling up in my favorite corner, I tug a blanket down over me and examine the envelope.

"Dinner is almost ready," Sam announces, coming into the room. He notices the envelope in my hands. "Oh, good. You got it. I noticed the return address. I'm assuming you are Penelope VanWinkle."

"That would be me," I say. "The first one was addressed to Percival Vincent-Willard."

"At least he has a theme going," Sam cracks. "Maybe next time he'll address it to Phillipa Vanderley, Lady of Winthrope Manor."

"You've been watching too many BBC period dramas."

"What can I say? I love the costumes."

The letter is from Xavier. The return address of the prison would tell me that even if the names he's concocted didn't give it away. He doesn't want to write my name on the outside of an envelope and risk having anyone in the prison see it. Several of his fellow inmates are behind bars with him because of my investigations. We also can't discount the reality that the reason he's in there at all is Jonah's escape, which means chances are high he still has people loyal to him on the inside.

And if anyone has encountered Jonah and spent enough time with him to become one of his followers, they know about me. I'm a popular topic of conversation for him.

If one of those people were to see that Xavier is writing me letters, they would get suspicious of him and his presence there in the facility. Not only would that ruin any chances of him getting the information he went in there to find, but it could also greatly lessen the chances of him getting out alive. That part is far more important to me.

I still think he could probably just address them to Sam and it would be fine, but he insists people would recognize my husband's name. Besides, it would be unseemly to address a letter to him that's meant for me. Apparently, Penelope and Percival are just fine, though.

Opening the envelope, I take out the letter and read through it. Xavier's handwriting is just like the rest of him: you never really know what you're going to get. Sometimes it's tight, controlled, and so small, it's hard to discern the white of the paper between the ink. Other times it's freeform and flowing, taking up almost too much space like each letter is trying to make itself seen. Then there are times when it's rushed and chaotic, toppling off the lines and crowding up together in the margins.

I wish I could interpret the meaning behind the shifts in the lettering. It should be simple. There should be some sort of direct line between his mood or his state of mind and the way his handwriting ends up on the paper. Unfortunately, also like Xavier, it really isn't that easy. It can vary from moment to moment, showing up differently even when he's in the same mood each time he writes, sometimes even shifting in the course of the same piece of writing for seemingly no reason.

The handwriting analysts at the Bureau wouldn't have shit on Xavier.

He could be four or five different people for all they know. It's one of the many reasons we are all very lucky Xavier hasn't gone the way of the serial killer. If he ever actually killed someone, he'd never be caught.

"How is he?" Sam asks.

"He sounds good," I tell him. "The crochet group is going well. He says it started with just a couple of guys, but it's really picked up popularity. He even had some of the volunteers who came in join up for a session."

"Leave it to Xavier to start a crafting revolution in the prison," he cracks.

I chuckle. "It sounds like everything is going well. Comparatively speaking, of course. So that's at least good. He says there are a few things that have caught his attention, but he's not sure what they mean yet." I sigh. "I just wish I knew exactly what he was thinking and going through. Everyone keeps saying he sees things other people don't. He feels things and recognizes things and thinks differently."

"You haven't noticed that yet?" Sam raises an eyebrow.

"Of course, I've noticed that. Don't forget I'm the one he brought to a vending machine within five minutes of me meeting him and asked which snack wanted to be me. First interaction with him. Trust me, I noticed. It's just—" I pause, trying to figure out exactly how I want to say this and knowing I'm probably going to say it the wrong way. "He's going to find out something. He's not going to come out of there without some detail, some insight that could completely change things."

"Isn't that what you want?" Sam asks.

"What if I don't know?" I ask.

"What do you mean?"

I'm surprised by the tears that come to my eyes and the crushing feeling in the center of my chest. I spent so much of my life being unemotional. Out of habit. Out of necessity. I needed to push it down to do what needed to be done. To survive. Now the emotions come more easily. But I'm not always ready for them.

"What if I can't understand what he's telling me? What if he comes out of there and knows he's figured something out, but when he tells me, I don't know what it means? Or if I think it means something it doesn't? What if I can't make any sense of it? I'm the one who put him in there."

"He put himself in there," Sam interjects.

"No," I say, shaking my head. "You keep saying that. All of you keep saying that. But he wouldn't be in there if it wasn't for me. He's doing it to find something out for me. I'm the one who had my father call in the favor. I'm the one who got Eric to vouch for the investigation and give clearance. This is on me." I draw in a breath. "I want him out. I'm going to shut this down."

"Why would you do that? He's doing fine. There hasn't been any trouble. After everything you went through and everybody who helped pull this thing off, you can't just stop it because you're worried you won't know what to do with the information he gives you. Which, by the way, you will. He can be difficult to follow, but he's not going to do an interpretive dance for you and expect that to give you all the wisdom he gathers. He'll make sure it's clear."

"I sent him in there because I got pissed off at Jonah for breaking out and no one being able to figure out how. I convinced myself it's important to know how he did it. But it's not. It doesn't matter. He's out. And I'm done chasing him. I'm done playing with him. I want him out of my life once and for all, Sam. And trying to sniff out his trail through the prison isn't going to do us any good."

"I don't think you actually believe that," he replies gently. "I believe you want him gone. And I believe he will be. Soon. But you know there's value in knowing what happened."

"If I can't take what he tells me and make something actually come of it, all of this will have been for nothing."

"You know that's not true," Sam insists. "It's not about Jonah. It's about what he did to get out and how many other people might have been a part of it. It's about security and about what happened to Serena.

And for what could happen the next time he's behind bars when you catch him. And you *will* catch him."

I give him a skeptical look, but the sincerity in his eyes melts through that.

"Stop second-guessing yourself, Emma. You did this for a reason. So did Xavier. He's not a child. He knows what he's doing. So let him do it. And take what comes out of it for what it is."

"I don't want him to be in danger," I protest. "Jonah's not worth it."

"He's not. But you don't need to worry so much about Xavier. It's not like he has years of a sentence ahead of him. Just don't have a snap reaction and end this now." He leans down and kisses the top of my head. "At least let him stay in there for a little longer. He told me in my letter he's making me a blanket."

"You got a letter, too?" I ask.

Sam nods. "Yep. R. Hood of Sherwood at your service."

CHAPTER EIGHT

T HE NEXT DAY IS THE RARE OCCASION THAT SAM AND I BOTH HAVE the day at home. It's his day off and I don't have any appointments or anywhere urgent I need to be, which means we get to spend the day together.

As much as we always have visions for the fun things we'd like to do when we have more time together, the day is taken up primarily by all those adult types of responsibilities we like to pretend don't exist. Cleaning. Laundry. A couple of minor repairs around the house, including finally replacing all the bulbs along the top of the bathroom mirror so they are the same kind rather than the jumble of random shapes that resulted from swapping them out at different times. That one probably isn't all that important, but it makes me feel better.

Grocery shopping is the highlight of the afternoon. Enough time has passed that I can go into the nearest market again without feeling like Gretchen is going to appear in front of me and launch into her woefully misled campaign of shame again, still blaming me for the death of an associate who—as I've reminded her a thousand times—tried to run me down and kill me with his car. I don't miss her. Great store manager. Terrible judge of character.

Being with Sam makes grocery shopping far more fun, and when a familiar song comes over the speakers and he gathers me into his arms to dance with me in the middle of the frozen food aisle, I catch an admiring gaze from an old couple walking by. It fills me with a warmth that carries through the rest of shopping, putting away the groceries, and even doing some meal prep for the week.

This is one of those things that Sam and I don't see eye-to-eye on. I love having a refrigerator full of little boxes, meals, and snacks ready to grab and prepare or eat. Sam says it makes him feel like he's living inside a convenience store's chilled display case. I try not to take that as an insult to my food preparation skills.

We compromise by only partially prepping, but there's enough else to do around the house that when we finally settle onto the couch that evening, I'm feeling accomplished and ready to relax. Curling up in his arms makes me feel at ease and comfortable.

The feeling doesn't last long.

Sam and I get through two shows before the news comes on. We always talk about how we shouldn't watch the news so much, that it's bad for our mental health. But that's fairly futile to argue. As a third-generation sheriff and an FBI agent, we're drawn to the crime reports. It's in our nature.

Tonight, as soon as the reporters announce the headline cases, my happiness starts to drain. My muscles tense and I can't seem to make the bones of my spine detach from each other so I can move.

"How could they find a body right behind a courthouse and no one saw anything?" Sam wonders.

I'm fixated on the screen, watching the footage of the DCPD crime scene investigation team swarming around the street just on the edge of the parking lot behind the courthouse. It's obviously not showing anything gruesome, but a flash of a shape covered in a sheet is impactful enough for most viewers.

It's not the fact that there was a murder that has me cold. It's not the gruesome crime that has rendered me unable to pry my eyes away from the screen. It's what they described in the tagline, the juicy little detail the newsroom wanted to use to get the audience champing at the bit to see how it was all going to unfold.

A tag on the corpse's toe.

It sounds like a sick joke. A toe tag on a body found dumped on the street. Like the morgue somehow lost one of its temporary residents. But that's not the kind of tag police reported finding. This one was a simple piece of cream-colored cardstock cut into a curved rectangle with a single word written across it.

Greed.

"That spot is just beyond where the security cameras for the parking lot would cover," I point out. "Whoever did it knows that. They left the body right there on purpose."

"A message to one of the judges?" Sam offers. "Maybe that's what the 'Greed' tag means?"

I shake my head. "I don't know."

The uncomfortable feeling brought on by the report stays with me even after the reporter finishes giving the barebones information about the murder and moves on to the next story in the lineup. It isn't until Sam jostles me gently and suggests we turn in for the night that I realize I'm still staring at the screen, the weather reporter predicting several days of rain invisible to me.

I don't sleep well that night. My mind is filled with thoughts of the cream-colored tag and the word written across it. The body was left where it was for a reason. It wasn't an accident or a coincidence. It means something, just like that tag does. I just don't know what.

I'm on my second cup of coffee in the morning when I can't wait any longer and call Eric. It's early enough that I'm not sure if he's in the office and will answer, but he does.

"Did you see the news last night?" I ask.

It's not a real question. I know he did, but even if he didn't, he knows what I'm talking about. It's an introduction to the conversation, a way for me to get more information.

"It looks the same," he says.

"That's what I was worried you were going to say," I groan.

"Were you?" he asks.

"What do you mean?"

"You've been waiting for years, Emma. Every time a body is found. Every time the police say there are details they're keeping from the public, you think it could be him," Eric says.

"I know. But it doesn't mean I wanted someone else to die."

"I know."

We both fall silent, our minds drifting back to another time, one that feels like a different life. It was so many years ago, but the memory feels fresh and bright.

"They don't seem to know much," I finally say. "It's like they aren't even making the connection."

"They might not be," Eric acknowledges. "Those murders and the attack were a long time ago."

"And they were never solved," I add. "No one ever even had a suspect. You would think something with this kind of similarity would stand out."

"That case is cold, Emma. Frostbitten, if you ask the detectives now. Some of them probably don't even know it ever existed because it never went anywhere."

"And this one isn't going to go anywhere, either, if we just pretend it's not the same guy. Or at least someone who knows about the cold case and is trying to revive it. The detail about the tags was never made public before. But they decided to talk this time. That's going to cause a stir."

"I don't know if they decided to talk, or if the media got a hold of it before the detectives could shut it down. Reporters are ruthless these days. Cell phones and social media have made it so they can essentially report crime and initial investigations in real time. It can be a great thing but can also be detrimental to keeping elements of investigations confidential," Eric muses.

"That might work in our favor," I say.

"How?"

"They aren't mentioning the past attacks. Whether the media knows about the link and are just choosing not to say it, or they don't even realize the link, as of right now, this murder is being presented as something completely new. A standalone murder with a totally fresh beginning of the investigation," I say.

"How is that a good thing?" Eric asks.

"Because someone's going to know it's not. And if they slip, we'll catch it."

"Does this mean you want to take this on?" he asks.

There's no hesitation in his voice. He's not trying to discourage me or make me feel like it's something I shouldn't be thinking about. He knows this case has been on my mind for a long time. Since the very beginning of my career, when I was just getting started in the Bureau. I'd found my place, but I was still trying to reconcile my life with it. I hadn't even taken the lead on my first major case yet.

These murders weren't my case then. The FBI didn't even get involved until after the third attack. I watched the case from the outside and waited for something to happen. I craved every detail, every drop of information they could squeeze out of the tiny pieces of evidence they found. But there was nothing. Cream-colored tags with words that didn't make sense. No video. No photographs. No fingerprints or DNA or fibers.

This wasn't someone acting frantically or on a whim. Every death, every attack was carefully orchestrated. The targets were specifically chosen.

Only no one could figure out why. Or by whom.

Even when the Bureau did get involved, it was brief and cursory. There wasn't anything to go on, and I wasn't allowed to be a part of the investigation. No one knew me then. My name didn't mean anything. And soon the case faded into oblivion. I haven't heard anyone mention it in so long.

Until now.

"I have to. It was bad enough before when we couldn't solve it. Now it's happening again. And if there was one victim, they are going to be others. You know that as well as I do. This is a serial killer. And he's not going to pop back up for one more go-round. There've been enough victims and enough time for the Bureau to get involved. We have to do this, Eric."

"Consider it done."

CHAPTER NINE

S AM IS STANDING IN THE DOORWAY OF THE KITCHEN WHEN I GET off the phone. He steps in with a concerned, quizzical look on his face.

"What was that all about?" he asks.

"That was Eric," I say.

"Talking about the Seers?" he asks.

"No," I tell him with a shake of my head. "There hasn't been anything new about that. We were talking about that body that was found yesterday in DC behind the courthouse."

"That's up in his neck of the woods. Does he know something else about it?" Sam asks.

"Not about that victim," I say.

"Why does that sound like you know something else?"

"Because I do. The FBI is taking the case."

"This fast? I know the victim was found near the courthouse, but there haven't been any other developments or anything that make it seem like the Bureau would be interested. Why would you be involved?"

"It's something I have to do," I say.

"Doesn't he have you working on enough right now?" Sam asks. "Not to mention everything you're working on by yourself."

"Sam, it's something I have to do. It's not just about the man yesterday. We think the person who died yesterday was another victim of a serial killer," I tell him.

He seems shocked by the revelation. It stops the protests I know he's already about to make. Not because he doesn't think I can handle the cases, but because he knows how easy it is for me to take on so many cases I forget to come up to breathe. Something that's happened all too often in the last few years.

My name is known now. People know who I am. They want me involved. And I want to be involved. This is what I chose for my life, and I'm as devoted to it now as I was the day I walked into the Academy for the first time.

But I have to keep my head above the water. I can't let myself completely sink into the depths of thinking of nothing but the cases in front of me, and constantly adding more. It's what I've done before and it left me on the brink. It's not that I don't think I could come back from it again. It's that I don't want to have to try.

But I can't turn away from this one. I can't pretend it's not happening, or that the details don't line up. This has been following me for a long time. I can't just turn my back and let others take care of it the way I was forced to do so long ago. This one is mine.

"A serial killer? I haven't heard about any other victims that seem connected," Sam frowns. "And they didn't mention anything about other victims on the news report."

"Not from recently," I explain. "There was a case years ago. Back when I had first started at the Bureau. There were two murders and an attempted murder. All of them involved tags like were found on the man yesterday."

"Tags that said 'Greed?'" he asks.

"The same kind of tags, but they didn't say the same thing. And they weren't all tied on the toe. Both of the first two victims had tags around their wrists that said 'Lust,'" I explain. "A man and then a woman."

"And the third?" Sam says.

"There was a blank tag found on the ground next to the survivor," I say.

"But it was never solved?" he asks.

I shake my head. "There was an investigation, but it never went anywhere. I can barely even say there were leads. There was a witness to the attack on the third victim, but she wasn't able to give much information. Just that it looked like a man. He was wearing a dark jacket. She didn't see his face and when he ran, she wasn't able to catch up with him."

"That sounds like a generic response," Sam frowns. "Are the police sure that was accurate?"

"Yes," I tell him insistently. "The attack happened in a parking garage not too far from the courthouse where this victim was found. The attacker followed the victim and was trying to kill her, but there were other people in the garage and heard the shouts. The attacker ran when they came around the corner. He managed to escape off the top level and the responding officers couldn't track him down."

"There were no cameras?"

"Not that caught anything. The garage had some on the outside, but none on the inside."

"That doesn't seem like great planning," Sam mutters.

"It's not. But unfortunately, as ubiquitous as cameras seem to be, they weren't nearly as prevalent a decade ago, and they still aren't everywhere, even now. You'd be shocked at how often I've encountered businesses that seem like they have a robust security system only to find out the cameras are dummies," I say.

"Dummies?" Sam raises an eyebrow. "Like the fake cameras Old Man Huff has around his front porch?"

I can't help but laugh. "I love that you are a grown man and you still refer to him as Old Man Huff."

"I've been calling him that since I was a kid," he protests.

"I know," I say. "But has it sunk in yet that when you first started calling him that, he was only about five years older than you are now?"

Sam opens his mouth to say something, then snaps it shut and walks over to the coffee maker. Apparently, he is not willing to let go of his mind's belief that the reclusive, paranoid, and occasionally aggressive man who lives on the outskirts of town, more in the woods than in the town itself, is perpetually ancient.

He shakes the thought out of his head as he sits down at the table with his coffee. "Fake cameras," he says, prompting me to continue.

"Yes," I nod. "They're actually sold that way on purpose. It's cheaper than having an actual functioning system but the average person doesn't know they're fake. They assume they're being watched."

"The same idea as having a sign for an alarm system but not actually having the system," Sam says. "Deterrent rather than any actual function."

"Exactly. I can understand the thinking behind it, but in practice, it's not the best approach. Especially for a business or somewhere public like the parking garage. That's the kind of place you actually need to have the security footage, but at the time, that garage didn't have it. There was no way of knowing who did the attack."

"And no fingerprints, hairs, anything?"

"No," I shake my head. "The… victim managed to scratch the guy's cheek but they weren't able to pull DNA from it. And she was in no way connected to the first two victims."

There's a lot more to the story, but those details can come later. They can come out once I've pried open the evidence and done a thorough examination with the new evidence.

I can't let this monster slip through my fingers. Not again.

"It's one of the most frustrating cases I've ever encountered in that way," I continue. "None of the victims had a shred of hard evidence. Not even a breadcrumb. The only thing that pointed to them being the same attacker was the shared M.O."

"So, it could actually be more than one person," Sam offers.

I shake my head. "No. I mean, I guess technically, yes, it's possible. There's no DNA or other evidence to conclusively show they were committed by the same person. But I can't imagine this is a copycat situation. It doesn't make sense. Why would anyone want to copycat a crime like this? They were, I hate to say it, bog-standard murders. There was no particularly gruesome or sensational method to them. And there was no clear rhyme or reason to the victims.

"Then there's the detail of the tags. That was never shared with the public, so someone would have to have very close knowledge of the case in order to replicate that. I'm sure there will be comparisons done on the handwriting to see if it was likely the same person who wrote the words. That's not conclusive, but it would be something."

"You said there was no rhyme or reason to the victims. But two of them had the word 'Lust' on their tags. A man and a woman. That seems fairly self-explanatory."

"You would think," I say. "But they didn't know each other. They weren't connected in any way, and the third victim had no connection to them either. There was no secret relationship, no affair, not even any indication that they'd ever met or even come across each other online. There was nothing. They were separated in age by quite a few years, came from totally different backgrounds, and there was no indication at all they'd ever crossed paths in any way."

"Alright," Sam says. "So why lust? There was a reason that particular word was chosen for their tags. It wasn't just a signature."

"That was considered, though," I tell him. I finish my coffee and bring the mug over to the counter. I'm tempted to have a third cup but put it in the sink and fill it with water instead. Grabbing a bag of bagels from the pantry, I take out two and drop the halves into the toaster. "There was a theory that maybe 'Lust' wasn't supposed to be a label for those people, but a label for the killer."

"It doesn't seem like a great name to choose if you're going for a serial killer signature," Sam says.

"I'm not sure there's really anything that's particularly good in that context, but I know what you're saying."

"Did that go anywhere?" Sam asks.

"Not really," I shrug. "I guess I can't say that it was proven wrong because the case is still unsolved, but it didn't lead anywhere. There were no common friends or family between the two, much less lovers. And their lives didn't overlap. They didn't go to the same places to eat or have coffee, didn't work anywhere near each other. Didn't use the same hairdresser or housekeeper or dog walker. Trust me, they tried to find a way that the same person could have lusted after these two people, but there was just nothing."

"Well, clearly there was some kind of overlap that was missed. There had to be some way the two of them were killed by the same person. And let me guess, the third victim didn't fit in either?"

I give a slow nod. "No connection to either of the two. And the tag was blank so nobody could figure out what kind of pattern would be made. And that's where the investigation stopped then, and where it still is now," I say.

"And they were absolutely sure the third victim didn't know the first two?"

"One hundred percent," I tell him, a little harsher than I meant to. "But with this new murder, there's reason to open it up again. There's still no new evidence, but the tag—it's different. We might not be able to tell why just looking at the murder, but something changed. The reason behind the deaths, the way the killer chose the victim, changed. And if we can figure out what is different about this victim, it will get us closer to finding the killer."

"Do you have any theories?" Sam asks.

"Nothing concrete. The one thing that has stayed with me all these years later is the tags. I think the Bureau was looking at the word too literally. There's never been a real explanation for what it meant. Neither of the victims were particularly lustful. They weren't having affairs. They weren't promiscuous. One was a married man who had worked with the same company for his entire adult life. The other was a woman who had a personal brand that might have been described as brash in some ways, but not inappropriate or suggestive. Even forensic dives into their computers didn't find anything scandalous," I say. "Trust me. I had to dig through internet histories."

"Maybe that's it? The killer thought they needed more lust in their lives?" he suggests.

"That's a possibility. The killer could be choosing people he considers unworthy of continuing to live because they haven't been making the most of their lives. It wouldn't be the first time I'd seen a killer who chose victims based on some perceived notion of wasted potential. But that's usually personal killings. Parents murdering their children for not doing well enough in school or not excelling at specific activities. Children killing parents for trying to restrict them. Spouses killing other spouses for not living up to their ideals. That's a personal type of killing."

"And these deaths weren't personal."

"It doesn't seem like it," I note, my voice low. "So, there's the possibility the word is meant differently. It's being used in a different context. Or it's less literal and meant to mean something else. I just don't know what."

"What has you so tense about this?" Sam frowns.

His eyes are focused on the counter in front of me where I'm trying to butter the bagels. My hand grips the knife so hard I've broken one of the bagel slices in half. I set them down and take a deep breath, willing the tension away from my shoulders.

"I hate cases that go cold," I tell him. "I want an answer."

I take another deep breath as memories float to the surface.

CHAPTER TEN

THE EDGE THE MURDER PUT ME ON FADES OVER THE NEXT COUPLE of days as I wait for more information, more details from the crime scene investigation unit, and the results of the autopsy. I have no choice but to go back to my life and think of other things.

By the time Saturday morning rolls around, I'm thinking about blueberry waffles and if the smell of them might help spring come along a little faster. Even if they don't, eating them would be worth a couple extra weeks of cold. I missed whether or not the groundhog saw his shadow this year, so I don't know if I should be continuing to bundle up or if I can feel hopeful for daffodils and robins soon. I'll just make my waffles and start planning a trip to the beach.

Sam ended up working the overnight shift last night to help out a buddy at the station whose wife suddenly went into labor well before anyone was expecting it. So while Christian was at the hospital helping her through her breathing and hoping the baby comes out healthy, Sam was prowling the streets, waiting for the wayward drunk driver or a kid ready to wreak havoc with a can of spray paint.

We often joke about how quiet and uneventful Sherwood is, and how his days as sheriff rarely reach a peak of excitement any higher than a couple of speeding tickets and a rumble in the parking lot after a football game.

In a way, the teasing is like a talisman. Like if we can be silly and joke about Sherwood giving Mayberry a run for its money, we can convince the universe that's the way it should be. Like we can keep anything more from happening.

We both know a lot more can happen on these streets than the drunk drivers and the bored teenagers seeking out some adrenaline. We were brought back together by a horrible child kidnapper ripping across the town, and only a couple of years later we were nearly torn apart by a twisted killer. Sherwood isn't safe from the horrors that exist in other places. If anything, when they come here, they're more concentrated.

But we can keep the thoughts of them out of our minds. We can pretend they are nothing more than case files and that being home here means stepping into a postcard of the perfect small town. Some people still get deliveries from a milkman. Farmer's markets and little stands selling summer produce and the fall harvest abound. Women still wear hats sold in boutiques on Main Street. I don't, but I've seen them. And we prefer to keep our crime petty and our deaths from natural causes.

At least I can dream. It's easier than letting myself worry about my husband every time he leaves for work. He has to do enough worrying about me.

When he walks through the front door into the smell of blueberry pancakes, the sun is just getting around to fully coming over the horizon behind him. He's on the phone. He raises his eyebrows at me when he comes into the kitchen and sees a platter of bacon already sitting in the middle of the table and a pitcher of orange juice waiting on the counter.

"Alright, I've got to go. Emma either didn't sleep last night or got up really early and is about to tell me bad news," he says. "Thanks again."

He hangs up and I scrunch my lips up at him. "Why do you think I'm going to give you bad news just because you come home to a nice meal?"

"It's the crack of dawn," he replies.

"That's not true," I counter, taking a waffle out of the iron and pouring in new batter. "The crack of dawn was like half an hour ago."

"It's still really freaking early. I'm used to you not sleeping when you have a lot on your mind, or when something bad happens," he says.

"Alright, I'll give you that. But other women make their husbands dinner when they come home from work. You're coming home from work in the morning, so I made breakfast," I smile.

He comes over and tucks a hand behind my head to pull me in for a kiss on my forehead.

"Listen to you pretending to be a housewife who spends your days haggling with the butcher and making dinner," he says.

I wave my batter-covered ladle at him. "Listen here, bud. Being a housewife and doing stuff like that was my dream before I detoured into the FBI, so watch yourself."

Sam holds up his hands like he's demonstrating his innocence.

"Hey, far be it from me to reject a waffle and some bacon. And my mama was that housewife, so there's no disrespect from me," he says.

I fish the final waffle out of the iron and bring the plate over to the table.

"The Seers posted about me again," I tell him.

"And there it is," he says.

"What?" I ask.

"What do you mean, 'what?'" he asks. "That's where the waffles led. You made me blueberry waffles and bacon so I'd be doped up on carbs and fat and wouldn't be thinking all the way clearly when you tell me some group of whackos has published a rundown of your daily activities so it's easier to find you."

"No," I protest. "This is not a weaponized breakfast. I made waffles because they sounded good and bacon because you like it, and then I was going to try making conversation. I guess my involvement as the current subject of a conspiracy group is not the right topic for when you've been up all night. Noted. Speaking of which, was that Christian? How's the baby? Was it a boy or a girl?"

"The baby is doing fine. She was born a couple of hours ago and is apparently really tiny but strong. They're keeping her for observation, but they don't think there are going to be any problems," Sam says. "But that actually wasn't Christian. That was your cousin."

"Dean?" I frown, surprised.

"Do you have any other cousins you haven't told me about?" he asks.

"I seriously hope not," I say. "But what is he doing up and on the phone with you this early in the morning?"

"He told me he's doing something for Ava involving sourcing some footage from Europe, so he has to be up early due to the time zone."

That gives me pause. "Europe? When the hell did he get contacts in Europe?"

"I dunno. He kept the details light. But anyway, it worked out because while he was waiting for the decryption, he finished working on Marie's cloud storage for me," he explains.

Asking Eric to try to break into the password-protected cloud storage Sam found out his cousin Marie had wouldn't have been great usage of FBI resources, so we went with the next best thing: Dean. As a private investigator, he's developed a wide range of impressive skills that enable him to delve into cases and get information no one else can. Including, apparently, international connections. I didn't know that.

He can't always promise everything he does is totally above board, but he's told me he doesn't do the kinds of things that might one day actually make him the target of those Bureau resources. I take that as a plus.

"Did he find anything?" I ask.

"Well, kind of," he says.

"Kind of? What do you mean 'kind of?'"

"It's more what he didn't find," Sam says.

"I really don't like when you try to do the riddle thing," I say.

"Alright. Remember how Aunt Rose was getting the bank statements for me because she's on the account?" he asks.

"Yeah," I nod. "But the bank has been giving her the runaround because of everything."

"Right. Well, she finally got them and I was able to go over them. Turns out, Marie was getting regular deposits."

"Payoffs?" I ask.

"Paychecks," he corrects me. "Direct deposit. And the information on the statements traces straight back to a news website."

"Marie was writing news articles?"

"Apparently," Sam shrugs. "It's not that much of a surprise, really. When we were kids, she used to say she wanted to be a journalist. But it never went anywhere, and we all just figured she'd changed her mind."

"Evidently not," I say.

He makes an agreeing sound. "So, I got in touch with the site and they confirmed she had been writing for them for a good while. Usually under a pen name or ghostwriting for their other reporters, which was why we never caught onto it. They gave me a list of things she'd done. A lot of fluff pieces, an advice column, filling in for some other theme columnists when they needed time off, so the content didn't have a gap."

"Doesn't sound like anything exactly hard-hitting," I say.

"Definitely not. Which is what brings me to Dean. Since I know now that she was writing for that site, I assumed that was why she had the cloud storage. It was for work. She'd keep her articles in there, maybe research she needed to do if she ever needed to do it. Her source notes. That kind of thing. Dean told me when he got into it, there was even a folder marked 'Work.'"

"That seems pretty to the point," I note.

"You'd think. But when he opened the file, it was empty," he goes on. "Everything had been deleted."

"That's really strange. You said that she was doing just kind of fluff pieces. Nothing too intense. Why would it be so important to delete all of that?"

"I'm not sure," Sam says. "But he says even when it looks like there's nothing, sometimes there's still traces. He's going to do some more digging and talk to some people he knows to see if there might be any recoverable traces on her devices. Any documents that were kept in the cloud storage system had to be created somewhere. Even if she also deleted them from the device, there might be something there that can still be extracted."

"Sounds like a step in the right direction," I note.

"Or at least some direction," Sam adds, reaching for the bottle of syrup. "Anyway, I'm starving. Thanks, honey."

We've eaten our way through the pile of blueberry waffles and bacon and I'm considering laying down for a nap with Sam when my phone chimes to tell me I have a text. By now it's a far more decent time of morning, though still really early. That means I'm not surprised when I see the message is from Bellamy.

Little Bebe isn't a tiny baby anymore, but she still tends to wake up way before her parents would necessarily want her to. And because she's at the age where she can just scramble around the rails on her bed and walk around, it's important for her parents to be awake when she is.

Bellamy: *I bet you never thought you'd be on the cover of this magazine!*

There's an attachment, and when I open it, I can't help but laugh. It's my face taking up half the cover of the kind of glossy tabloid found on the shelves next to grocery store registers. The headline is in bright yellow lettering, the font bold to make sure that no passersby could possibly miss it.

"Look, babe," I grin, turning my phone to show him the image. "'FBI Agent Conspires with Underground Extremist Group.'"

He barks out a laugh. "Man, they must be getting some really good yoga in with all that stretching of the truth."

"The subtitle says I'm going to strip away everyone's freedoms and reestablish Puritanical laws and punishments." I zoom in closer on the dramatic picture, trying to figure out where it was taken. "That's unfortunate."

I type a response to Bellamy and just as I send it, my phone rings. I see Eric's name across the screen and answer it, still giggling at Sam's reaction to the cover.

"I already saw it," I say by way of greeting. "Your lovely partner sent me a picture. You know, I thought my Bingo board was full before, but now I think that really tips it over the edge. I have officially been featured on the front of a tabloid. The ultimate achievement."

"Emma," he starts.

"I might have to go to the store and buy a copy of it so I can find out what kind of extreme rules and guidelines I'm going to be enforcing soon when I manage to take over as supreme ruler of the country. I mean, I assume that's the position I'll have. I have a feeling the underground extremist group doesn't have a specific hierarchy in place that would allow them to select their own leader."

"Emma."

"And if they did, why would they need to work with me? Other than my obvious government ties, which I guess would be helpful for the whole coup aspect of this plan."

"I'm not calling about the tabloid," Eric cuts in, his voice sharp.

"Oh," I say. "Sorry, I— "

"There's been another murder."

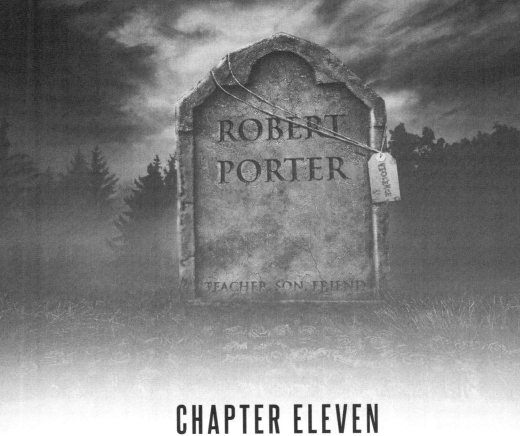

ROBERT
PORTER

TEACHER, SON, FRIEND

CHAPTER ELEVEN

"Do you want me to go with you?" Sam asks.

I toss my pajamas into the hamper in the corner of our bedroom and shake my head as I pull on clothes.

"No. You need to get some sleep. Parson is only about an hour from here. Maybe a little further. I'll be back tonight. You rest. You still have to go back to work for a shift later. I'll call you and let you know what's going on."

I throw on some makeup and coil my blonde hair up onto the back of my head so I can clip it out of the way. With my gun strapped to my hip and my bag on my shoulder, I kiss Sam, give him a tight hug, and kiss him again before rushing out of the house.

Even with the scene not being too far away, the drive to Parson seems to stretch out far too long. The sparse details Eric told me on the phone only make my mind spin faster. As soon as the other body was found, I knew there was a chance for more. It was unlikely the killer would surface again just to kill one more person. Chances were—are—

high that there are other planned victims. I just hoped we would have more time. I hoped we could have the possibility of finding the killer before someone else died.

When I arrive at the scene, it looks similar to the news footage of the scene behind the courthouse. The area is cordoned off and officers are milling around, trying to take it in, making notes, and waiting for the medical examiner to come and move the body.

A detective looks up as I approach. He has that look on his face that says he's ready to claim the scene as his own and defend it against a random onlooker, but that expression lessens as a hint of recognition flickers across his eyes. We haven't worked together before as far as I can remember, but he's likely seen me on new reports. Or maybe even the tabloids.

I take out my badge and show it to him.

"Agent Griffin," I say. "FBI."

He nods. "I heard the Bureau might be coming in. Detective Mavis."

He doesn't sound particularly exuberant to have me around and he doesn't acknowledge my introduction beyond that. But he doesn't push back, and I've learned to take that as a good thing when walking into an investigation like this. It's better if the local police department is willing to cooperate with the Bureau when we handle a case. Even reluctant cooperation is better than defiance, which I've encountered on more than enough occasions.

I'll take his feathers being ruffled at having to accept outside management of the case over him making my life hell by refusing to communicate and giving me the runaround any day.

"I'm sure you know by now this case is being investigated as a potential serial killer," I tell him.

I hate even saying the word "potential," but that's officially what this is. Until we can absolutely prove the murders are related, and that the same person committed all of them, I can't conclusively label this the work of a serial killer. But it is. It's the only explanation that makes sense.

"I've heard," he nods. "I admit I don't know much about the original victim."

"Victims," I correct him. "There were two murders." I naturally pause, the hesitation so subtle that I'm sure I'm the only one who picks up on it. "And an attempted murder. Years ago."

He nods as if urging me to continue.

"In all situations, there were tags present. The first two victims had the tags tied to them and the word 'Lust' written on them. An additional tag was found at the scene of the third attack, but it was blank. We figured the perp waited until after killing the victim to write it."

"Lust, huh?"

I shrug. "Nobody's ever been able to figure out what the word has to do with the victims or how they are connected. There've been no suspects."

"The Bureau was involved the first time, right?" he asks.

"Yes. Briefly. But nothing came of it," I tell him. "The case went cold and there hasn't been any progress on it since. Not until the murder a couple days ago."

The detective nods. "From what I know about that one, this is looking very much like it. I was just getting ready to get the details from the CSU."

"I'll go with you," I say.

He nods, his lips tight. I choose to ignore the reaction.

I lift the tape for myself and duck under it, following Detective Mavis across the pavement to a cluster of officers off to one side. While we wait for them to turn to us, I look around. The body was found in the parking lot of an old, abandoned photography store. There doesn't appear to be anything notable about the area and I don't see any of the typical signs of it being used as a dumping ground.

I hate to make the association with Marie, preferring not to think about her in that way at all, but I can't stop the link that immediately forms in my mind. She was found in a warehouse that was left behind by a business many years ago. Left behind, but not empty. The building was stripped of the equipment and supplies that had enough value to bother selling or scrapping before the company walked away, leaving it with gaping holes and scars across the cement floor.

The doors were locked and a chain was padlocked over the handles as if that would keep anyone out. I couldn't imagine that lasted for long. It was likely only a matter of days before someone discovered the hunkering building and recognized it for what it could be.

It may have been just a shell to others, an outdated mass that couldn't serve its original purpose any longer, but to the people who took over, it was a haven. A place for them to find shelter when they had no homes or their homes weren't hospitable to the lives they wanted to live. A place where they could meet with like-minded people, where they would be hidden and could wallow in the altered reality of their choice. It was a place of their own for as long as they could hold onto it. Which was why we found Marie surrounded by years of refuse, syringes, bottles, and other shreds and discards of the lives spent in and out of that hollow shell.

This parking lot doesn't look like that. It's sun-bleached and cracked, the fractures spread like veins across the surface and filled with grass and weeds growing up from underneath. But there's no trash. No tossed aside shopping carts or mounds of clothing and blankets left behind when they got wet or too burdensome to bring along while wandering.

It looks like this place was just forgotten. I can't pinpoint how long it's been sitting here or even what it used to be.

"Agent Griffin, good to have you."

I look over in the direction of the voice and see an officer who looks familiar enough for me to know I've encountered him before. I can't place him exactly, but that's not all that unexpected. I've crossed paths with far more officers and detectives in my career than I can count. It's far more likely for them to remember me than it is for me to be able to recall their names. I try not to admit that.

"Thank you," I say.

"Brandon Conner," he says, releasing me from the search through my mind to hopefully find him. "I was on a case you worked about five years ago."

That's enough to make the memory pop into my head.

"The Claire Vreeland murder," I say. My eyes narrow. "But that was in South Carolina."

"I moved up here a couple years back when I got married," he tells me. "My wife's family lives in the area."

"Oh," I nod. "Well, congratulations on the marriage."

"Thank you. I hear you got married recently as well."

I nod again. "A little more than a year ago."

"Congratulations."

The exchange tapers off into awkwardness and the silence passes back and forth, waiting for one of us to say something else. But I think we're in the middle of two different conversations. I finally lean slightly forward toward him.

"What can you tell me about this?" I ask.

"Oh," he says, snapping a look back over his shoulder and then back at me. "Right. Female, thirty-eight, Paisley Graham."

"You already know all of that?" I raise an eyebrow.

"She had her identification on her," he admits. "Along with her debit and credit cards, cash, and jewelry."

"Robbery isn't part of the motive," I state.

I feel like I'm telling him more than I am confirming it as a part of the case. The other victims had plenty of valuables on them as well. It's one of the significant details of the murders. None of them appeared to have any other motivation or exacerbating circumstances with their deaths. No theft. No sexual battery. None of the added elements that people often expect to be a part of a violent death.

"As of right now, cause of death appears to be blunt force trauma."

"Was she beaten?" I ask.

"No," he says. "There's no damage to her face and there doesn't appear to be any other injuries or damage. Just a severe blow to the back of the head. But the body hasn't been moved, so there might be things we haven't seen."

"And the tag?" I ask.

I expected it to be the first thing he mentioned, but it almost feels like the officer is skirting around the issue, trying not to talk about it.

"Tied around her neck," he says.

"What does it say?" I ask.

"Gluttony." He glances back again. I look where he is and see the black mass of the body covered with a tarp. "Which is strange. She isn't fat. Not even overweight."

"I'd like to see the body," I say.

He brings me over to it and I introduce myself to the officer standing nearby.

"The body has already been photographed?" I ask.

"Yes. But it hasn't been moved. The medical examiner hasn't arrived."

"Let me see."

She moves the tarp out of the way. The woman's body is curled on its side on the sidewalk, almost like she's sleeping. I can see the horrific damage to the back of her head. Even without extensive examination, it looks like the kind of blow that would result in death within seconds, if not instantly. At least that provides some solace. This woman didn't suffer.

Her face is turned up toward the sky and her eyes are closed, furthering the appearance of sleep. I wonder if her killer lowered her eyelids after her death or if it was a reflex at the moment she was attacked.

I can see what the officer told me about her injuries. Her face is as pristine as can be expected on a corpse. There are no visible bruises or cuts. It doesn't look like there was any kind of fight or scuffle. As far as I can see right now, there doesn't even look like a scrape where she would have hit the ground when she was hit.

There's very little blood on the ground. What is there looks more like transfer than like it actually came out of the injury. These details tell me she was killed somewhere else and brought here.

I crouch down and carefully tilt the tag up, not wanting to disturb anything about the body.

"Gluttony," I murmur. My eyes scan over her form. "Definitely doesn't look it."

Officer Conner hovers beside me.

"Why would someone in good shape be called a glutton?"

I shake my head. "I don't know."

I stand and let out a breath. I glance back and forth between the officers. "Thank you, officers."

Conner gives a single nod of acknowledgment and I make my way over to Detective Mavis where he has walked away and seems to be getting more details from another of the officers.

"Get me her phone," I hear him saying somewhat under his breath.

"I'm glad they found her phone," I say. "It will make contacting her next of kin and tracing her recent movements easier and faster."

The detective looks over at me and gives the kind of bob of his head that tells me there might be more of a clash happening than I wanted to think.

"Yes," he says. "I was thinking the same thing."

"Good," I say. The officer brings over the phone in a bag and I reach for it. "Thank you. I'm going to the precinct to find a room to act as headquarters for this particular murder. Since I'm handling multiple sites in several locations, most of the investigation will be handled from my home base, but I want a place here in Parson where I can manage evidence, interviews, and research about Paisley's murder.

"Please photograph and record the entire area. I want footage of the entire parking lot, the sidewalk, and the building. Chances are slim, but survey the surrounding area for surveillance cameras or other recording devices. Find out if there are any businesses or even residential locations nearby that might have recordings or could have witnesses. If there's any way to pinpoint when this body was placed here and what type of vehicle was used, we need to find it.

"Keep me updated on all progress and all evidence. I don't want any decisions made without putting them through me. No interviews. Do not discuss any details of the case, including the tag, the word on it, or the potential for serial killer activity with anyone."

I look around at every person present to make sure they are all not only listening to me, but that they have fully internalized what I'm saying to them. "I mean *anyone*. With the exception of the medical examiner, no one who is not here at this time is to receive any details of the case.

"It is critical that details are kept confidential for the sake of the investigation. I need every one of you to understand there are aspects of this case and the cases related to it that have not been shared and will not be shared except on a very strict need-to-know basis. Speculating or discussing details could greatly compromise the investigation. No one is to speak to the media. No one is to answer questions. If there are any, send them to me. Get in touch if you need anything. Thank you for your work."

I stalk back to my car and get inside. A chill rolls through me that has nothing to do with the weather outside. The case is getting more difficult, and this new murder means the chances of another coming soon are higher. It's on my shoulders to decode what's happening and find the killer before his next target becomes a victim.

CHAPTER TWELVE

MY PHONE RINGS AS I'M DRIVING TOWARD THE POLICE STATION. It's gripped in the holder attached to my dash, so I hit the button to answer and put it on speaker.

"Agent Griffin."

This is the phone I use when I'm investigating and need to be accessible by others working the case. I learned many years ago not to give out my personal cell number to people I only work with. The separation helps to keep my life balanced and prevents work, or the less savory side effects of it, from seeping into moments of my existence that should belong just to me.

My personal phone is still sitting in the passenger seat beside me, ready to bring me communication from my husband, my cousin, my father, or my closest friends. A handful of others have the number as well—neighbors and some associates I need to be able to keep in touch with but aren't necessarily linked to work—but for the most part, it's kept for those close to me.

The exception is Jonah. I don't know how he got my personal number and now that I hear his voice coming through the phone on the dash, I am even more confused about how he could have gotten this number. It's not advertised or spread around, and I can't imagine he spends too much of his time talking with the police officers and Bureau agents who have the number.

"What do you want?" I demand angrily. "You know what? I don't care. I told you not to call me again. I'm hanging up."

I reach for the phone, but before I can hit the button to end the call, he asks me to stop.

"I'm not calling to ask you to do anything for me. This isn't about Miley or Serena or Marini. Those don't matter. You were right. I've been asking too much from you. I shouldn't be relying on you to handle these things. And you don't have to anymore. I'm going to figure it out."

His words make me pause. The second I heard his voice, I prepared for a fight. Now he's fallen back, relinquishing the hold he feels he has on my time and my energy.

"Then what is it?" I ask.

"I know you say you don't care, but I wanted to talk to you about the Seers," he says.

"Jonah…"

"Just listen to me." He doesn't have the same sharp, aggressive tone he had the last time he talked to me about it, so I resist the urge to cut him off. "I know you don't think this is important, but I want to know you aren't trying to put this aside. That you really are thinking about it clearly."

"What do you mean?" I ask.

"You might not want to acknowledge it, Emma, but I know you. Maybe not because I've spent time with you, or because I've gotten the chance to get to know you—and I know that's my own doing, so you don't have to remind me. My point is, I know you in a way that goes beyond that. I know you because I know your father and your mother. I knew your grandparents."

"Don't talk about them," I say, hating to even hear mention of them on his tongue.

"You want to pretend I didn't exist, but you can't. They're my family, too. Don't you ever forget that. I knew them well before you were here. And it wasn't always bad, Emma. The division wasn't always there. And when it wasn't, I knew them all. And I know myself. I can see those things in you. Your eyes. Your hair. The way you walk. Your laugh. Your stubbornness.

"You don't want to let anything in. It's far easier for you to pretend everything is fine, that this isn't serious and that you can control it better if you don't think about it, than it is for you to acknowledge the possible reality of it."

He's right and I hate to admit that. I don't like to think about the time he spent with my family. I know it's ridiculous, but I feel a sense of protectiveness toward them, even in the past. It's like I can some-how defend them from him in the years before I was born by separating them in my thoughts. Like if I don't acknowledge that he was a part of the family and not a memory boarded up into a room in the attic, I can stop him from hurting his parents and his brother.

But there's nothing I can do about it. Those years existed. The dam-age was done when I was only a baby. Now he's using them against me in a new way and I'm fighting to stop the angry feeling crawling along my skin.

"I know the reality. I've seen the magazine cover. I know what they're saying about me."

"Did you read the article?" he asks.

"Yes," I say. "Did you?"

I'm not sure why it shocks me so much to think Jonah would have read the tabloid, but I can't imagine him kicking back with a drink and the glossy pages, absorbing his daily dose of gossip and trash like a vitamin.

"Yes. It's getting worse, Emma."

"It's getting more ridiculous."

"And that just means it's getting more dangerous. The more extreme the claims, the more extreme the believers. They're the ones you have to worry about. Not the ones who think critically. Not the ones who make sense. You need to worry about the ones who are willing to let someone pour these ideas in their throats and drink them down. The ones who can bring themselves to look at lambs and see monsters."

"I'm no lamb, Jonah."

"You need to be more careful. Stay out of the spotlight. Don't get involved in anything high-profile," he presses. "I'm not saying not to work. Just stay with cases you already know."

"Wait. Why would you say that?" I ask.

"Say what?"

"That I shouldn't get involved in anything high-profile," I say.

"It's what you do. When there are big cases, you handle them. You end up in the news and in articles about the cases. People can see you. They hear your name. They know where you are. And that's all they think about. The ones who are reading those articles and believing what they say, that's what they're focused on. They aren't thinking about a serial killer. They're thinking about you. And they'll use every tiny detail they can pick up on to trace you."

"It isn't like the media publishes my address or that it shows where I am in real time. They don't do live broadcasts of my murder investigations," I say.

"People like the Seers don't need that much," Jonah says. "That's what you're not understanding. When you're doing investigations that keep you further under the radar, you're protected. Cases that aren't massively covered in the media or written up keep you out of the public eye. People don't know where you are. But when you're doing the high-profile cases, you're giving them a target.

"They don't need specifics. They don't need a map drawn for them. These people are creative, Emma. They aren't afraid to dig, to put effort into tracking you down. You've always prided yourself in your observation skills. You can read people and you notice things about what's around you. Other people do the same thing, and when they really put effort into it, they can glean a tremendous amount from what may seem like the tiniest details.

"Right now, I could tell you so much about the people around me. For example, just looking out the window, I see three women walking together. One of them is carrying a bag from Brogan's, but it looks worn, like she's using it as a tote, not a shopping bag. That tells me that's from her area, not this one. Another is carrying a bag from Storm. She just bought something. The way they're posing with the statue means they probably haven't been around here for long. Possibly just arrived today or yesterday.

"They're heading for the set of steps that leads to the back but they keep pausing. They can't see the same view. One's pointing out that thing like the Eye on the boardwalk. She seems excited. The others are nodding. That narrows the options for where they are staying down by more than half and gives me a good idea of what they'll be doing over the next few days.

"I'm able to figure all of that out just by watching them for a few seconds. And I don't care about who these people are or what they're doing. Imagine what I'd be able to notice if one of them were someone I was trying to track. Those little details can add up to so much. I don't want anyone doing that to you and that leading to them being able to find you," Jonah says.

"This isn't for you to worry about, Jonah."

The conversation ends without him pushing me any harder, but I still feel the adrenaline as I get into the police station.

ROBERT PORTER

TEACHER, SON, FRIEND

CHAPTER THIRTEEN

OMETHING IS TICKLING THE BACK OF MY MIND AS I DISCUSS THE case with the chief and get set up in the conference room that will act as my de facto office during this investigation. Having offices out in the field is helpful when I'm investigating sprawling cases that have several crime scenes, especially when there are no identifiable suspects. It gives me the chance to stay organized and have a place to go when focused on that particular piece of the case.

I still tend to do much of the work at home, but at least this means when I'm in Parson interviewing people or canvassing the area, I'll have a centralized location set aside to keep evidence and brainstorm. As I'm setting up the space and taking notes about what I've already found out, I can't stop thinking about the conversation with Jonah. Something he said has burrowed itself into my brain and is digging deeper.

I was trying so hard not to let myself overreact and get too emotional that I wasn't fully processing each thing he said to me. It means what's getting to me is staying just out of reach. I can't even remember the exact words. There's just something my subconscious clung to and is trying to force forward.

"...however they possibly can."

I realize the chief is talking and I missed what he said.

"I'm sorry," I say. "What?"

He gives me an understanding look that says he thinks I'm distracted by the details of the case from this morning.

"I was saying I will, of course, have a team at your disposal that will help you however they possibly can. You can utilize them for whatever footwork might be needed for this here in Parson, or whatever you need done from a distance when you return to Sherwood or Quantico."

Or Harlan or Saltville or Feathered Nest or Breyer or Cold Valley or Michigan or Myrtle Beach.

The destination sticks itself to the end of my string of sarcastic thoughts without me recognizing it was coming, and for a second I don't even realize it was there. When it sinks in, my heart starts pounding.

"Thank you," I say, trying not to let on what's going through my head. "I appreciate your cooperation and will definitely be taking advantage of the help you have to offer. This is a complex case, and I'm currently handling other matters as well. In fact, I actually need to leave."

"Oh," he says, obviously surprised at my sudden departure. "I thought you would have been here for the rest of the day."

"I need to see to something very time-sensitive," I explain. "But I've given the team at the scene specific instructions for how to process the scene and what information I need from them. I'll be back as soon as possible to go over everything. Until then, if there's anything pressing or you need to ask me anything, you can get in touch with me on my cell or through email."

He's confirming my contact information and trying to say goodbye as I hurry out of the room and down the hall toward the exit of the building. As soon as I step foot out of the precinct and break into a jog toward my car, my hand is already on my phone.

By the time I'm at the airport, I have a ticket to the next flight to Myrtle Beach. It isn't direct. I'll have to transfer flights in Richmond, but that will save me several hours. I prefer not to have to go through multiple takeoffs and departures when I'm flying, but I can't be that choosy with this. I need to get there as soon as possible, something better than the ten hours it would take by driving. I'm lucky enough to find a connecting flight that will put me on the ground in just under four hours.

It'll be an extremely close shave to get to the airport before takeoff, and the four hours still seems far too long, but it's the best I can do.

I keep a small bag packed in the trunk with very basic supplies and I grab it as I leave my car with the valet to park. Full-out running gets me through pre-check security and to the gate just in time, and I take my seat moments before the doors close and the attendants start their safety spiel.

My fingers itch to call Sam and explain more thoroughly what's going on. I was able to briefly get in touch with him after booking my ticket to let him know where I'm going but couldn't get into detail about it. Now that I'm sitting here, strapped to the seat and staring out the window at the tarmac, I want to pick up my phone and tell him everything.

The fact that I can't ratchets up my anxiety even more. Even with my phone in airplane mode, I can't make a voice call. Like most airlines, this one has a policy prohibiting voice calls while onboard the aircraft. I might blur some lines when it comes to adhering to the strict letter of policy and law in some instances, but I'm not about to play that game aboard a flight. The last thing I need is to add to my collection of tabloid covers and sensational articles with headlines about a federal agent grounding a flight.

Instead, as soon as I'm allowed, I take out my computer and start an email to him. I don't want to tell him everything this way. The flight isn't full, but I'm very aware of prying eyes and nosy neighbors any time I'm in public. The people in the row behind me could easily peer through the gap in the seats to see what I'm writing. I carefully craft the message so Sam can understand it, but it doesn't offer the kind of information that might compromise anything.

"*On board. J is in Myrtle Beach. Please send picture of the back of Marie note. Explain more when I land. I love you.*"

It's very little more than I said when I called, but it's something. For the next hour, I research the area, taking notes about what he'd said on the call and trying to narrow my scope while waiting for Sam to get back to me. I'm not positive, but I think getting the picture from him will offer me a critical detail.

While I wait, I run a search of the names Jonah had mentioned. The first thing I look for is Bogan's. Jonah had mentioned that name when describing the women outside his window. He'd specifically said it looked wrinkled and heavily used, so she'd likely brought it from home.

That tells me she's a tourist. My first clue. It turns out Bogan's is a chain located in several places, but not in South Carolina. It confirms she is visiting from somewhere else, but not from where. That isn't important. I don't need to know where she came from. All I need to know is that she was here.

Jonah had confirmed that with the mention of Storm. A tiny shop frequented by tourists, it specializes in more off-beat beach accessories and clothing. This is not the kind of store visitors go to in search of that bright pink, palm tree pattern bikini and matching board short combo so they can look cute as a couple walking down the sand. It caters to a more alternative aesthetic. It also happens to be somewhere I visited often during the stretch of time my family lived in nearby Conway and again when I traveled back during college breaks.

His mention of it makes my skin crawl, but I'm trying to see this for what it could be. My chance.

The switchover in Richmond is mercifully quick, and less than two hours later, the landing gear grinds and squeals to a stop. The muscles in my legs bounce and twitch with the energy built up in them. I want to be running, to be bounding up stairs, to be kicking in a door. Not standing in an airplane seat waiting for the passengers in front of me to clear the aisle so I can move.

My rental car is waiting for me when I get to the terminal, but there still isn't any reply or message from Sam. I head for the downtown area anyway, taking the tiny droplets of information Jonah gave me to show me where to go.

It's getting into the latter half of the afternoon, but that doesn't mean anything is winding down. If anything, the town is starting to wake up.

If he's here, I'll find him. I have to.

CHAPTER FOURTEEN

IT'S BEEN MANY YEARS SINCE I'VE SET FOOT ON THIS BOARDWALK. Memories flit past as I make my way down to Storm. Part of me is actually surprised the store is still here. Some shops in tourist areas cling hard and become legendary, never leaving even when they become run down and irrelevant, while others seem popular and different enough to stand out, yet still fade away with the trends and tides.

Storm has stood the test of time. Nostalgia rushes over me as I approach the door. It looks almost identical to what I remember from my last visit. There are a few new band names on the stickers plastered to the front windows and doors. Bumper stickers and patches visible on a display in the window include a few political and social references that wouldn't have meant anything all those years ago.

But for the most part, it's the same. The smell is even the same as the door opens and a group of laughing, babbling young vacationers tumble out together. The weather here is far warmer than it was in Northern Virginia, but I still question the practicality of cutoff jeans so short their pockets don't even have room to hide combined with a string bikini top meant for a far less endowed woman. The whole ensemble is barely concealed under a gauzy white crop top meant to just barely skirt the rules of wearing clothing over bathing suits in most establishments around here.

Of course, practicality likely wasn't her goal when she got dressed this morning.

I wait for them to pass, then step inside. The smell is wafting over me now. Salt and sand. Incense and dark wood. Sugar and coconut.

It's so familiar it's like walking into frozen time. I almost expect to see myself come around the corner with a young Bellamy, her skin darkened even further by the sun and her hair wild with the salt water and wind.

"Can I help you?" a woman a couple of decades older than me asks.

I know her face. It's older and etched with the time that has passed and the sunlight it soaks in so frequently. But laughter has been kind to it. I can almost see her younger version talking to me through the veil.

She doesn't remember me. There's no reason why she should. It's been so many years and thousands of people flow through the shop every season. I'm just another face. She doesn't realize that this face is one that used to belong here.

"Agent Emma Griffin," I introduce myself, walking toward her with my hand outstretched. "I'm with the FBI."

Her eyes widen a bit, but she takes my hand and shakes it.

"FBI," she frowns. "Is something wrong? Something with the shop?"

"Oh, no." I shake my head. "I'm sorry. No."

"Good," she exhales, sounding relieved. "You never know these days."

"I can attest to that," I say. "I'm in the area looking for someone and they mentioned the name of your store. They said they saw a woman carrying a bag from here earlier today and taking a picture in front of a statue."

She looks a bit taken aback. "A bag from here? They must be frequent customers."

"Why do you say that?" I ask.

She walks over to the counter and pulls out a plain black paper shopping bag. It's completely different than the plastic bags emblazoned with the name of the store I remember from when I shopped here. I probably still have one of them folded up in a box somewhere.

"I started using these a little while back. Fully recycled materials, made locally. They don't have any identifying marks and a couple of businesses around here have started using them. As far as I know, I'm the only shop that exclusively uses the matte black version, but that's still pretty narrow," she says. "I don't know if just a tourist would be able to identify it that easily."

It's a sign of the popularity of the shop. She doesn't need the identifying information on her bags to lure in customers. There's already enough buzz to ensure her business stays regular. But it makes Jonah's comment stick more sharply in the back of my mind.

"Alright. Thank you. I appreciate your time."

I glance around as I'm stepping back from the counter.

"You look like you know the place," she observes. "You've been here before?"

I offer her a hint of a smile. "In another life. Have a good day."

As I'm walking toward the door, she calls out to me.

"You said there was a statue?"

I turn back to her, nodding. "The person I'm looking for mentioned the women he saw posing at a statue like it was their first day on vacation."

"Obviously, there are statues in a lot of places around town, but if she'd just bought something here and seemed to be a tourist, I'd take a look at Plyler Park."

"Plyler Park?" I ask.

It sounds familiar but only in that hazy, passing way that means I might have overheard it from nearby chatter or seen it on a sign. It doesn't hold any particular significance for me.

"It's a park where they do live music and entertainment. Events for families and such. It's not far from here. There's a really popular statue in there. A couple of dolphins. Maybe that's what they were talking about," she tells me.

"Are there hotels nearby? Maybe apartments or condos?"

"Sure," she nods.

"Thank you."

I'm on my phone getting directions by the time my feet hit the sidewalk. It turns out I don't really need them. It's so close I could have found it just by walking a little further down the boardwalk. Around me, I hear the sounds of people sinking deep into the promise of spring. It's not quite that time yet, though. The peak of spring break won't be for another month or so, and Beach Week will come another couple of months after that. But this is the sweet spot for locals and opportunistic vacationers willing to brave lower temperatures to also get lower crowds and lower costs. Later in the year, it will be too loud to hear the waves and the smell of fresh waffle cones won't be as strong as the alcohol in the air.

But there's still life. Still excitement. There's a hint of danger, but not the kind that makes my hand reach for the gun on my hip. It's the danger that comes with new teenagers trading the grains of sand they once pressed together into castles for extra seconds on their curfews, stacking them up and seeing how many minutes they can construct before it all comes crumbling down. The danger that comes with calling in sick to work to get on the road sooner, with skipping a day of school and avoiding questions from the teachers. The danger that comes with affairs in the hotel rooms and lust in the dunes.

I draw in a breath, my mind going to cream-colored tags and words that don't make sense.

It doesn't take long for me to get to the park and when I see the statue, I know it's what Jonah was talking about. People pause to snap pictures in front of it like they can't walk past it. But it's more than that. Beyond it, close enough to draw in visitors looking for another thrill, is the SkyWheel.

His voice echoes through my head. *The thing like the Eye.*

He knows I would immediately know what that means. It's another flex of his familiarity. He's slithering past what's on the outside, what people who see me on TV or have casually encountered me know about me, and into the center where I keep what I hold dear. He can't know the actual feeling that goes through me when I see the Eye, whether it's from a plane getting ready to land or as I'm driving down International Drive. But he knows it's an anchor point. It's something I would immediately recognize, and he's using the former name purposely. It isn't the Eye anymore. It's the Wheel. That doesn't change that it's planted right in the heart of somewhere I love dearly.

The mention of Florida was a tactical move. But this is what he was talking about. The enormous Ferris wheel, already lit up and glowing against the late afternoon horizon. It towers over the city like the other does in Orlando, offering those courageous enough to soar that high above the ground incomparable views of the area.

Jonah mentioned the girls were looking at it like they were planning to take that ride. I look around. If he was seeing them, he had to be close. I stare up into the windows of the hotels around me. Part of me is waiting for a chill, for the creeping feeling that goes through me when I know he's watching me. I want him to know I'm here, and yet, I don't.

Not until I know for sure where he is and can trap him.

My phone rings in my pocket. I take it out and see Sam's name on the screen.

"Hey, sweetie," I answer. "Sorry I had to go so suddenly. I just…"

"Don't worry about it," he says before I can figure out how to properly explain everything. "Where are you?"

"In Myrtle Beach," I tell him. "I told you."

"I know," he says. "But where in Myrtle Beach? Where are you?"

"I'm in Plyler Park. It's near the SkyWheel, right off the boardwalk. This is where he is."

"Okay. Stay there."

"What do you mean?"

"I just landed. I'll be there in five minutes."

ROBERT
PORTER

TEACHER, SON, FRIEND

CHAPTER FIFTEEN

I CAN'T HIDE MY SHOCK AS SAM JOGS ACROSS THE GRASS TOWARD ME a few minutes later.

"What are you doing?" I sputter.

"You got on a plane without packing and with nothing more than a voicemail to tell me what was going on. You seriously think I wasn't going to come?"

"I sent you an email, too," I point out.

"That just made it worse. I drove to DC and got a flight. What are you doing here?"

I realize he must have been on the road toward the airport almost instantly in order to be so close behind me. A direct flight from DC got him here less than two hours after I landed. I can't believe he went to that extent, but I also completely believe it. This is Sam.

"Jonah is here," I tell him. "I know it. I just have to figure out where."

I explain the entire situation and all the details I picked up on from the call with him. I point out the hotels close to the park.

"You think he's vacationing?" Sam asks.

"No. I think this is the most recent stop on his don't-get-caught tour. He's bouncing around, not staying anywhere for too long. Whenever he calls me or messages me, I try to listen for any sounds in the background or anything he says that might give away where he's been. It doesn't happen often. He's careful. But there have been a couple of times when he's mentioned things or I've heard sounds that give me clues. Nothing that has ever been enough to pinpoint it, though."

"Then why now? Why would he be so careless about giving those details this time?"

"Because he's on edge. He's worried about this conspiracy group. It's really throwing him off. I guess the idea of someone else having an illogical obsession is just too much for him," I say.

"Well, considering he knows where that kind of thing can lead, I would think it would be a touch disconcerting," Sam says.

"Which is why he called me. He said it wasn't about the cases he's trying to get me to handle. He doesn't want me doing anything high-profile. He knows about the case."

"With the tags?" Sam asks. "I thought that wasn't being released."

"It's not," I confirm. "But he mentioned me working on a serial killer case. Granted, that could just be using the past as a reference for the future, but it seems very convenient he called me while I was leaving the scene of the latest murder in a string. He knows what I'm doing, and he's using that as proof that these Seers can find me. He wants me to stay away from them. He was worked up enough to let details about this area slip." I look around again. "I just need to figure out the exact place."

"Or maybe he wanted to lure you here for a reason," Sam offers. "It's not like him to just slip."

"I'd considered that. But either way, he's here. I know he is. And I have to find him, whether he wants me here or not."

"Have you called the police?" he asks.

"No. And I'm not going to, Sam. Before you start arguing with me, this is mine. When the time comes, I'll get back up. For now, it's us," I say.

"It was going to be just you," Sam points out.

"What?" I ask.

"It was going to be just you. You're doing it again, Emma. You didn't know I was coming. You had no idea I was going to be here. You were going to do this by yourself. With everything that has happened, you were still going to confront him by yourself," he says.

There's anger in his voice, but it's weighed down and dampened by the worry and disappointment. Being on my own felt far more comfortable to me for a long time when I first joined the Bureau. I didn't want anyone too close. Even my friends. Even the man I was dating at the time, who thought we would spend our lives together. I whittled my world down to being just about myself and let the chaos in my mind take control.

It spiraled me out of reason. It stopped me from thinking things all the way through and doing them the way they should be done. I threw myself into danger. I trusted only myself and didn't bother with anyone. It nearly cost me my life several times.

I won't say I stick tight to the line now. I still do what others think I shouldn't do. I follow my instincts and my skills before protocol when I need to. But I've tried to lessen that. I keep my gun on my hip. I keep my phone in my pocket. Most of the time, there's a knife in the hidden pocket in my bra. My FBI credentials allow me to take both weapons on a plane with me, so I didn't have to stash either when I grabbed the spontaneous flight.

What I didn't bring with me was other people. I know I shouldn't do it this way. I shouldn't go into situations that could be hazardous with only myself. It's taken time, but I've learned to always think twice before investigating on my own in potentially dangerous situations in other cases. I bring Sam or Dean or I call the police. I do what I need to do to protect myself.

It's different with Jonah. He's a separate entity, an entirely unique circumstance. Jonah is mine. He's out because of me. He's a threat because of me. It's not up to anyone else to stop him. I don't want to put anyone at risk, but I also don't want to answer to anyone. I don't want to wait.

But I know Sam doesn't see it that way.

He sees me putting myself in danger. He thinks I'm doing exactly what the people I'm chasing want me to do. They want me alone, isolated, and vulnerable. He just doesn't understand that I don't feel vulnerable. I'm not afraid. I might be dangling above shark-infested water, but I won't flinch. I'll willingly let one swallow me whole and kill it from the inside.

"Did you take the picture?" I ask.

He glares at me for a second, obviously frustrated at me pushing the conversation forward without acknowledging his concerns. We'll talk about it later. I'll do everything I can to comfort and reassure him. For now, this is what I need to do.

Sam reaches in his pocket and takes out his phone. He pulls up an image and shows it to me.

"What does this have to do with anything?"

"When I first saw the note, I noticed something on the back," I explain. "This piece of paper was torn from a larger one that had something printed on it. There isn't much left, but I think it could mean something."

"Like what?"

I turn the phone around to different angles so I can examine the image. Sam had put the note face down on the kitchen table when he took the picture, which lets me see the full piece. One edge of the note is slightly fuzzy from where it was carefully torn. It makes me think about being in school and folding pieces of paper, then running my fingernail down the seam to make it as sharp as possible so the paper would tear into a smooth, even piece. I can see Jonah doing the same thing.

I know you, Emma.

"Right here," I show him, pointing out the teal ink on the edge of the note. "The way the paper was torn makes it look like this is the top of a piece of stationery or letterhead. The ink is a logo or the name of a company. Maybe a hotel. It's just the top of it, but it could help us find where he was."

"He left that note in December. You really think he would stay in the same hotel for that long?" Sam wonders.

"We don't actually know that he left it in December," I point out. "As a matter of fact, I can pretty confidently say he didn't. Remember, when he left that note on the front porch on Christmas Eve, it said that my Christmas gift was delayed, but it was coming. If he had hidden that ornament in the front yard at the same time, why would he say it was delayed? He put that out in the yard at some point after Christmas. I didn't get around to taking down those decorations until the beginning of February. He could have put it in there any time between Christmas and then."

"Which means he was watching the house," Sam says.

"Or at least had some way of paying attention. And if I don't miss my guess, the ornament wasn't the only plan he had. I'm sure if he'd gotten to Sherwood and found all the decorations gone, he would have had something else to hide."

Sam seems to think about this for a second, then shakes his head.

"Why would he be so careless? He takes so much effort to cover up where he is, but then uses a piece of stationery from the hotel where he's staying to leave a note? That doesn't sound like him."

"It sounds exactly like him. It isn't carelessness. It's arrogance. He didn't think I would notice. Or at least that I wouldn't be able to piece it together. "

I look around, taking in all the signs and logos of the hotels, condos, and other buildings within close enough range for Jonah to be looking out the window and see the spot where I'm standing. I don't see anything that looks exactly right. Frustration builds inside me. Then I remember the next part of what he told me about the women he was watching through the window.

I look around until I see the closest sidewalk that leads to one of the hotels. He described them walking around the building and that the direction they were going indicated which side of the hotel they were staying in. I explain this to Sam as I take off toward the sidewalk, following it at a quick enough pace to keep my mind from chasing out in front of me. I struggle to keep myself from breaking out into a run. I don't want to alarm anyone around who might be watching.

My clothes already stand out against the crowd of vacationers in bathing suits and Hawaiian shirts. Anyone paying attention would be able to see my gun. It's already enough to put people on edge. I don't want to cause even more trouble for myself by making a scene. Or possibly worse, by intriguing people drunk on either brightly colored drinks or the inhibition of travel enough to follow me and take out their phones to chronicle my every movement.

The description Jonah gave and the way the sidewalk moves away from the park only gives one clear option of a hotel. Nothing about it matches the logo on the paper, but I can't see any other option. This has to be where he is.

CHAPTER SIXTEEN

SMASHING DOWN THE DOOR WOULD HAVE BEEN MORE SATISFYING. The feeling of my boot making contact with wood and splintering it away from the frame is always a rush. It gives emphasis. Punctuation to the message I'm sending to whomever is on the other side of the door.

But I don't get that moment. The manager at the desk confirms to my badge and not my face that someone by the name of Ian Griffin is staying on the eighth floor in an ocean view room. The badge doesn't earn me possession of a key to the room, but the manager agrees to come up with us and open it with a master key.

She reaches out to knock when we get there and I cringe at the pleasantry. Her announcement of our presence is almost laughable. I wonder if she expects him to sing out a cheerful "come in," or if she just thinks he will come to the door and swing it open. I have to remind myself that she has no idea what's at stake here, but it doesn't do much to calm my racing nerves.

The silence from the room feels like a taunt. It takes far too long for the manager to swipe the key card and open the door. The instant it's open, I barge in with my gun in my hand and my heart in my throat.

Everything is quiet. There's no sign of Jonah, or anyone, in the space. The suite is divided into separate areas with double doors in an antique shade of dusty pink separating the living area and small kitchenette from the bedroom. I go to the bedroom doors and lean my ear against the crack between them to try to hear movement on the other side. Nudging them open with my shoulder, I sweep my gun through the space. There are a few items on the surfaces. A cup on the side table, a discarded food wrapper on the table. Enough to show there was once a person here.

My anger and adrenaline make the edges of my thoughts blurry as I stalk across the room to the closed bathroom door. It opens to the smell of body wash and aftershave but nothing else. The closet is empty except for an empty plastic garment bag with a receipt from the hotel's laundry service. I tear it down furiously.

"Shit!"

Sam lets out a frustrated sigh, stepping toward me to try to comfort me.

Shoving my gun back into its holster, I stalk over to the desk and open the drawer.

"When are these rooms cleaned?" I ask.

"This room isn't," the manager replies. "There's a note in the system specifically requesting no housekeeping services. Mr. Griffin put it in when he checked in. He occasionally requests towels and fresh linens, but he doesn't want to be disturbed. He noted he's here on business and needs to be allowed to work."

The short, bitter laugh that comes out of my mouth feels like bile in my throat.

Inside the drawer, I find a stack of letterhead and stationery from different hotels. My hand tightens around them, but I stop myself from ripping them into the tiny shreds I want to.

"The man staying here was not Ian Griffin," I tell her. I touch my hand to the coffeemaker. "It's still warm. He was just fucking here."

"What do you mean it wasn't Ian Griffin?"

I whip around to face her. "It wasn't Ian Griffin. The man staying here who asked that you don't have your housekeepers interrupt him was not Ian Griffin." I take out my phone and pull up a picture of my father. "This is Ian Griffin. Notice the scar and you can tell the difference. Know anything about either of them and you can tell even better. Ian Griffin is in Virginia right now. He hasn't been anywhere near here."

"Mr. Griffin checked in with a credit card and an ID. That's standard procedure for all guests."

"Those were fraudulent," I tell her. Fury pulses inside me again. "That motherf—" I take a deep breath and exhale. "He knew exactly what he was doing."

My eyes land on the doors to the balcony and I run out onto it, scanning the ground and everything I can see from the vantage point. He has to be close. The heat of the coffee and the smell in the bathroom would only linger for so long. Jonah got out of the room just before I got into it, and that means he's still close.

"Close down the hotel," Sam tells the manager. "No one leaves. It needs to be searched."

"Sir, the guests, I can't…"

"Yes, you fucking can," I tell her through gritted teeth. "I don't care if the Queen and all of her corgis are taking up the top level of this hotel throwing a rager with tea-filled kegs for diplomats from every known nation on this planet, you are putting security at every exit and not allowing anyone to leave until this building has been searched."

My phone rings and I snatch it out of my pocket.

"Griffin," I bark into it.

"You were close, Emma. Very close."

The sound of Jonah's voice coming through the phone makes heat surge up my face until it feels like my skin is going to bubble and peel away. I turn back onto the balcony and walk to the edge.

"Where are you?" I growl.

"You know, it's always better to take the stairs when you can. It's good for your cardiovascular health."

"Where are you, Jonah?" I demand.

"Your hair is getting long. It suits you. I always liked your mother with longer hair."

Behind me Sam is on the phone with the local police, calling for a team to come and search the hotel. I stay on the balcony, my hand so tight around the wrought iron edge I can feel it cutting into my skin.

"You did this on purpose."

"It's a nice view, isn't it? I always ask for a balcony. I think it adds so much to the room. It's a wonderful place to drink coffee and look out over the ocean. Or people watch. You never know who you are going to see strolling around beneath you."

I stare down, my eyes frantically surveying the entire area beneath me. I look at every face, search every person, trying to find one who looks even vaguely familiar. Someone who moves like him or stands like him.

"What the hell are you doing? What is this?"

Sam comes out onto the balcony beside me.

"How valiant of your knight in shining armor to make sure you're not alone," Jonah crows, the cruelty in his voice increasing with every teasing, prodding comment. "He wouldn't want you in danger, either, you know. Doesn't that mean anything to you?"

"Don't you dare talk about Sam," I seethe.

"Is that him?" Sam asks, sounding both shocked and angry.

"You wanted me here so much, you step out and show yourself, coward," I demand.

I'm pacing back and forth along the balcony like a caged animal. Rage makes every inch of my body sting and tingle, and my vision red around the edges.

"Where is he?" Sam asks. He leans over the edge like I did, trying to find him. He cranes his neck, looking at the roof of the building beside us, checking corners and walkways.

"I'm not a coward, Emma. I'm in charge. I'm in control. You need to remember that. I told you to get away from the cities, to stay out of the spotlight. But you couldn't. You have to be in the middle of everything. You don't care who can see you, who wants to find you. You think you know who's around you, but you don't. I am in control, Emma. This is my game."

"This is not a fucking game!" I scream into the phone.

He laughs under his breath. "But you'll play. Because you have to."

"I don't have to do anything, Jonah. I'm not your tool."

"We made an agreement. You gave me your word."

Sam grabs onto my arm. "Emma."

I follow where he's pointing. A figure has stepped from behind the statue in the park. From the distance, I can't see features. But I can see the shape of the body and the way he's standing. I can see he's holding a phone and appears to be looking directly at me.

Without another word, I run off the balcony and through the room, out into the hallway, and down the steps so fast my feet nearly buckle beneath me. My phone is back in my pocket and my hand is on my gun. When I reach the bottom, I see security standing beside the door. The man steps slightly in front of me, holding up his hand.

"No one leaves," he says. "I'm under orders to keep this door shut and not allow anyone to leave."

I pull out my badge and show it to him.

"You're under my orders. Get out of my way."

He steps aside just before I kick the center bar of the door to open it and run out. Being down on the ground rather than looking at it from above is slightly disorienting, but I run in the direction we came. I don't care who sees me. I don't care if they notice my gun.

Before I'm at the statue, I can see Jonah isn't there anymore. There's a group of smiling couples trying to fit themselves into one picture on one side and a small child trying to climb up onto it on the other. As I descend on the statue, the child's mother scoops him up and the couples scatter. I whip around, my eyes slicing through the crowd, trying to find him. He was just here. I saw him.

I look up at the hotel and see Sam still on the balcony. He's pointing to the side and I run in that direction. The people in the park split to let me through, but I can't see Jonah anywhere. I stop, spinning around rapidly, trying to find him. But he's gone.

I take my ringing phone out of my pocket.

"You aren't going to find me, Emma," Jonah says. "I told you, I'm in control. I brought you here. You are going to uphold your end of this agreement. Until what needs to be done is finished, I stay out."

"Emma," Sam calls to me from somewhere behind me, but I don't know where he is.

The rage has washed over me in such a torrent I feel like I'm losing grip.

"I'm done!" I scream into the phone. "I told you before. You're on your own. I'm not doing this anymore. I don't care what you want. You didn't allow me to take you in the first time, and I don't need your permission or help this time. I will hunt you down. I don't care how long it takes."

I feel Sam's arms wrap around me, squeezing me close to him. I fight against them instinctively, not wanting to be held. He only holds me closer, pulling me away from where I'm standing and back toward the hotel.

"Happy St. Patrick's Day, Emma. May the luck of the Irish be with you."

"You sick son of a bitch!" I shout, still struggling against Sam. "Come out and face me."

I know he's not there anymore. Sam takes the phone from my hand and puts it in his own pocket. That's when I realize he's gotten me out of the park and I'm back on the walkway to the hotel. People around us watch as he ushers me to the door and puts me in the elevator. I rest my cheek against the cool metal of the interior, waiting to either pass out or feel better. My knees finally give and I crouch down close to the floor, my hands buried in my hair behind my head.

"He did this on purpose," I mutter into my thighs. "I am so stupid."

"You're not stupid, Emma," Sam says.

I look up at him. "I let him manipulate me again. He mentioned a store I used to go to all the time and said he saw a woman holding a bag from there and that she'd just bought something. He knew I would know the name of the store and where he was, but I went to the store. I talked to the owner. They don't use bags with the name anymore. They just use plain black bags. He wouldn't know it was from that store. He made it up. He talked about the statue and the wheel. He left just enough bread-crumbs for me to follow him right to his gingerbread house. He knew I was going to figure it out. He made sure I did. I was either going to end up here or in Orlando."

"Why would he do that?" Sam asks.

"To get me away from the Seers and the serial killer case. To make sure that I could do as he says and focus completely on what he wants me to do. He wants me to chase him so no one can chase me." I let out an exasperated sound. "I fell for it. I can't believe I am so stupid to fall for that."

"Listen to me. You aren't stupid. You didn't fall for anything. You did what you do. Whether you want to give him that power or not, you are wired to fight. You're wired to unravel problems and make things right, to do everything you can to scrub the earth of the people who don't deserve to be walking on the streets. Or at least to put them in cages where they belong. You can't help that."

"But I let him get under my skin."

"He lives under your skin," Sam says. "And he'll stay there until this is over."

"I am going to end this," I say. "I am tired of him. I'm tired of his manipulation. I'm tired of his interference. I'm tired of never really being able to rest because I'm waiting for the next moment he's going to show up and fuck something up for me. I'm tired of it."

"I know you are."

"I've given up enough of myself for him. He's defined me for too long. Even before I knew he existed, he was a part of me and my story. I'm done with that. I have far too much to think about, far too much to do to give up more of my life to his whims. I won't chase him. I won't do his dirty work to keep him on the end of a line he thinks he can control. And I won't bite at his cryptic little messages."

"Cryptic messages?" Sam asks.

I nod, taking a step toward the elevator door that has just opened. "He doesn't use riddles, but that doesn't mean he hasn't mastered the art of being vague as hell. He likes to see if he can make me scramble to get to the point of it. This time he wished me a Happy St. Patrick's Day. Luck of the Irish and some other nonsense. That's not even for another few weeks."

"I don't think you need to look hard to find the meaning behind that," Sam says.

He reaches into his pocket and pulls something out, holding it up so it dangles in front of me. I step out of the elevator and take it from his hand.

"What's that?" I ask.

"It was hanging from the statue," he tells me. "A woman nearby said the guy on the phone asked her to tell 'Sam or Emma' to take it."

I look down at the necklace in my hand. The delicate silver chain draped across my palm holds a small round pendant. Encircled with a delicate band of gold, the resin inside glints in the overhead light. Inside is a preserved four-leaf clover.

"It's Miley Stanford's," I say, touching my fingertip to the pendant. "I saw it in a picture of her."

CHAPTER SEVENTEEN

I T TAKES THE NEXT COUPLE OF HOURS TO STRAIGHTEN EVERYTHING out at the hotel and file reports with the local police. I call Eric to catch him up on what's going on and make sure everyone involved in the investigation into Jonah's escape is kept up to date on the details.

By the time it's all finished, Sam and I are starving and exhausted. The manager offers us a room and I take her up on it gratefully. After what she, the guests, and the staff just went through, I would have understood if she let Sam and I know in no uncertain terms that we weren't welcome on the premises.

Instead, she made sure we had a comfortable room and pointed out the room service menus to us. We eat to the sound of each other breathing and the TV droning on. I don't even know what's on the screen. It doesn't matter. I only have it on so the sound can fill the silence and I won't be tempted to fill it myself.

Not right now. Right now, I need to think.

Sam is asleep within seconds of me turning off the lights in the room, but I lie awake beside him for a few more minutes. I stare through the balcony doors we have open so I can listen to the sound of the waves. I can also hear people still out on the boardwalk, laughing and cheering without a care in the world. At the very edge of my plane of vision, I can see the glow of the lights from the SkyWheel.

I think about the necklace carefully wrapped in a handkerchief and stowed in the corner of my bag. I wonder how Jonah got ahold of it and what he knows about it. I know he's waiting for me to ask. And I know I won't.

Early the next morning, we board a flight back to Virginia. We'll fly into DC together and I'll ride with Sam back to the airport where I left my car. It'll give us at least a few more hours of quiet together.

By the time we get back to my car, I already have a series of messages from Detective Mavis and the chief. They have information to share with me. It's time to get back to this case.

I kiss Sam goodbye, promise to keep him updated, and head to the Parson police station.

"I'm sorry for the delay," I announce as I walk into the room I'm using as my office. Both men are waiting for me at the conference table. "I needed to handle something about another investigation. So, what do you have for me?"

I sit down and make eye contact with each of them, waiting for one to start the conversation.

"We heard from the victim's mother this morning," Chief Calvert tells me.

I nod. "I was able to call her yesterday but could only leave a brief message. I've been out of contact since then."

"Yes. She mentioned she attempted to call you, but you didn't answer. So she got in contact with us. We made the official death notification to her and asked some basic questions about her daughter. I know you specifically instructed that you didn't want any interviews being done without your approval, but this was standard background information. Nothing intrusive. Just finding out basic aspects of her daily life, her relationships, that sort of thing."

I nod again. "Alright. These are still things that I would like to be a part of because there are specific questions I need answered, but I appreciate you taking the initiative to get the ball rolling. What did you find out?"

"The last time she spoke with Paisley was the night before her murder. They have a fairly close relationship and communicate regularly.

Usually, every other day at least. Mrs. Graham said she didn't sound upset or strange in any way. She didn't mention being worried about anything or scared. It was a perfectly normal conversation. She didn't say she had any plans that night or that she was going to be going out. As a matter of fact, her mother said it sounded like she was planning on just having a quiet night in and going to bed early."

"They have the same last name. Was Paisley married?" I ask.

"No," Calvert says. "She was several years ago, but she got divorced. She changed her name back to her maiden name right after."

"I'm guessing that means the end of the marriage was fairly contentious?" I ask.

I often find that women who change their names when they get married hang onto their married names, even after the divorce. Especially if they've been married for more than a short time, they will have established themselves under that name. It can be unduly complicated and frustrating to go through shedding that name and reasserting herself with her maiden name, not to mention a bureaucratic nightmare.

For some people, it's worth it. They want that reassertion. They want to communicate to the world—and to themselves—that whoever they were during their marriage is no longer who they will be in the future. It's a sign of showing that they are an independent person, not tied to their husband's identity.

For others, they feel like that name is theirs, for better or worse. They feel that shedding it is almost akin to giving up a piece of themselves after the marriage, like their former husbands lent it to them only on the condition they stayed married, but now that they weren't their wives any longer, they took it back. Like getting stripped of your uniform after being fired from work.

In a way, it's like the opposite of what I've done. I changed my last name to Johnson after getting married, but in my professional sphere, I still use Griffin. That's how I'm already known and it makes it far easier to divide up the two parts of my life. Griffin is now a title, right along with "Agent."

"It was," Calvert confirms. "But her ex died in a car crash almost a year ago, so he's not a suspect."

"Well, at least that's an avenue down," I note.

"And it doesn't leave many other options. Apparently, she was very popular."

"That's not exactly unusual in murder victims," I tell him. "Once someone is killed, everyone suddenly remembers all the wonderful things about them and the bad things disappear. They become the kindest, sweetest, most beautiful, and most loving person to have ever crossed paths with their friends and family, and no one can even begin to imagine what could have happened to make someone want to hurt them."

I don't mean to sound cynical or unfeeling. That's just the reality of the situation. In my career, I've encountered countless families and groups of friends who have lost someone. With very few exceptions, it's always the same. Particularly in the earliest days after the murder, everyone who was a part of the victim's life clings to the most positive aspects of that person and their relationship with them.

Whether it's because it takes away some of the pain to only think about the good things, or because they feel guilty thinking anything even somewhat negative about someone who has met a cruel and unfair fate, the people closest to a victim are often some of the most unreliable when it comes to actually gauging who they were and how they impacted the world around them.

This tends to shift as the investigation continues and a more realistic picture of the victim will emerge. Right now, I'll need to sift through all of what I hear about Paisley and try to determine what is the most accurate depiction. Something as simple as uncovering a feud with someone in the neighborhood, a bad breakup, or a bad habit can shed light on details of a victim's life that help point the investigation in the right direction. I don't expect her mother to tell me about a neighbor she's arguing with over pine sap dripping onto a car and have that solve the murder for me, but the more I know about her as a person, the more directions I'll have to go in my search.

"That's definitely the truth," Detective Mavis says. "But this time, I think it's actually true."

"Did you interview someone?" I ask.

I wouldn't put it past him to have "not heard" my instructions, or to just think he was doing what he should do because I wasn't there.

"No," he says. "But someone who already has a candlelight vigil planned for them less than twenty-four hours after they're murdered can't be all bad."

"A candlelight vigil?" I raise an eyebrow.

The chief nods. "Her mother said a member of the church group Paisley attended got in touch with her and said they are planning a memorial and celebration of Paisley's life for tomorrow evening."

"How did Mrs. Graham feel about that?" I ask.

"She was touched, obviously. She says Paisley had been talking about her parish over the last couple of months. She hadn't been very involved in the church for years, but recently decided she wanted more direction in her life. She was struggling a lot with her ex-husband's death, even though the divorce was nasty. The group apparently gave her the support she was looking for, and she'd made a lot of friends."

"Can you send me the details for the vigil?" I ask.

"Absolutely."

"Thank you. I asked that all information about the tags on the victims be kept strictly confidential, so I'm assuming you didn't ask her anything that might have involved that detail."

"Right," Calvert nods. "I didn't mention the tag or the word."

"I appreciate that. I'll talk to her about it when I go to meet with her. But as far as either of you know, there's nothing about her, her life, her habits, anything that might make the word 'Gluttony' make sense?" I ask.

"No," they both respond.

"She was in great shape," adds Calvert. "There wasn't anything on her person or in her immediate surroundings that made any connection. Her mother didn't mention anything. I can have my team search her social media and see if they find anything."

"Please do," I tell him. "But don't contact any of her friends."

"Of course."

"Thank you. I'll be in touch if I need anything," I say. I gather up the written notes they've given me. "I'll be accessible. I'll likely be back in the area tomorrow."

I leave, but instead of making my way back to Sherwood, I head for Breyer.

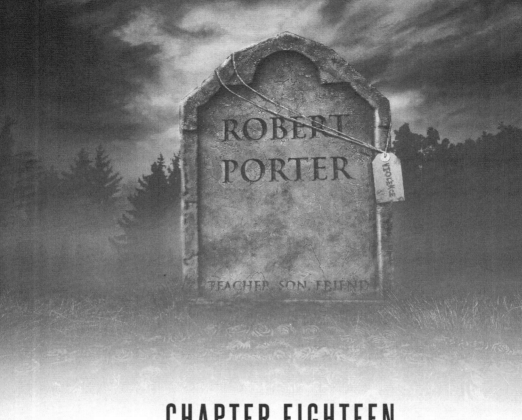

CHAPTER EIGHTEEN

T HE MESSAGE FROM LOUISE CAME AS A SURPRISE, BUT I'M NOT
going to waste time and risk her and the others she mentioned losing their interest in talking to me.

I follow my GPS instructions to the address she gave me in Breyer
and find a small, welcoming-looking home. Even in the cold gray of
in-between winter and spring, the lawn looks loved and tended. A
flower garden flanking either side of the cement stoop has tiny buds of
flowers in front of the box hedges, ready to come up in a few weeks and
fill the space with an explosion of color.

I point them out from the porch when Louise opens the front door.

"I love your flower beds," I tell her. "My husband made some for
me back home and I think I've managed to kill every variety of flower
meant to grow well in the Virginia climate."

"Eggshells," a voice says from the depths of the house behind her.

"I'll have to give that a shot."

Louise steps back and gestures for me to come inside. The home feels as warm and comfortable as it looks. There's a deep, rich smell coming from the back of the house where I assume the kitchen is, and a TV show several years older than I am playing in the background. It almost feels like when I would visit my grandparents as a small child.

They weren't always the most conventional of grandparents, and I found out the extent to which that went the older I got, but one thing I could always rely on about my grandfather was that when evening would roll around, he was going to find his place in the yellow and green recliner in the living room, prop up his feet in his favorite slippers, and watch episodes of shows he watched when he was young.

Those slippers are actually one of my earliest memories. In it, I can't remember his face. All I remember is the sound of his voice singing along to the theme of an old detective show and his feet bouncing on the footrest of the recliner in those slippers. He often talked about how well made they were and that they were going to last forever because he wore them all the time and he never had to throw them away.

What he didn't know was my grandmother noticed his devotion to the specific style and brand early on and bought up several pairs. She rotated them regularly so they always felt broken in but didn't wear out. After he died, she gathered them all up and put them in his recliner. That was the first time I saw her cry.

"Thank you for being willing to come out here," Louise says. "I don't get a lot of time off, and when I do, I like to be home."

"No, thank you," I say. "I really appreciate you having me in your home. And for being willing to talk to me more."

"Come in and sit," she says, gesturing to a blue corduroy sofa. A polished coffee table sitting in front holds a platter of cookies and a pot of coffee. "Help yourself."

Looking at the homemade cookies makes me realize how hungry I am, and I eagerly reach for one, taking a couple of bites before pouring myself some coffee.

Two men come into the room from the back of the house. One is holding a bowl of nuts that he places next to the cookies. They both look familiar.

"This is Peter, and this is Angelo. They worked for Marini as well," Louise says.

"Hello," I say.

They both greet me and sit down in chairs opposite the couch. Louise takes a spot at the end of the couch and turns to me with a serious expression.

"We want to help," she says.

"Good," I nod. "I appreciate that."

"But we need to know what's going on."

The declaration cut off what I was about to say and I have to swallow down the next words with a bite of warm pecan sandie.

"Alright," I say. "What do you mean?"

"You know what we mean," she replies. "No one is telling us why there's so much fuss over his death. Or even why he was going to prison."

"He didn't tell you?" I ask.

She shakes her head. "That would require him to have a conversation with any of us. That wasn't something he did. All we know is we were fired because he was going to self-surrender to prison. He gave no details and we haven't been able to find out anything."

"The only things we've been able to find about him online are about his death," Angelo adds. "I can't find any details online. Just that he took a deal that prevents the information from being public. I didn't know that was legal. I thought everything like that was public record."

"There are some shady areas," I admit. "What I can tell you is that he was going to prison for a very long time, but that the crime he was self-surrendering for was not the only element of our investigation."

"That's not enough," Louise says.

"Not enough?"

"We know something big had to have happened," Peter says. "Marini was a powerful man. He was rich and people did what he said. People like that don't end up in jail unless there was something big. And the FBI doesn't go after them even after they're dead for no reason."

"We worked for him for years," Angelo says. "Whatever he was a part of, it was happening right around us. We deserve to know."

"And to make sure our names aren't linked up with any of it," Louise adds. "Eventually, things come out. You can't keep everything a secret forever. People are going to know what he did, and if they know we worked for him, they might think we had something to do with it. I don't want my future at risk because of him. I already had to deal with him ruining enough. If he was smuggling something or selling drugs or embezzling, it might fall back on us, and I can't have that."

The three nod at each other. It seems they've already discussed this at length. They came to the agreement they would continue to cooperate if I was willing to give them the details of what happened. They already knew Marini was an awful person to work for. They just wanted to know what kind of monster they were really dealing with.

The trouble is, they can't even imagine.

I'm torn about telling them. The details have been kept extremely closely guarded and so far haven't been leaked. But there are no legal barriers stopping me. Nothing is formally keeping me from telling them. The police investigation into Marini's death is officially closed and eventually, the details of the Emperor's crimes will come forward, just like they said.

Something of this magnitude doesn't just stay buried. Victims are going to be identified, families will be notified, further investigation will be needed. If everything was kept so secretive, there would never be answers.

Finally, I decide to tell them.

"Marini wasn't going to prison for theft or embezzlement or drugs or smuggling," I start. "Not specifically, anyway. We may still under-cover elements of all of those crimes as well."

"What's that mean?" Louise says.

"What I'm going to tell you isn't going to be easy to hear. You'll have to understand that I can't share every detail of the story. There are things I'm going to leave out and questions I'm not going to be able to answer. And I have to ask that you not discuss this with anyone else. Please keep in mind there is an active investigation with the Bureau and it could be severely damaged if this information falls into the wrong hands. Do I have your discretion?"

They all nod and I take a breath. Setting my coffee down on the table in front of me, I start the story.

CHAPTER NINETEEN

"HOLY SHIT," PETER WHISPERS.

His eyes are wide and it seems he hasn't blinked in the couple of minutes since I stopped talking.

Angelo is shaking his head, glancing every few seconds over at Louise, where she sits with her hands over her mouth. Tears have pooled in her eyes and her cheeks have gone red as she fights the emotions washing over her.

"We didn't have anything to do with any of that," Angelo finally says. "Nothing."

"We didn't know," Louise says.

I shake my head, holding up my hands to stop them before they continue.

"You don't need to worry. No one thinks you did. Everything from our investigation so far shows he did this very carefully and very separately away from the rest of his life. The Emperor was his alter ego. He went to great lengths to make sure those activities didn't interfere with his daily life. None of you, none of any of the staff, are considered related in any way," I reassure them.

"Thank God," Peter says.

"I just can't believe what I just heard," Angelo says. "I knew he was horrible. But…it makes me sick to think about any of that actually happening."

I'm glad I kept some of the details to myself, knowing they would be too much for them to take. They were difficult for me to stomach, and I barely had any interactions with the man. I only met him a few times. These were people who had worked with him for years. Though they weren't friendly by any stretch of the imagination, the idea of being in close proximity on a regular basis with someone capable of doing the things he did is difficult to take.

"How could I not have known?" Louise wonders aloud. "I was there at his house every day. I saw him. I spoke with him. Maybe it wasn't much, but…"

"Louise, I need you to hear this when I say it to you. There's nothing you could have done about this. And there's no reason you should have known. I know that's hard to wrap your head around, and you think you should have somehow intuitively been able to tell there was something wrong about him. But I promise you, that is not the case.

"You don't just automatically know these things about people because you are in the same space with them every day. People like him are masters at hiding what they do. Part of the joy and the fulfillment for him was to be able to go about his normal life, working, engaging with other people, earning admiration and respect from people, all the while carrying on with this other half of his existence no one knew about. He prided himself in being able to cover that up and never let it show.

"The fact that you couldn't suspect anything like that was going on just shows that you don't have the capacity for evil that he did. No one should be able to think that way. The kinds of things he did should never cross a person's mind. You are not to blame. None of you are to blame. I'm not asking for your help because I think you need to make up for something, or that you did something to contribute to this. I'm only asking because you were the ones who were in his orbit. You knew things about his daily activities and his life that might be able to clear some things up."

I want to tell her what I know, what I've been through, but the space doesn't feel right for it. Enough of the air in the room has already been taken up with horrific words and images none of us will ever be able to rid from our minds. I'm only glad those images are only in their imaginations. I have many of them etched in my memory.

"When did all this start?" Peter asks.

"We can't be absolutely sure. There's still a tremendous amount of investigating to do to get all the details straight. I'm positive there are still many victims that haven't been found or identified, and until we can do that, we won't know for sure when this happened or what started it. But I became aware of it because of one specific death."

I take out my phone and bring up a few pictures. Turning the screen toward them, I first show an image of Serena. "Do you know this woman?"

I turn the phone so each of them can see the picture clearly. They all shake their heads.

"No," Louise says. "She doesn't look familiar. It's not one of the women he used to bring around."

"So, he would bring women around?" I ask.

"Yes. we usually didn't see the same one more than a couple of times, and there were never any introductions. He would bring them by for drinks before they went to the opera or some gala. Sometimes they would come back afterward and go right to his suite. I wouldn't call any of them a relationship. That wasn't what he was in it for."

I nod. Those words are significant. I remember the way he talked about Serena. There were feelings there. He thought she was special. That would make him even angrier when he found out the truth about her.

I change the picture to one of Miley Stanford, the woman who Serena was pretending to be and who has—as of now—remained missing.

"How about her?"

Louise and Peter shake their heads immediately just like they did with Serena, but I notice Angelo hesitate for a moment. It's only brief, but there's a flicker across his face. An expression like he wants to say something. But he rethinks it and shakes his head like the others.

"No," he says.

"Are you sure? She doesn't look like any of the women you saw around here?" I ask.

"No," they all confirm again.

"Alright," I say, disappointed not to have gotten at least some confirmation of recognition. "How much do you know about the house? Would you know if there are things like safes or vaults? Anything where he might have hidden things?"

"Yes," Louise says immediately. "There are several in the house. But none of us have access to any of them. He didn't allow the staff to know passcodes or anything else. We weren't even in the room when he would open them. To say he made it very clear we weren't trusted would be an understatement."

"I can see that," I nod. "And you have no idea what he kept in them?"

"I'd assume the usual things," Angelo says. "Money. Jewelry. Documents."

It's the documents I'm particularly interested in. I make a note in my mind to get a warrant for the safes and vaults. It might take creative convincing to get a judge to grant me the ability to open them, but I need to know what's in there. There would be one way to work around that, though.

"What happens to his estate now?" I ask. "Do you know who his beneficiary would be?"

"I don't know," Louise says. "As I said, we didn't have a close relationship with him. We didn't know much about his personal life. I know he didn't have children and was never married. I would assume he had a will, but I don't know who he would have left everything to."

"Not knowing who inherits also means we don't know who is in actual control of his house and possessions," I say. "Which might make further investigation more complicated."

"If we find out anything, we'll let you know," she tells me. "I can ask around to see if anyone knows about any family or anything."

"Thank you," I say. "Just remember to not share any of the details I gave you."

"Of course."

"Is there anything else we can help you with?" Peter asks.

"No, I think that's it for right now. Thank you. I really appreciate you taking the time to talk with me."

I let my eyes linger on Angelo for a moment, trying one last time to wrestle something, anything out of the group. "Is there anything else any of you can think of?"

They shake their heads. I nod, feeling a little defeated. "Well, if you think of anything, please don't hesitate to get in touch with me. I'm around."

At Louise's insistence, I finish my coffee and take a couple of cookies for the road. With them sitting on the seat beside me, I make my way to the police station.

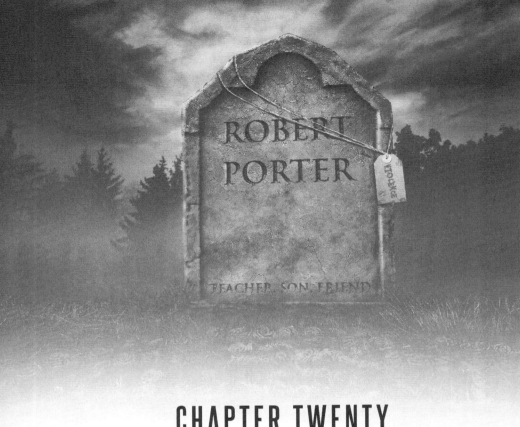

CHAPTER TWENTY

"EMMA, WE'VE GONE OVER THIS. THE INVESTIGATION INTO SALVADOR MARINI'S DEATH IS CLOSED," DETECTIVE WHEELER SAYS, WALKING AROUND HIS DESK AND SITTING DOWN HEAVILY. "THE MAN HAD A HEART ATTACK. AND WHO COULD REALLY BLAME HIM? AFTER EVERYTHING HE DID, KNOWING THE WELCOMING COMMITTEE AT FEDERAL PRISON WAS WAITING WOULD GIVE ANYONE A HEART ATTACK."

"I've told you, I don't think he just had a heart attack. There's more to it than that," I insist.

Simon comes over and I can see in her eyes she's not happy to see me there. It isn't personal. She and I get along fine. She's just as tired as Wheeler is of going over this with me again and again. She wants it behind her. Serena's death was hard on her. It was her first case of that magnitude and having to face a woman frozen to the ground who then spent nearly a year in the morgue without a name or an identity dug deep into her. In a lot of ways, it seems she is still struggling to recover from it.

But I can't be gentle with her. And I can't let my longstanding friendship with Wheeler cloud my judgment and make me simply trust what he says. I'm more convinced than ever that Marini didn't just drop dead of a heart attack. There's something more to it.

"Hey, Agent Griffin," she says. "I thought we were overdue for your next visit about a closed case."

I turn a withering glare in her direction and she immediately steps back. We're not that familiar.

Turning back to Wheeler, I lay it all out for him.

"I want everything," I say. "If this case isn't going any further here, I want everything you have about him. Medical examiner reports, autopsy photos and notes, statements. Everything."

"Emma," he starts, but I flatten my hands on his desk and lean toward him.

"This is out of your hands. I'm sorry. I tried to keep you in the loop because I know it meant something to you, but I can't keep scrambling around trying to get you to cooperate. The Bureau will handle this now. You might have the authority to declare the investigation closed here in Breyer, but you don't have that power with the FBI. You can't stop us. He killed in more than one state. He conspired to kidnap and traffic human beings, and engaged in torture and imprisonment. Not to mention attempting to kill an FBI agent. There's more than enough here for us to sink our teeth nice and deep."

"Then why did you even bother to talk to us?" Simon asks.

I look over at her, my eyes scanning her carefully before landing on his.

"Courtesy." I turn my attention back to Wheeler. "You've been there since the beginning of this investigation. Your information and insights might be helpful. But if you aren't going to be a part of it, I'll relieve you of it. Get me everything."

I walk out of the station and get into my car. My personal phone shows a missed call from Eric, so I call him back.

"What are you doing?" he asks.

"Leaving the Breyer police station. I was talking to Wheeler about Marini, trying to convince him to look deeper into it. But he says it's closed, so it's all about us now."

"I really need to get someone to check my business cards for me," he comments.

I make a face at the phone even though he can't see me.

"Why?"

"Because I could seriously swear they say I'm the one in the superior position and should be making decisions like that, but clearly they must have been printed wrong," he says.

"Do you not want to investigate his death?" I ask.

"I do," he says.

"Then stop throwing your tantrum."

"I should be allowed to throw a little bit of a tantrum."

"Alright. A little one. Go ahead," I say. He whines and complains for a couple seconds. "You done?"

"Yes," he admits with a chuckle.

"Feel better?"

"I do. And it's actually good timing. I happen to be in possession of the reports from the fitness tracker. And it seems like there is some pretty interesting information on it."

"Really?" I ask. "Like what?"

"Just some inconsistencies. Changes in his respiration and heart rate. Indication of erratic activity. Stuff like that. I'll send the report over to you to look at."

"Thanks. I'm going to be at Dean's tonight, but then I have to head back up tomorrow. If I can think of anything else, I'll let you know."

We get off the phone and I drive to Xavier's house. Dean's car is in the driveway and I use my key to let myself in. I can hear him in the kitchen, and when I go in, I find him leaning over a massive mixing bowl, seemingly investigating what's inside. I stand there for several seconds waiting for him to acknowledge me, but he's just poring over the thing without so much as a glance in my direction.

"Is it coming to life?" I finally break the silence.

He jumps slightly and snaps his head up to look at me. When he sees it's just me, his posture relaxes and he returns to his examination of the bowl's contents.

"Technically, it's already alive. It's supposed to be sourdough pizza crust. I'm just not sure if I did it right," he says.

"I know you were tasked with feeding them and drying out one of them, but were you given authorization to actually bake something with Xavier's starters?"

"Yes," he says. "But only recently. In my last call with him, he said he was starting to worry about their psychological health and wondered if not having anything made out of them would cause them to question their identity and their purpose for existence."

"So, pizza," I say.

"So, pizza," he echoes. "I figured that was the easiest way to make sure the starters felt good about themselves. Or whatever. What are you doing here?"

"I was just at the station in Breyer, and before that, I was talking with Marini's staff. They're willing to help, but it turns out they don't really know anything. I gave them some details about his crimes, and all of them insisted adamantly that they knew nothing about that and weren't a part of any of it."

"Didn't we already know that?" Dean asks.

"That was the assumption, but it makes me feel better to at least see them and hear them say it, and actually believe them. They seemed genuinely sickened and shocked hearing what he did."

"Do you blame them?"

"Definitely not," I say. "And right after I left, I talked to Eric. He sent me the final records for Marini's fitness tracker. I thought we could go over them. He said there were a couple of inconsistencies and other strange things."

"Sure," he says. "Let me get this rolled out and in the oven and I'll look it over with you."

I go into the library and set up my computer. I'm surprised to see I already have an email from Detective Wheeler with attachments of Marini's autopsy and other records. The message notes that some of the information has been redacted for transfer over email, but most of it is fairly self-explanatory. If there is anything I need to know, I can get in touch with him to pick up hard copies if necessary.

I send back a message thanking him. I don't want to alienate my old colleague. I hope he isn't taking it too personally that I won't take his decision about the case at face value. It isn't just this case or how I feel about the facts that are coming up. Wheeler hasn't proven himself to be the most reliable in the past few years after his son's death. He fell hard into a bottle and has struggled to crawl all the way out. His rage and despair have whittled him away to far less than the man I used to know, but there are glimmers of him coming back.

Dean comes into the room a few minutes later.

"Mushrooms, onions, and peppers with extra cheese," he announces.

"Way to balance it out," I say.

He sits beside me and I pull up the report. At first, it's difficult to understand exactly what I'm looking at. When the numbers and graphs start to make sense, I begin to notice what Eric was talking about.

"Look at this," Dean says, pointing to the day three days before Marini's death. "It looks like something was going on here."

"A workout?" I ask. "Maybe he went to the gym to clear his mind?"

"I don't think he was the kind of guy who actually needed his mind cleared. And it doesn't look like the same kinds of reactions as when he was working out. His heart rate is extremely high. There isn't a break. It just suddenly went up and stayed up there for a while."

"The morning he died there's something similar," I note. "It's not as long or as intense, but something happened right here," I point at the shift in the readings. "Something made his heart spike up and his respiration go really erratic. Then everything was fine until right here, when everything stopped. I'm guessing the moment of his death."

"Except for right here," Dean says. "There's a break in the readings."

"What do you mean?"

"They aren't completely consistent. The readings report at regular intervals, right? But right here, there's a jump. It's only off by about a second, but during that second, there's no readings of any vitals."

"Could he have suffered more than one heart attack?" I wonder. "Is that possible? He could have had the first attack and his heart stopped. Then it started again, only for another one to come a little while later and finally kill him?"

"I don't know," Dean shrugs. "That sounds like a stretch."

"I'll have to talk to a doctor about it. But this is definitely strange."

I sit up late that night going over the lives of the tagged victims. I feel like I could write the biographies of the first two killed by now. Jay Bradley and Lori DeAngelis. I've gone over their lives so many times. I've reread all the statements from their friends and families. The information collected about their last days. Their work records. Online histories. Everything the investigation gathered.

And none of it has any more significance now than it did then. I still can't find anything about them that shows why they would become victims of the same serial killer, or what would inspire someone to tag them with the word 'Lust.' Now I have to add the apparent greed of a man of moderate means and by all reports a boring life, and the gluttony of a woman in great health who was seeking more and trying to find her path.

I finally drift off on the couch and dream of pavement and blood and cream-colored tags.

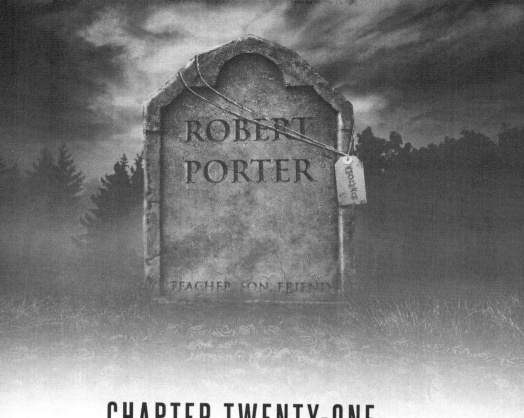

CHAPTER TWENTY-ONE

I WAKE UP WHAT FEELS LIKE MINUTES LATER TO THE SOUND OF THE clock chiming and Dean fussing under his breath in the kitchen. My neck and back ache from being curled up on the couch at a strange angle. I stretch and twist them as I make my way to the kitchen, thankful that most of Xavier's devices and traps have been deactivated.

"What's going on in here?" I ask.

"Just the coffee maker and I having our regular morning conversation," he says.

"Sounds like a bit of a one-sided conversation," I remark.

The machine lets out a hiss and a puff of steam, then rattles ominously. Dean points at it.

"Every morning," he says.

"Didn't Xavier leave you notes on how to work the coffee machine?"

"He did," Dean says. "But he didn't tell me how to deal with the automatic brew timer he put on it. So, no matter what I try to do, it attempts to make coffee at four-thirty every morning, then again at seven every morning. And it is always angry. Not that I blame it. I'm not so chipper myself at either of those hours, either."

"So, what is the coffee situation?" I ask.

"Just give me a minute," he says. "After it goes through its little fit here, I'll be able to make some."

"Why don't you just ask him next time you talk to him?"

"I tried to," Dean says. "But he told me that is an issue of the home, and he is not currently a part of the home, so he can't comment on it. And yet, he can comment on how he does not like the new air freshener I got."

"How could he possibly know he doesn't like the new air freshener you got?"

"He saw the box on the counter behind me when we had a video call and he didn't like the sound of the name," he admits.

"What was the name?"

"Vanilla."

"Well, that is pretty offensive. You should have known better," I laugh.

The coffee maker stops making noise and Dean goes about making cups for each of us. When he's done, he goes to the freezer and pulls out a box of frozen waffles. Four of them go into the toaster oven.

"I noticed you fell asleep on the couch," he says. "What were you doing all night?"

I let out a sigh. "Just trying to figure out this serial killer case. I know there's something I'm missing. And now there are two more victims."

"That's not your fault," he says, stepping in to assuage the guilt I don't even have to voice for him to know is there.

"But I can't piece it together. It's not making any sense. Why are these people being targeted? And why would the killer put a tag on them? What's the point of that? And the words on them. Lust. Greed. Gluttony."

"It's the seven deadly sins," Dean offers. "Each of them is being labeled with a sin."

"I know that's what it sounds like," I say. "It's the first thing that pops into anybody's mind when hearing those words. But that's exactly why I don't think that's what it is. A killer going after people because of them falling victim to the seven deadly sins is so much of a cliché. It's straight to the point of being laughable."

"That doesn't mean somebody wouldn't do it," Dean says. "In fact, that might mean it's exactly what somebody would do."

I shake my head. "I just don't think so. I don't think somebody wanting to punish people for engaging in these sins would take so many years away from murdering, only to come back and start up again. And even if it is what they did, why these victims? None of them seem to have anything to do with the sins they've been attached to. I feel like there's a piece missing. I just can't find it yet."

"You will," Dean says. "If anybody could, it's you."

His words twist in my gut and I force it not to show on my face.

"There's a vigil for the most recent victim tonight near where she was found. You want to come with me?" I ask.

"Sure," he says. "It'll be nice to spend a couple days in Sherwood. Right when I think I've figured everything out about this house, something changes. I don't want to think Xavier managed to rig it to actually alter its own structure or be self-aware and communicate, but I swear I went around a corner yesterday I've never seen before."

Before the vigil, I stop at the home of Cassie Graham, Paisley's mother. I spoke with her on the phone when Dean and I stopped for lunch during our drive up from Harlan and she asked me to come by so we could talk about Paisley. When she opens the door, it's like I'm looking at a reflection of her. She's not all there. It's just the outside of her, the part that people can see. But everything that was once inside is gone.

"Thank you for coming," she says, stepping aside to invite me in.

"Thank you for having me," I say. "This is my cousin Dean Steele. He's a private investigator."

Cassie nods. "Is he going to help with Paisley's case?"

The words come out with a veil of tears. She doesn't try to stop them. She has no reason to.

"I'm going to do everything I can," he tells her.

I haven't specifically talked to Dean about helping with the investigation, but I knew he wouldn't turn it down. This is why he became a private investigator. It's the same tug that led me to the FBI. He can't bear the thought of things like this existing in the world and not doing anything about them.

"Come in," she says. "Sit."

We go into the living room and she gestures at a floral couch. We take our seats on it and she drapes herself down into a rocking chair with matching cushions. Her body starts rocking back and forth almost instinctively. Her arms curl onto her lap with a slight curve and I can't help but wonder if she used to rock Paisley as a baby in that very chair. The thought makes my chest ache.

"First I want to say how sorry I am for your loss," I start. "And tell you I am the lead of this case. I will put everything into finding out who did this to your daughter."

"Thank you," Cassie says. "I know who you are. I'm sure you hear that all the time. But I want you to know how much better it makes me feel to know you are here. I know you'll do all you can for her."

I reach forward and take her hand. "I will. This case matters a lot to me. All of my cases matter to me, but this one is especially significant. I…" I draw in a breath and pause. "I am going to work as hard as I can to figure it out." She nods. "What can you tell me about Paisley?"

I listen as she talks about her beautiful, talented daughter. This isn't the phenomenon of the victim. I see the pictures and the awards. I know everything she's saying is true. One thing that stands out to me is that she was always thin. Athletic when she was young and a runner as an adult. She never struggled with her weight and never showed any signs of having an eating disorder of any kind.

"The end of her marriage was really hard on her. They tried to make it work. They really did. I just feel like they got married too fast and didn't know each other well enough to actually make the commitment to keep trying. It wasn't that they didn't love each other. Maybe they loved each other too much. I'm not even sure what that means, exactly. It was like they couldn't be apart, but they really couldn't be together. In the end, the divorce itself got really nasty. They were both hurting so much, they did whatever they could to hurt each other.

"I thought it was going to destroy her. But she got through it. A little by little, it seemed like maybe she was going to be Paisley again. I was going to get my daughter back. I didn't want to push her. I never wanted to try to minimize what she went through or be that mother who says to just get over it or just be happy. I wanted her to be able to work through it so she could really heal. I wanted her to be able to find love and happiness again.

"And just when it seemed like things were getting better, William died. It completely crushed Paisley. Looking back on it now, I think there was a part of her that still believed they were going to get back together. Even if it took years, they were going to find each other again. Then one drive down the road at the same time as a drunk driver and it was all over. She was crushed beyond description. It hurt her so much I was worried I was going to lose her."

The words choke in her throat and I squeeze her hand.

"You can take a break," I tell her softly.

She shakes her head. It's the determination of a mother wanting to speak for her daughter. The more she talks, the closer Paisley stays. When she goes quiet is when her child starts drifting away from her.

"She seemed like she was completely at a loss. She was just going through the motions and I didn't know where she was going to land. Neither did she. But a few months ago, she found the church group. We were pretty active in the church when she was younger, but I guess you can say life happened and we stopped attending and it became less a part of our lives. But when she found it again, it really seemed to click. It was like she was rediscovering part of herself, and things were getting better."

"What can you tell me about this church group?" I ask. "Did you ever meet any of the people? What are they called?"

"A few of them," she says. "The Parson Community Parish. They were nice. That sounds so silly to use as an actual description of somebody, but it's accurate. They were just nice. They seemed to really care about Paisley and what was going on with her. They wanted to help her. But none of them ever looked down on her. There was no sense that they pitied her or were trying to change her in any way. They just wanted to be there for her and encourage her. That's why I thought it was so wonderful when they contacted me about doing the vigil for her tonight. I feel like it's as much for them as it is for Paisley and me."

"I think it is," I nod. "Gathering together like that can be very healing in a situation like this." I glance over at Dean. He knows what I'm thinking and gives a slight nod to encourage me. I look back at Cassie. "There's something I need to talk to you about specifically. And it probably won't be easy for you."

Her eyes widen and more color drains from her face.

"About Paisley?" she asks. "What is it?"

"You know there are elements of the investigation that haven't been disclosed," I say.

She nods. "Yes. The officer I spoke with said some things are being kept from the public for the purposes of the investigation. He wouldn't even talk to me about them. I don't understand why. I'm her mother. That is my child lying there. How does anyone deserve to know more about what happened to her than I do?"

I nod and give her a sympathetic look. "I don't have children. I can't tell you I understand how you're feeling, or that I know what you're going through. If I said any of those things, I would just be giving you the same kinds of platitudes other people are going to. And I'm not going to do that. I'm here to find out what happened to your daughter. And I'm also here for you. Which means I'm going to be honest with you. That doesn't mean I can tell you everything.

"I know that might be hard to hear. But it's important for some things to be kept just within the investigators so that we can identify suspects or other potential details about the cases. Do you understand?"

"Cases?" she asks. "As in multiple?"

Dean slides closer on the couch, knowing she might need more support through this.

"Yes," I confirm. "As I said, I need to talk to you about something that might be hard to hear, but I need you to listen. You might know something that could help."

"I've told you everything," she says. "I don't understand what else there could be."

"Cassie, we believe Paisley was the victim of a serial killer."

She shudders so deeply she looks like she's going to be sick. I wait for a second.

"A serial killer? You think my daughter was a victim of a serial killer? I—how? Was it just random?"

"I didn't say that," I clarify. "Right now, we don't know all of the details. There are no suspects. But the cases that we believe are related have been cold for many years. The killer has only recently reemerged. Did you hear about the victim found behind the courthouse in DC a few days ago?"

She nods, her face drawn. "It's the same person?"

"I can't confirm anything right now. As of now, we don't have any suspects. There's still a lot of investigating to do. But the details of the cases do seem like they were perpetrated by the same person. One of the most important details left out of coverage of Paisley's death is the tag."

I show her a picture of the tag found tied around Paisley's neck. It was taken carefully to show as little of her body as possible. "Does this mean anything to you?"

"Gluttony?" she asks, her voice betraying the same kind of confusion that I've felt trying to decipher these tags. She shakes her head adamantly. "No. Why would that be left on her body? Paisley wasn't... she took such good care... I don't understand."

I can see her starting to crumble and I turn off the screen, taking the image away from her.

"We're not sure what these tags mean. It was not our intention for this particular detail to be released in the media about the last victim, and it will not be discussed in Paisley's case. The fewer people know about that detail, the easier it would be to identify someone who knows something they shouldn't. These words mean something. I don't know what yet. But they do. And finding out what will help lead to the killer."

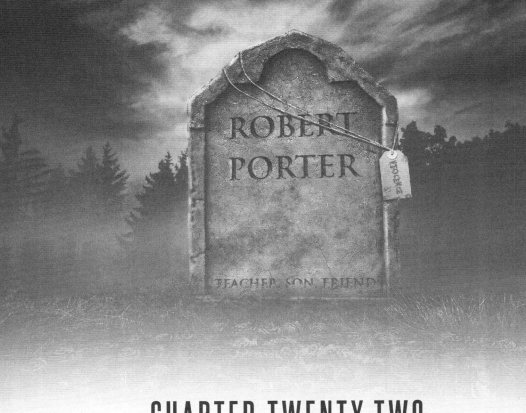

ROBERT
PORTER

TEACHER, SON, FRIEND

CHAPTER TWENTY-TWO

A FTER THE CONVERSATION WITH PAISLEY'S MOTHER, IT FEELS cathartic to walk into the vigil set up in her honor. A group has gathered at the corner of the parking lot, staying just outside of the police line and spreading out along what was once a pedestrian sidewalk.

There's a slightly surreal feeling that comes with standing there among them, looking at the line I dictated be put into place. Before this moment, we saw this space differently. They see only the tragedy that happened here, the site where Paisley's body lay on the cold ground. I see a puzzle, a conglomeration of countless tiny pieces waiting to be swept together into something cohesive.

But right now, we are all here together. We're experiencing it together. It's a living, breathing space we're existing within, and for, and because of.

Someone hands me a candle stuck through a paper cupcake liner and then holds one out to Dean.

"Thank you," I say.

The woman nods and starts to walk away, then pauses, looking at me with something curious and close to suspicion in her eyes.

"You're a detective," she says.

"FBI agent," I tell her.

She nods. "I thought I recognized you. Are you here for Paisley?"

"Aren't we all here for Paisley?" I ask.

"She was wonderful," the woman says. "So sweet and caring. I don't understand how anybody could do something like that to someone like her."

"I'd like to think it's hard to understand why anyone would do something like that to anyone," I say.

But even as the words come out of my mouth, they feel disingenuous. Death isn't fair and it isn't equal, and while it's not popular to say, some deaths are simply far more difficult to accept and to rationalize than others.

"That's true," she notes. "No one should hurt anyone like this."

"How did you know her?" I ask. "Were you part of her church group?"

"Yes," she nods. "Are you investigating me?"

"No," I say, trying to smile. "I'm just getting to know her."

The woman relaxes. "I'd only known Paisley for a few months, but I could see what a good person she was. Being in our parish was doing amazing things for her. She was even considering going into leadership. There's a training program that guides those wanting to delve deeper into their journeys to provide comfort and counsel to members of the community."

"She was going to become a pastor?" I raise an eyebrow.

"Not exactly," she says. "But that is an option for those who find their calling. I've known a few members who have gone on to join the ministry. But for Paisley, it was more about being a friend. Someone others could come to talk about their problems and have a kind ear to listen."

"That's really beautiful," I say.

"Agent Griffin?" a voice says behind me.

I glance toward it, then look back at the woman. She smiles at me.

"It was nice to meet you. Thank you for coming."

"Of course," I say. "I'm glad you did this for Paisley."

She walks away to hand candles to other people who've arrived. In the gathering darkness, I wonder when someone will be around to light them. I turn back around to the woman who said my name.

"It is you," she says. "Right?"

I nod. "It is. It's good to see you, Seema. It's been a long time." Dean steps up beside me and I gesture to him. "Dean, this is Seema Bradley."

Seema eyes him, trying to discern who he is.

"Emma's cousin," he clarifies, recognizing the look as well.

Seema nods and I hold my hand out toward her, not sure how to introduce her. She speaks before I can.

"She's another one, isn't she?"

"Another one?" I ask.

"Paisley," she says. "She's another victim. It's him again."

"How did you ... ?"

"You're here," she says. "I know there was another victim. That man behind the courthouse. It's happening again. You wouldn't be here if Paisley wasn't part of it, too."

A man touches Dean on the shoulder and when he turns, I see the glow of the candle in his hand. He touches the flame to the candle in Dean's hand. As the man walks away, Dean steps closer to Seema and me. He tilts the flame toward our candles and the wicks catch the light. I meet her eyes across the glow.

I nod. "Yes."

The faint smell of the candles still lingers around us as Dean and I drive to Sherwood after the vigil. Between the words of the speakers and the flicker of the flames in Seema's eyes, there isn't enough space for words in the car. But Dean doesn't need the silence.

"Do you really believe it's the same person?" he asks.

"What do you mean?" I ask.

He glances over at me with an expression on his face that says he doesn't understand why I asked the question.

"The murders. The original ones and these. Do you really think they're the same person? Or could it be a copycat?"

"Why is everyone asking that?" I ask, my tone a little more aggressive than I intended. "I don't understand why a copycat is the first thing anybody is thinking of."

"It's not the first thing," Dean says. "But it makes sense to ask."

"Why?" I ask, my voice hot. "Why does it make more sense to ask if somebody else is copying a person who committed murder a decade ago than it does to think it's the same person? The details are the same. The method is the same. Details that weren't released are the same. This is the same person, Dean. And he has to be stopped."

"Okay," he relents, holding his hands up in surrender. "Okay, Emma."

We arrive to a quiet house and I take a shower, my head tilted back into water hot enough to make my skin sting. I don't want to feel or think of anything else. When it starts to run cool, I get into pajamas and crawl into the bed beside my sleeping husband.

He's warm and solid and real as I wrap around him. My body folds around his so my head rests against his back and my hand is over his heart. I let the smell of him cover the wax and burning cotton. I let the rise and fall of his chest balance the surge of sobs from the crowd.

I let his presence pull me to sleep.

He's still there in the morning. I kiss the soft dip behind his ear and whisper that I love him, then get dressed and make coffee while I wait for him to get up. The freezer has been emptied of the tin pans that once filled the shelves, so I cope with the thoughts rolling through my mind by taking out my favorite mixing bowl and falling into a batch of cinnamon rolls. They take hours to rise and then bake, so they won't be ready for breakfast this morning.

Instead, I cover them with plastic wrap and stash the tray in the refrigerator. There they can rise throughout the day and be ready to bake tonight. The smell of them will welcome Sam home. I'll have to make sure some of them remain after Dean gets his fingers into them. Upon second thought, I wash out the bowl and make a second batch.

"Good morning," Sam smiles, coming into the kitchen dressed in his uniform and glowing from having just shaved.

I straighten from putting the second batch in the refrigerator and return his smile.

"Good morning."

"I didn't even hear you come in last night."

"You were asleep," I say.

He leans down to kiss me, smiles, then rebounds and kisses me again. "Is Dean here?"

"He's upstairs. I guess he's still asleep. I have a feeling he's not getting the best sleep at home. Apparently, the house has been changing on him," I say.

"Well, that happens," Sam notes, pouring himself coffee. "Last time I was there, there were at least three rooms I'd never seen before." He takes a sip and looks at me with narrowed eyes over the lip of the mug. "Are you okay?"

"What do you mean? Why wouldn't I be?"

I crack eggs into another bowl and toss in some chopped onions and mushrooms I keep in the refrigerator for these kinds of mornings.

"I don't know. It just seems like something's bothering you," he says.

"I'm fine," I tell him, tipping the eggs into a frying pan and smiling at him. "Toast or an English muffin?"

An hour later, with Sam at work and Dean sitting in the living room watching the news, I walk down the hallway into my office. Closing the door behind me, I sit at my desk and look at my computer. For a second, I hesitate. I'm not even sure what's making me pause this way, but I finally break it and open my computer. I pull up a set of images and minimize them so that they fit on the screen, then go into a separate folder and pull up more, doing the same so the screen has four images. All closeups of the tags on the victims.

The top two are from years ago. Two tags emblazoned with 'Lust.' One stained on the edge with blood.

The bottom two are from the recent murders. 'Greed' on one. 'Gluttony' on the other.

I stare at them, comparing every detail of the images. I want to know they are exactly the same. I need to see the same curves, the same color, the same tilt of the handwriting. Four tags. Four lives.

Sitting back, I fight the heavy beating of my heart and force a trembling hand to open a drawer and take out an old day planner. So many of the pages are empty, the dates long since passed. I open to the last page with anything written on it. The thick black felt tip ink looks just as stark against the page as it did the day I made the notes. I read what they say as if they can distract me from where my fingertips came to rest.

They can't.

I slide the cream-colored tag from the seam between the pages and feel the cardstock for the first time in years. I set the book on the desk and put the tag in my palm, holding it up beneath the four images on the screen.

The same.

CHAPTER TWENTY-THREE

T HERE'S A CERTAIN LUXURY TO BEING ABLE TO WORK FROM HOME for a day when I've been driving around as much as I have over the last few days. I've gotten so used to making the drive within the triangle that has come to define my existence. Sherwood, FBI headquarters, Harlan. Adding in other destinations doesn't feel like that much of a stretch until a morning comes when I'm not hopping into the car with a cooler and a tote of snacks, ready to think my way through hours on the road.

There's also the luxury of silence that comes with it, and fortunately having Dean in the house rarely changes that. He works when he's here almost as much as if he were at home, and sometimes we'll go most of the day without crossing paths.

It's that way through the late morning and into the afternoon. With the blank tag tucked back into the day planner and returned to the desk drawer, I'm staring at my computer screen, reading through everything I can find about the victims.

A picture included with an article about one of the original murders catches my attention and holds it for a long moment. A much younger-looking Seema smiles at me from the grainy newspaper image. The picture was probably beautiful once. I can imagine it framed up on the wall in her living room. It would be brighter and in focus. But it seems almost appropriate to be captured this way: in black and white and almost faded.

The man beside her is Jay, the male murder victim found first. She never doubted him. Not for a single second. Not even when the investigators were making snide comments and suggestions about his lifestyle or what he might have gotten into when he was away from home. There was a strength in her, a steadfastness that didn't seem to match up with the quiet, almost meek exterior. It didn't matter to her what anyone said about her husband. She knew him. She loved him. And he loved her. Actively, deeply. He loved her.

And there wasn't a single fiber in her being that would question who he was and the dedication he had to their marriage. They might not have been the most exciting couple. They might not have lived a thrilling life. By all accounts, they were quiet and reserved, preferring to keep to themselves. But they were happy. They were in love. And she never stopped fighting for him. Even behind the fire reflected in her eyes at the vigil, I could see she is still fighting.

Next is the second victim, Lori DeAngelis. As self-described on the personal blog that brought in thousands of monthly readers before she died, she was a big woman with a big mouth and plenty of ideas to fill it. Though that sounded enticing, almost like it could have led to the lustful label, looking through all her postings showed nothing even vaguely suggestive. She never talked about sex. She never even mentioned attraction or affection of any kind. The only pictures of her were from the shoulders up and a look on her face that almost dared readers to come in and read what she had to say, then think about it for themselves.

Statements made about her by friends and family said she was strong and opinionated, but not as aggressive as she might have looked. If anything, she was goofy and awkward. She dated but didn't have anybody special.

There was nothing in any of the research done about them that showed they crossed paths at all. They came from very different walks of life and lived in very different ways. It didn't seem they could have known each other in any way, which begs the question of how someone else would have known both of them.

I even combed through Jay's internet history to see if he even so much as stumbled across her page one day. What I found was interesting, in the sense that any dead person's online history can be interesting, but it didn't give me any connections.

The only thing that seemed to connect them at all was their deaths, and even those were different. The medical examiner's report was inconclusive in regards to Jay's specific cause of death, but Lori appeared to have been hit by a car and thrown against a brick wall, which ultimately killed her.

What was interesting, at least in the absence of anything else that could be seen that way, was that both died during storms. In both instances, the bodies were found either during or immediately after a very severe thunderstorm, with the writing on their tags only surviving because they were covered with clothing or body parts that kept the rain from completely obliterating the ink.

Before I can go any further, my phone rings. I've been so tempted to turn off the ringer today. It seems like over the last few days it has rung nonstop. But I can't do that. I need to stay accessible, and that means listening to every ring and chime and chirp and buzz. This time, it's an unexpected number across the screen.

"Hello?" I answer.

"Mrs. Griffin? I mean, Johnson. I mean..."

"It's alright. Yes?"

"This is Bonnie from Sherwood Mini Storage," she says. "I hate to have to tell you this, but it seems your unit was vandalized last night. I was just doing my rounds and noticed."

"My unit?" I frown. "What happened?"

"I don't know," she says. "I was hoping you would come down here and look at it to see if anything was missing or damaged."

"Of course," I tell her. "I can be down there in just a few minutes."

"I'm sorry," she says. "I hope everything's alright."

"So do I."

I hang up and head to the living room. Dean is sitting on the couch with his computer on the table in front of him. He looks up as I lean against the door, stuffing my feet into my boots.

"Everything okay?" he asks.

"Probably," I say. "The storage place just called me and said my unit was vandalized last night. The office manager didn't seem to know if there was anything actually wrong but asked if I would come down there and check it out. I'm just going to run over and take a look. I shouldn't be gone long. You want to come?

He shakes his head. "I'm actually right in the middle of some stuff for Ava. Is it cool if I just stay here?"

Normally, I would raise an eyebrow at that information, but my mind is already racing with what could be waiting for me at the storage unit.

"Definitely. I took a tray of cinnamon rolls out and put them on the counter to warm up. They should be ready to put in the oven in about 20 minutes. If you want to preheat it. If I'm not back here by then, put them in. I'll make the frosting when I get back," I tell him as I grab my keys and head out.

It only takes a few minutes to cross town and get to the storage unit. I haven't actually gone inside the unit in more than a year. There's very little left inside, but I hold on to it just in case there's ever a need for it. It's one of those strange security blanket things. This is the unit where the property management company stored all of my grandparents' belongings when they emptied them out of the house so they could rent it out, by my father's request.

When he left and signed the deed over to me, there were renters, but the management company handled everything about it. I had literally nothing to do with it, and it wasn't until I needed to go back to Sherwood years later that I even put much thought into the house and what might have come of it. By then, the renters were gone, and it had been sitting empty for a while. I moved in, and when I decided to stay, I opened up the storage unit where my family's life had been stowed away and gradually restored it.

Keeping the unit feels like I'm still holding onto that part of the house's history, even though all that's left inside is only a couple of crates and a bulky piece of furniture I still don't know what to do with. I'm not sure why it's so important to me, but every time I think about letting the unit lapse, I can't make myself do it.

Bonnie is waiting by the gate when I get to the unit. I've known her for years, but only in passing. She's the daughter of the owner of the company and looks far too young to possess the title of "office manager," but I know she's actually older than she looks. Right now, most of what she looks like is terrified. This is probably the first time anything like this has happened on her watch.

People choose gated storage companies because they want to feel like their possessions are being kept secure. A unit being vandalized in the middle of the night doesn't look good. When the unit belongs to an FBI agent, it probably feels a lot worse.

I smile at her to try to reassure her I'm not preparing to completely fly off the handle and she gets in her golf cart to follow me to the back of the lot where my unit is located. The moment we turn the corner, I notice the door to the unit is standing open.

"Was it like this when you found it?" I ask, getting out of the car.

Bonnie nods. "It was. I didn't go inside or touch anything. I wanted to have you look over it first and see if you notice any issues."

"You mean other than the broken lock and open door?"

She flinches, her cheeks going red, and nods.

I approach the unit and peer inside.

"Is anything missing?" she asks.

I shake my head. "Everything looks to be exactly where I left it. Have you accessed the footage from the security cameras yet?"

She looks sheepish. "The cameras haven't been working."

I do my best not to roll my eyes or to ask if they didn't learn anything from the last breach. That was years ago now, but I would think they would pay attention. But this just harkens right back to the conversation I had with Sam about the dummy security cameras and ones that don't work. Most people assume a place like this has cameras covering all the units and that they are constantly working to make sure everyone's belongings are safe.

"You really should pay better attention to that," I say.

"I'm so sorry," she says again. She reaches into her golf cart and produces a lock. "I brought a new lock for the unit. And we'll make sure the cameras are fixed."

"I still expect a police report to be filed," I tell her. "I'll have Sam come by here tomorrow."

She nods. "Thank you."

I reach up and grab the handle for the door to tug it down and lock it. As it slides into place, the large purple spiral spray-painted on the door makes my stomach lurch.

CHAPTER TWENTY-FOUR

THE FIRST COUPLE OF PICTURES I TAKE OF THE SPIRAL ARE BLURRED because I'm shaking, so I video call Eric instead.

"Do you see it?" I ask.

"I do," he says. He lets out a breath. "Shit. It looks like the others."

"At least similar," I say.

"What's going on?" Bonnie asks. "I'm sorry I didn't notice that when I first looked at the unit. I told you I didn't touch anything. I didn't move the door, so I didn't see it."

I ignore her, but the anxiety brought on by the swirled shape marring the previously bright white paint of the storage unit door has me pacing in short exchanges back and forth in front of the still partially open unit.

"You got the picture I sent you of the scene behind the courthouse," I say. "And I just got the crime scene photos from Paisley Graham's murder this morning. I'll have to go over them again, but I'm sure I'll find one there, too."

A door slams and I look up to see Sam coming toward me in long strides. His face is tight, his eyes narrowed with concern.

"Emma, what's happening?" he asks.

"Sam, what are you doing here?" I ask.

"Sam's there?" Eric asks.

"He just got here." I look at Sam again. "I thought you were at work."

"I got done with everything a little early, so I decided to come home. Dean said you left for the storage unit but hadn't come back yet. What's going on?"

"The unit was vandalized," I explain. "Bonnie called me and said she found it today and wanted me to come look at it. When I got here, it was standing open."

"Alright," he says. "Was anything missing?"

"No. It doesn't even look like anyone went inside," I say. "When I closed the door, I found this." I gesture to the spiral.

"What is it?" he asks.

I look at Eric in the screen of my phone. His expression is intense and serious.

"You need to tell him, Emma," he presses.

"Tell me what?" Sam asks.

The words are lodged low in my gut where I've stashed them for all these years. I don't want to bring them up now. I can only talk to Eric about it because he knows what happened. He was there the day the police insisted I go to the hospital and the Bureau got involved. I swore him into silence in the same way I promised it to myself.

"Emma," he repeats, more insistently this time.

"I'll tell him," I say. "I'll call you back."

I end the call and put the phone in my pocket. Once I've secured the lock on the door, I tell Bonnie not to forget about the police report and the cameras and head back to my car.

"Where are you going?" Sam asks, his hands out to his sides as he tries to figure out what's going on.

"Home," I tell him. "Meet me there."

Nerves chew at my insides throughout the entire drive back to the house. This isn't something I ever wanted to talk about. In the years since the attack happened, I've wanted to solve it. I've wanted to find out what really happened and make sure it didn't happen again. But I wanted to keep myself at a distance from it. Now I can't and I don't know how to confront it.

We get home and I walk into the house without watching Sam's squad car pull into its place at the curb. Dean gets up from the couch when I come through the front door.

"Emma," he says. "Are you okay? Did Sam find you?"

"He found me."

Sam storms into the house and Dean's eyes widen.

"It looks like the two of you have something you need to talk about. I'm going to go up to my room."

"No," I say, holding my hand out to stop him. "You need to hear this, too. I should have told both of you to begin with."

Dean sits back on the couch, but Sam stays on his feet. He stares at me with expectation, but I'm still struggling to find the right words.

"Go ahead," he prompts. "What was that all about? What was that spiral on the door?"

"Spiral?" Dean asks.

"There was a purple spiral painted on the storage unit door," I tell him. "I didn't see it at first because the door was open, but when I closed it, I found it."

He thinks for a second and I can see the recognition starting to click in his mind.

"Wasn't there a spiral or something like that near the guy behind the courthouse?" he asks.

I nod. "Yes."

Sam's expression grows more serious. "Excuse me?"

"Okay," I say, holding up my hands to try to calm him. "Just take a breath. I'll be right back."

I run to my office and grab up the crime scene photographs and files from the murders, along with the day planner. When I get back into the living room, Sam doesn't look like he's settled down at all, but I can't keep trying to bring him down. I just have to push through this and let it happen as it's going to.

"One of the details about the murders that was never discussed is these spirals," I start. "I noticed them during the first investigation and brought them up to the team, but they weren't taken seriously. The detectives said they seemed like coincidences. Just random bits of trash or graffiti I was turning into spirals in my mind because I thought it might mean something.

"And I was still so new in the Bureau, and I hadn't built up much respect yet. There were still a lot of people in the FBI itself as well as on the police force who saw me as a little girl who was getting in over my head. They didn't want to I think I could have figured something out that they didn't. So they all but ignored the fact that they were there."

"At every scene?" Sam asks.

I nod. Spreading the crime scene photos across the coffee table, I point to a different place on each of the images.

"See? Here. And here. This one was painted. This one looks like it was carved. Then, the more recent murders, there they are, too. There was a piece of rope twisted into the shape of a spiral in a piece of grass near where the body behind the courthouse was found. It was photographed, but the crime scene unit all but dismissed it as just a piece of discarded construction equipment from a site down the street."

I move over to the last photograph. "This is where Paisley was found. I haven't examined the images as much. Haven't found it yet."

"Right there," Dean says, reaching over my shoulder to point at the glass door a few feet from Paisley's head. "Do you see it?"

It takes me a second at first, but then I see what he's pointing out. On the glass is what looks like a smeared handprint, but when looked at carefully enough, the smear forms the shape of a spiral.

"Yes," I say. "There it is. But, see, this is the perfect illustration of why the investigators didn't take them seriously. Every one of these spirals is different. They were made with different materials. They're different sizes. They don't have the same number of rotations in the spiral. And the difference in the rotations doesn't change in order numerically. It can't be a signature because it's not consistent, according to them."

"But that's bullshit," Dean says. "The fact that they aren't consistent makes them consistent. Something like this doesn't just show up out of nowhere. How often do you just walk down the street and see things like this all over the place?"

"Like on our storage unit door," Sam says, bringing the conversation back to what started it to begin with. "Why was Eric so intent on you telling me about the spirals?"

I hesitate.

"Emma, is there something else you're not telling me?"

I draw in a breath.

Time to let out the truth.

"A couple of weeks after the second murder, one of these spirals showed up in the parking garage I used. I wasn't sure if that was really what it was because it looked so different from the other ones. I tried to ignore it. After all, I was being told it meant nothing. But then... I was attacked."

"You?" Sam sputters, his eyes wide in shock. "You are the survivor of the attack from the serial killer?"

It sounds so absurd when he says it that way, but I can't do anything but nod.

"Yes," I confirm. "He followed me after work. I used to go to the library and study every day after work, which is why I used that parking garage. He must have known. He learned my schedule and knew where I was going to be. He followed me into the garage and when he saw there wasn't anybody else around, he attacked me. He tried to strangle me. I fought back, of course, but he was strong. It would have worked if it wasn't for a couple of people who came in right at the right time."

Dean and Sam are both staring at me with twin expressions of disbelief and horror. I give them a tight smile.

"They chased him off me, but he ran and got away before we were able to catch up with him. The police weren't able to track him down."

"And the security cameras weren't real," Sam gripes, bitterness and acidity now dripping from the words.

"Yes," I say. "The security cameras weren't real."

"Why didn't you tell me this? When you were talking about the attack and the security cameras, all of it, why didn't you tell me it was you?"

"Because it's something I don't want to think about," I defend myself. "It was horrible and traumatic. And I didn't want to worry you."

"Emma, you can't stop me from worrying about you. You know that."

Once again, I'm struck with how impossibly much this man loves me. I put my face in my hands and take a deep, shaking breath, finally letting the emotions out. This time, I let Sam wrap his arms around me and hold me close.

It takes a couple minutes, but I successfully gather myself and stand up straight.

"Thank you," I whisper.

Dean comes up and rests a hand on my shoulder, but it's not because he thinks I'm about to collapse into a crying fit. It's a prompt to continue.

"The guy didn't resurface after he attacked me. I waited. I've waited and waited for him to come back for me. Or for him to kill again. And he never did."

I look down at the photos again.

"After the attack on me, the Bureau got involved, but they weren't able to find anything out. And even with their investigations, I didn't

THE GIRL AND THE 7 DEADLY SINS

feel safe or secure. I was constantly looking over my shoulder. I was constantly waiting for the next spiral. The next murder. It got to the point where I was almost welcoming it. I thought about drawing a spiral myself. Like it was going to call out to him like the Bat-signal.

"I wanted to know who he was and why he'd come after me. But nothing ever came out of it. I was left with the blank tag that fell on the ground beside me and a hell of a lot of survivor's guilt. I couldn't figure it out. He killed right there in the city where I was trying to make a difference, then he attacked me, tried to make me his next victim, and I still couldn't figure it out.

"The years went by. I started to wonder if he was dead. Maybe something happened to him after he ran away from me that day. Or he crossed the wrong person when looking for his next victim. Either way, it seemed like we were never going to hear from him again. There were no other murders with the tags. There was no written communication. Nothing. I really believed there was a chance it was over.

"Then, it started happening again. It's humiliating to me that I couldn't find my own attacker. It's worse that I stopped and now two more people have died."

"That's not your fault," replies Sam.

"I know. But I needed to work through it without any of that hanging over me. Without it seeming like I was trying to put myself above the victims or get attention for myself. This isn't my origin story, Sam. It's not something I want capitalized on and blown up into some sort of folklore tale. This isn't about me. This is about the four people who have died because of this person."

"It *is* about you," Sam presses. "This is absolutely about you. You survived the attack, but not because he didn't try. Now he painted the spiral on your storage unit. He knows where you are. He's been right here. And he's sending you a message."

"He's right, Emma," Dean adds. "This is dangerous. He's threatening you."

"I still don't know what it means," I say. "I just know the spirals have been there. That doesn't mean I understand why he put them there."

"It doesn't matter," Sam says. "It means something. And for everybody else but you, it meant death. And I don't trust that he's going to stop with just a walk down memory lane."

"He has to know you're working on the case," Dean says. "The woman at the vigil said she knew you were working it. Who was she?"

"That was Seema. Her husband was the first victim. I came in contact with her after my attack when the Bureau had taken up the investigation. We lost touch after the case went cold, but she noticed the detail about the tag on the courthouse victim. Then it showed up on the news and she heard I was investigating. Then she heard I was in the area of Paisley's investigation and figured she was another of the victims. Even after all these years, she's not willing to rest. She wants to know what happened. I don't want to let her down again."

"You won't."

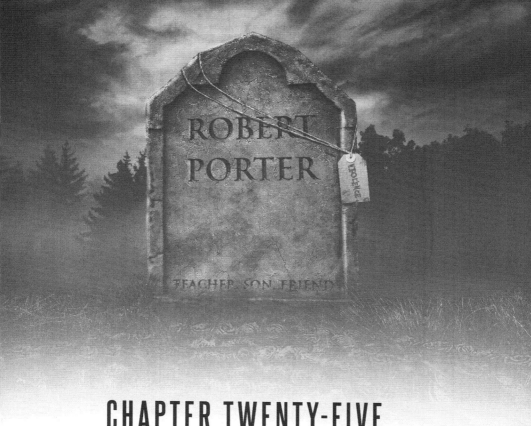

ROBERT
PORTER

TEACHER, SON, FRIEND

CHAPTER TWENTY-FIVE

"**Y**OU NEED TO LEAVE TOWN," SAM TELLS ME.

"What?" I ask.

"You can't be here. I can't believe I am actually about to say the words I am going to, but Jonah was right. You need to get out of Sherwood."

"He wanted me out of Sherwood because he wants me focused on the cases that mean something to him," I counter. "Because of this asinine conspiracy group he's positive is tracking me down."

"I want you to go because it's not safe here, and it's not. Whoever this guy is, he's close. Not just close enough to know what town you live in, close enough to be able to identify your storage unit. I don't understand the significance of that," Sam says.

"Neither do I," I reply.

"Even more reason to get you the hell out of here. He's sending a message and it's not one I want you answering. This is dangerous, Emma. I can't stand the idea of something happening to you. I already have to deal with that risk all the time. I don't want to try to deal with it even more."

"I have work I have to do, Sam," I tell him. "I need to keep working this case. And the Emperor."

"I thought you weren't looking into that anymore," he says. "I thought you were done with Jonah."

"Figuring out who Salvador Marini really was and what he did goes beyond why I started investigating him to begin with. There are countless victims, Sam. Literally countless, because we don't know how many there are or where they are or who they are. Their stories deserve to be told, regardless of who brought them to my attention. It's not for Jonah. I'm working that case because it needs to be worked."

"And you can do work somewhere else," Sam points out. He steps forward and takes both of my hands, pulling them up to rest them in the middle of his chest over his heart. It's what he does when he wants to make sure I'm listening carefully to him.

"Babe, you know I don't ever want you away from me. I would keep you right here all to myself if I could. But I can't even dream about doing that if you're not here at all. I need you to be safe. And until we can figure out who this person is and why they want to come after you, you're not going to be safe here in Sherwood."

"What am I supposed to do? Go to a hotel? Go hide in a bunker? I'm not going to run. He made me run once. He made me fight. I was scared, Sam. He nearly killed me, and it was because of mistakes I made and things I would do differently a thousand times over if I could go back again. He made me run once. I'm not running from him again."

"I'm not asking you to run," Sam says. "I'm just asking you to stay safe. Just spend some time at Eric's house. Or Dean's. Or your father's. Just go somewhere to throw him off. Please."

We go to bed that night with bellies full of cinnamon rolls and the next morning, I leave for my father's house. I haven't yet gotten around to signing the title and everything back to him yet, so it's technically mine, but even during all those years he was missing it still always felt like it was his house.

Dad greets me at the front door with a big hug and presses a kiss to the side of my head.

"It's good to have you here," he says. "I've missed you."

"I've missed you, too," I tell him. "I just wish I wasn't here under these circumstances. I hate this."

"I know you do, honey. But your husband is a good man. He's just trying to protect you. He wants you to be safe," he says. "He loves you."

"I know he does," I say. "And I love him. But I don't want to be away from home because I'm running away. I don't want to give this person more power and more satisfaction knowing he ran me out of my home. I'm not going to stay here long. Just until I can convince Sam that I'm going to be alright."

"That's fine," he says. "This is your home, too. You can stay here as long as you want. And right now, I need you to explain to me what's going on. I didn't get many details out of you when you said you were coming."

"I don't want to talk about it," I say.

"Unfortunately, that's not an option," he insists. "I need to understand what you're dealing with."

It's moments like these when I really remember how much my father missed. Of course, I remember missing him. I remember him not being around. I remember all the years I wondered where he was and what happened to him. I remember everyone telling me he was dead and choosing not to believe it. But what I don't think about often is what he missed. Not just being physically near me but having the chance to be my father. In these moments, he makes up for it within himself.

He gives me a little bit of time to bring my things into my old room and settle in. I hate being here instead of with Sam back in Sherwood, but I try to tell myself it's a little like summer camp. I'm packed up with my clothes in a duffel bag and I'm going to write to him every day. It will be through email and texts rather than paper, but the sentiment remains. And soon, I'll be back home with him where I belong.

When I'm done unpacking, I go back into the living room and find a sandwich and mound of potato chips my father has put together for me. I chuckle as I sit down in front of it.

"You don't have to feed me, you know," I say. "I'm still an adult."

"And my child," he corrects me. "I want to be able to take care of you."

I relent and pick up one of the chips, nibbling on the end. "Thank you."

"So, tell me what's happening. I have a basic idea, but I need you to fill me in more," he says.

I start at the beginning and tell him the entire situation. As I talk, I notice his face dropping and the color going gray. He looks pale and shaken when I finish.

"What is it?" I ask. "I'm here now. I'm fine."

"I know," he says. "It's just that I feel so horrible for not being there for you when you needed me. I made a decision when you were about to turn eighteen that I thought was the right one for both of us. I really believed it was the best way to protect you. But every time I think about it, I feel so much guilt and sadness."

"Daddy, I don't want you to feel that way," I say. "You did what you thought was right. And, honestly, it probably was. As hard as it is to think about, you knew what you were doing. You knew what was happening and believed you could stop things from getting worse by not being around. And you did. I'm still here. And I am this person because of the choice you made."

"And I am prouder of you than I could ever say," he says. "But that doesn't change that I'm your father. I was the only parent that you had left, and I walked away from you. I wasn't there for you and I didn't know what you were going through all the time. I did my best. I tried as hard as I could to keep up with what was going on and what you were dealing with so I could help in any way possible. But I wasn't always able to. And I'm so sorry."

"Stop," I say. "You have no reason to say you're sorry. You were dealing with your own stuff, and you had other people to take care of."

"I should have been taking care of you," he says. "You are the most important person to me, Emma. And I feel like I didn't always have the chance to show that to you."

"Yes, you did," I say. "You showed me by making a decision that was hard for both of us but that you knew was right. You didn't know what was going to happen."

"No, I didn't," he insists. "I had no idea you would go into the FBI. I know you had talked about it, especially when you were younger and I was putting you through all those martial arts classes. You talked about how you should just go into law enforcement because you were already prepared. And you started talking about it again when you were in college. But I didn't know for sure you were going to do it. And honestly, I hoped after I left you would choose something else.

"You were always so incredibly talented. Your creativity was beyond anything I'd ever seen. The only other person who came close was your mother. I hoped you would hang on to that. That you would use your art to help you cope, and that you would keep leaning into it so you could have a life outside of all of these dangers and challenges."

"I'm not afraid of the dangers," I reply. "Or the challenges. This is what I want to do."

"I know," he says. "And you're good at it. Better than I am."

"That's not true," I say. "But I'll keep trying to live up to it."

We eat and catch up on other things before the conversation gets back to why I'm here.

"You were telling me about these tags that were left with the bodies," he muses. "You said there was one at the site where you were attacked."

"Yes," I nod. "It fell out of his pocket when I grabbed his shirt. But it didn't have anything written on it."

"That means he usually had plenty of time when he was committing the murders," Dad notes.

"Why do you say that?"

"Because he wrote the tags after the murders, not before. He didn't write the words out, then go find somebody to kill to fit with it. Or have the tags ready to go when he went after his victim. It was a ritual, a ceremony. The actual writing of the tag and putting it on the body was an important step in the process for him."

I nod slowly. "But what about the spirals? I know they were part of it. I just don't understand what. What could they mean?"

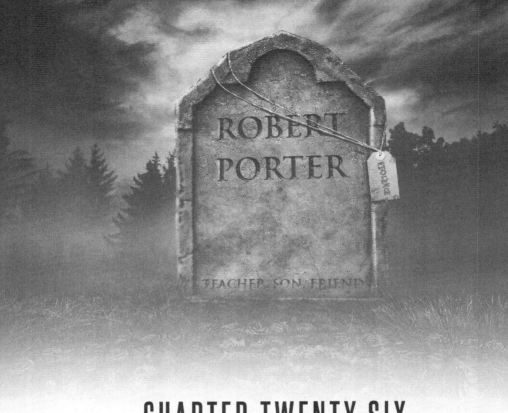

ROBERT PORTER

TEACHER, SON, FRIEND

CHAPTER TWENTY-SIX

"I DON'T UNDERSTAND," I FROWN, LOOKING OVER THE AUTOPSY REPORT FOR PAISLEY GRAHAM. "SHE WAS FOUND IN A PARKING LOT. SHE DIED OF BLUNT FORCE TRAUMA. HOW DID MUD END UP IN HER THROAT? I SAW HER FACE. IT DIDN'T LOOK LIKE THERE WAS ANY DAMAGE. NO BRUISING OR CUTS AROUND HER MOUTH. NO MARKS ON HER CHEEKS. NOTHING THAT WOULD INDICATE SOMETHING BEING FORCIBLY SHOVED DOWN HER THROAT."

"Not unless it happened after she died," Eric points out.

"Why would somebody who wanted to put mud in her mouth do it carefully enough to not cause any damage?" I ask.

"I have no idea," he says. "All I can tell you is what the medical examiner found."

"Thanks," I say with a heavy sigh. "I'll just add it to the list of everything else about these cases that makes no damn sense."

"Have you gotten anywhere?" he asks.

"I don't know," I admit. "That's the fun part about it. I don't know what I might have found out because I don't actually know what I'm looking for. All I remember about the person who attacked me is that it was a man. Or at least it seemed like one. I didn't see his face. I can't even tell you how big he might have been. I was so shocked by what was happening and so wrapped up in responding in what I thought was the right way that I didn't do the very basics of what I was supposed to do."

"You can't blame yourself for that, Emma. You can't look back on how you handle the situation and judge yourself for it. You were going through a lot right then," he says.

"That doesn't give me an excuse to completely freeze up the way I did. I really thought I was going to be able to outsmart and overpower him. Like he was some pathetic mugger who wanted to snatch my purse. And I was so far dug down into my training, and this idea that things happen within some sort of set parameters that let you choose one response or another, that I didn't even listen to my instincts. If something like that happened now, I would react in a totally different way."

"You aren't the same person you were then," Eric points out. "Of course, you would react differently. What happened to you that day is part of what shaped you into the agent you are. I know you don't like to think about that or acknowledge it, but it did. That was one of the moments that gave birth to the bullheaded agent who does what her gut tells her to over her orders. Who listens to her instincts before following the rules. And thank God you do."

"There is something I might have found," I tell him. "I don't know for sure if it means anything, but I'm grasping for every straw I can right now."

"What is it?" he asks.

"Paisley used to work at the camera store that was in the abandoned building where her body was found," I say. "It closed a while back, but she worked there for a few years when it was open."

"That is interesting," Eric notes. "So, whoever killed her must have known that about her. Maybe a former coworker? Or disgruntled customer? Were you able to look into anything about her work history? Any complaints?"

"I'm still working on that. But the friend I spoke to who told me about it said she never heard any complaints from Paisley about it. It wasn't like it was a thrilling job or something she was going to build her career on. Just something to pay the bills until she figured out what she really wanted. But she seemed to enjoy it just fine and never talked about any problems."

"Great," Eric says. "We need to find as many people as possible who worked there when she did. See if there was any drama we don't know about. Unless we can establish links to the other victims, it doesn't mean much, but it's a starting point."

A couple hours later, I'm still digging into the lives of the victims, trying to find links and piece together anything that could connect them when I get another call on my work phone. It's Chief Calvert from Parson.

"Good afternoon, Chief," I answer, holding the phone between my ear and my shoulder so I can keep typing.

"Agent Griffin," he starts, "where are you right now?"

"I am currently just outside of the DC area," I say.

"Can you get back here quickly?" he asks.

The tension in his voice makes my blood cold.

"I can leave here in just a few minutes. Is everything all right?" I ask.

"I'm not sure," he says. "But you're going to want to see this."

Rather than going to the police station or to another scene where investigators swarm around, the chief directs me to Parson Memorial Grounds. I'm curious and a little confused as I drive through the stone gates and follow his instructions to coil through the paved roadways until I reach a section up on a hill. This area looks newer than some of the other areas of the cemetery. The stones are a greater distance apart and look pristine compared to some of the ones that have obviously been weathered by time.

I park my car next to the curb and climb out, tugging my sweater close around me to ward off the cold wind rolling off the heavy dark clouds overhead. Several yards ahead of me are a group of people gathered around a grave. If it wasn't for one of them taking pictures and most being dressed in police uniforms, it would look like a funeral.

Chief Calvert notices me over the shoulder of Detective Mavis in front of him and waves me over.

"Agent Griffin," he calls. "I'm glad you made it."

"I can tell you this isn't where I expected to end up today," I comment. "What's going on? You said there was something you think I would want to see."

"Right over here."

He walks me over to where the others are gathered at the grave. They step aside to give me space and I immediately see what he wanted to show me. The stone in front of me is new, the dates etched into it indicating the man beneath it died only a few weeks ago. But it isn't the dates that I'm paying attention to, or even the name. Instead, it's the cream-colored tag hanging from a long piece of twine wrapped around the stone.

And a spiral of roses lying in the grass on top of the grave.

My vision blurs a little bit and a rush of emotions starts deep in my belly and crawls up my throat. I lean closer to read the tag.

Violence.

"What is this?" I demand. "What the hell is this?"

"No one knows," the chief says. "The caretaker found it this way and called us. He assumed it was some kids—"

I shake my head as I take several steps backward away from the grave.

"No, it's not that. This isn't a prank. This is sick," I mutter. "Send me the photographs and get in touch with the family. I want to know who that man was and what he has to do with any of this. And while you're at it, find out where your fucking leak is and fix it."

I stalk back to my car, angry and frustrated. Someone is taunting me and I want to know why. As I drive out of the cemetery, I pay attention to everything around me. I want to know how someone could have gotten in and out without being noticed. This grave is in an out-of-the-way spot, but there's only one entrance. Its location would make it difficult to see someone leaving the card and roses behind, but they would have to go through the stone gates to get there.

In the distance, I notice a white truck moving slowly along one of the paved pathways. It finally stops and several people climb out across the grass and leave flowers on a few different graves before getting back in the truck. Interested by what seems like just a random act of compassion, I try to let go of the immediate surge of anger I felt when I saw the tag on the grave. Maybe whoever did it wasn't willfully trying to be cruel.

But no matter how much I try to convince myself not to be, I'm angry. Furious, actually. This can't have been a prank. This was deliberate.

It's a statement. One designed for my attention.

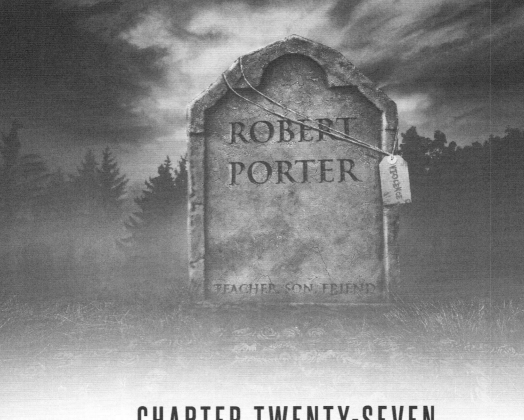

CHAPTER TWENTY-SEVEN

M Y FATHER ISN'T HOME WHEN I GET BACK TO THE HOUSE, SO I GO into the kitchen to make a cup of tea, then change into lounge clothes and curl up in the corner of the couch to call Sam. I have plenty more work to do for the day, but I intend to do it here, and that means there's no need to be anything but comfortable.

"Hey," he says. "I called you just a bit ago. I was worried when you didn't answer."

"I know," I say. "I'm sorry. I got a really strange call today and I just got back to the house."

"What happened?" Sam asks.

I describe the scene out at the cemetery for him.

"That's disturbing," he notes.

"A bit."

"But it also worries me that you're still out going around to places by yourself," he adds.

"I'm working, Sam," I say. "I told you. I have to handle these cases. I can't just pretend they don't exist because you want me to go into hiding."

"I don't want you to go into hiding," he counters. "I just want you to be safe. Especially when it comes to this case. The man who drew that spiral on the storage unit door could be after you again. He could have known you were going to go back to Parson."

"Anyone who knows I'm investigating the cases would know I was going back to Parson," I reply. "But I wasn't there today until they called. And I don't know if this actually has anything to do with the case at all. Keep in mind I have been put on the hit list for a government conspiracy group. For all we know, this is just someone who believes they're trying to make a statement and it just isn't coming across."

"I don't think you actually believe that," Sam says.

"The thing is, in either of those scenarios, somebody with inside knowledge of the case is talking. The existence of the spirals wasn't released to the media. In either set of murders. No one has known about them except for the investigation team and the people I've told. So, whoever put those things on the grave knows about the case."

"I'm worried about you," he says.

"Don't be," I reply. "I promise, I'm fine. I'm being vigilant and paying attention. Nothing is going to happen to me."

"Why didn't you have your gun?" he asks.

The question startles me slightly. I didn't expect that to come from him in this conversation.

"When?" I ask, even though I'm pretty sure I know what he's asking.

"The day you were attacked. You said he tried to strangle you and he almost did, that you fought back, and you weren't able to stop him. You were already in the Bureau. Why didn't you have your gun?"

"I did," I tell him. "It was in my bag and when he jumped on me, I dropped it and couldn't reach it."

"Why did you have it in your bag? Why wasn't it in your holster?"

"I hadn't learned yet," I admit. "I know now."

The next morning I go back to the cemetery. I feel like I acted too rashly. Even if everything has been removed, I feel the compulsion to show my respects to the man and the grave. When I get out, parking in the same spot I did yesterday, I notice that the tag has been removed from the stone. But as I approach, the spiral of roses is still clearly visible in the grass on the top of the grave.

I resist the urge to scoop up the petals and toss them into the air so they will scatter. I spend a few moments at the side of the grave. I didn't know the man, so I don't have much to say, but I hope my quiet presence will have some meaning.

Robert Porter. Teacher, Son, Friend.

I notice the grave doesn't say anything about the man having a spouse or children. I haven't yet had a chance to really delve into this man's life and find out how he fits—or doesn't—with the other victims. According to the scant amount of information I could find, he died in a one-car crash after driving under the influence, but I've read enough police statements to know there's more to the story than that.

I turn so I'm standing beside the grave, looking out over the rest of the cemetery in the same direction as he is.

"You have a good view," I tell him. "This is a beautiful resting place."

The grounds are huge and rolling, taking up what feels like everything I can see all around us. It's such a contrast to the cemetery where my mother is buried alongside Eli, the man who devoted his life to keeping her safe. That's a much smaller spot, tucked far away from the busy, touristy areas. They rest among trees dripping with Spanish moss and the smell of orange groves.

I'm still looking out over the grounds when I notice the same white truck I did yesterday. This time, it's in a different area from before. I go down to my car and drive over to where the truck is parked. The group is heading back toward it when I get out of the car. A familiar face catches my attention: the woman from the vigil.

"Good morning," I call out to her as I hurry in her direction.

She looks up and smiles.

"Hello," she says. "This is a surprise."

"For me as well," I say. "I don't think we were properly introduced the other night. I'm Emma."

"Violet Henher," she replies.

She gestures for me to follow her over to the truck and opens the doors. Inside are several containers of flowers designed to leave in the small stands on the graves. I watch as she tugs two of the pots over to herself.

"It's nice to meet you," I say. "Officially, that is."

"You, too. What are you doing here today?" She cringes and gives me an apologetic look. "I guess I probably shouldn't ask that so casually

THE GIRL AND THE 7 DEADLY SINS

when we're in a cemetery. Sometimes I forget how sad visits here are for other people."

That strikes me as a strange response, but Violet just keeps right on gathering up the flowers before turning back to the rows of graves.

"Are they not sad for you?" I ask.

"Sometimes," she admits. "But far from all the time. I find it peaceful here. It's why I volunteer here."

"Oh," I say. "You're volunteering."

She nods. "It's a program I developed for the parish. A few of us come out here three days a week to put flowers on graves. Sometimes there's a burial that's going to be unattended, and we act as the witnesses. We believe no one should be buried without people who truly care around them."

"But you don't know them," I say.

"That doesn't mean we don't care," she shrugs. "They're human beings just like us. And no matter who they are or what happened to them in this life, we are connected just because we were here. We may never have met them, but it's significant that they existed, and we want to acknowledge that."

"That's beautiful," I say.

Violet offers me a soft smile. "I think you feel the same way, Emma."

I nod. "I do." An idea occurs to me. "Did Paisley volunteer here?"

Violet shakes her head, already dashing that possibility. "No. She didn't like the idea of coming out here to the cemetery. It didn't give her the same kind of comfort and peace it gives to us. But that's the joy of what we do in the community. There's something for everyone, a way that everyone can give back to others. You just have to find what speaks to you and use that."

"Tell me, Violet, does your group ever put anything other than flowers out on the graves?" I ask.

She looks slightly baffled by the question. "Anything else?"

"Like notes or decorations," I explain.

"Sometimes during holidays we put wreaths, or if we know of a birthday or the anniversary of a death, we'll do something a little special," she says. "But that's about it."

"How about recently? Have you done anything special recently?" I ask.

"Not that I can think of."

"Did you happen to put flowers on the graves over there this week?" I ask, gesturing in the direction of the grave that had been tagged.

"No. The cemetery is so large we have to break it up into segments so that everyone is visited once a month. Those graves will be in our rotation for next week."

"Okay," I say. "Thank you. I'll let you continue. If you think of anything more about Paisley, anything she told you, or anyone she interacted with, that might have some significance for the investigation, please get in touch with me."

I give her my card and she reads it, then smiles. "I will."

I start to walk away, but she calls my name. I turn back around to see her holding up two sprays of flowers. "Would you like to help?"

I break into a grin, coming back toward her. "I would. Thank you, Violet."

CHAPTER TWENTY-EIGHT

B ECAUSE DEAN CAME TO VISIT MY FATHER AND ME THE NEXT DAY, I get to be a part of his video call with Xavier. I have to sit behind the computer so I'm not visible, but it's good to hear his voice. I really don't think it's as necessary for me to stay hidden as he thinks it is. Other inmates who have calls scheduled may walk past his screen and could catch a glimpse of me, but the high population of the prison makes it unlikely that someone who has encountered me would happen to walk by.

But it makes him feel better, and I'm willing to relent to a clandestine call if it reassures Xavier.

Dean has been filling him in the murders with each of his calls, and he talks about them casually now, not wanting it to sound like it's an investigation but rather just him talking about the news. Xavier stays quiet except for the little listening sounds we've all come to recognize. When Dean is done, there's a short stretch of silence.

"It can't be the seven deadly sins," he states matter-of-factly.

"Emma doesn't think so, either," Dean tells him. "She thinks it's too much of a cliché and that no serial killer would use that as their signature. Besides, the sins written on the tags don't correspond with the victims."

"That's not what I mean," Xavier says. "Clichés are clichés for a reason."

"See?" Dean prods, looking over his shoulder at me.

"They exist," Xavier says, "and they continue to exist because they existed before. Simply because something has been overdone doesn't preclude it from being done again. You give far too much credit to the creativity and intellect of the average killer. Keep in mind that for the most part, someone who is willing to begin a campaign of serial murder lacks something."

"What about Ted Kaczynski, Jeffrey Dahmer, Ted Bundy? All of them had IQs that were far above average," I point out.

"They lack something, Emma," Xavier says. "Not necessarily intelligence. But very smart people can be very dumb. They can also be very narrow in their view. Sometimes they see tremendous innovation and creativity in something mundane and trite. I have no issue with the possibility that someone may grasp onto the seven deadly sins as their modus operandi. But I do take issue with the tag that says 'violence.' That isn't one of the seven."

I look at Dean and he gives a knowing nod.

"As of now, we're not sure how this one fits in. It may not even be related."

"Why not?" he asks.

"He wasn't murdered," Dean explains. "Robert Porter died in a traffic incident after driving drunk. In every other instance, the murder happened and then the tag was written. Why would a tag be placed on a grave of someone who this killer clearly didn't kill?"

"But the spiral of roses," Xavier counters. "You said no one knows about that detail."

His voice has dropped as he tries to conceal what he's saying.

"It was never released to the public," Dean clarifies. "Which means whoever put those things on the grave knows about it."

"If it was just some sort of joke or meant as a message to Emma, how would whoever did it know to put that detail in?" Xavier asks.

I nod.

"That's something that's sticking with me. It's odd. And it could definitely mean something. I just don't know what. When it comes to the tag, any number of people could have leaked that. The only one that's gone public is the 'Greed' tag found on the victim by the courthouse. The most recent crime scene, as well as the first two from years ago, are locked down. Meaning someone has to have leaked it. I hate to think anybody would, but it happens."

"You think it could be somebody in the police department?" Xavier asks. "They would know about the spirals."

"No," I say. "They wouldn't. That's the other side of it. I can see them leaking about the tags, but the spirals were never acknowledged as an actual clue in the first murders. It hasn't even come up yet in the new cases. The only people who would even know are the ones I've told personally. I've specifically avoided mentioning them to the police."

"Maybe you shouldn't be so quick to think you understand," Xavier says. He says it matter-of-factly, but it's one of those casual bits of wisdom he has a habit of throwing off like they're nothing. I'm almost stunned to speak for a second.

A small beep emits from the computer speakers, indicating that the timer has started to count down the seconds until his time is up. We begin our goodbyes and I get that same strange hectic feeling I did the first time I was part of one of these calls. It's a strange reaction to the seconds counting down. Like I have to make sure each one of them is adequately full.

"Let me know if you need anything," Dean says.

"Still no," Xavier says.

"Write to me," I implore him.

"I will. Oh, read the prison newsletter. I hear it's on the website. They did a profile of my crochet group," Xavier says proudly.

Dean and I both chuckle.

"We will, I promise."

The call ends and I get up off the floor to walk around the coffee table and sit next to Dean on the sofa.

"It's always so strange when those calls end," Dean muses. "It's like he just kind of stops existing."

"You sound like him," I remark.

He nods. "Somehow I feel like I understand him better now."

"You've always understood him better than anyone," I point out.

"Differently now," he says.

I nod and reach over to pat his back. Glancing at the screen of his computer, I realize it's later than I expected it to be.

"That press conference is about to air," I say, reaching for the remote and turning on the TV. With the channel tuned, I call Sam. "Are you on your break?"

"Just got to my office," he replies. "I'm turning on the stream of the conference. Why is it pre-recorded?"

"I'm guessing since this guy is supposedly one of the more influential figures in that Seers group, he's a target himself. Doing it live would just be asking for someone to come take him out," I say. "Remember, this conference is supposed to be all about him denying he has anything to do with the group."

"Do you think that's true?" Sam asks.

"I don't think that matters," I say. "Whether he is a member or not, if he gets up in front of thousands of people and rejects the Seers and their beliefs, he's going to offend anyone dedicated to the cause. That's not a particularly safe position to be in."

As soon as we heard that one of the supposed leaders of the conspiracy group targeting me was going to speak out about the group and its beliefs, we knew we needed to watch. There have been rumblings of anticipation over the last couple of days. No one is quite sure whether he'll actually refute the things said about him, or make the conference into a platform.

The prevailing theory is the latter. There are so few avenues for these people to get their potentially dangerous beliefs out in front of the mass public in any genuine, meaningful way. But a televised press conference could give him just the stage he's looking for.

"But if it's pre-recorded, doesn't that mean the channel could just decide not to air it if he says anything that isn't what they expect? If he starts going off spinning their theories and calling people out, they could just stop recording and never air the footage," Sam wonders.

"If they catch on to what he's saying," Dean points out.

"What do you mean?"

"These people are masters of deceit and misdirection. They can say one thing and mean something completely different, and it's up to the person listening to wade through and find that kernel of purpose. The thing is, what they find is up to them, too. They can take it to mean whatever they want it to, depending on what they believe. This guy could get up there and say the sun is shining, it's a beautiful day, and some of the people listening are going to take it as a call to arms and a blistering condemnation of the Bureau and its unequally applied policing and biases," Dean shrugs. "That's what makes it so dangerous."

"So, you're saying no matter what he says in this conference, it can't be taken at face value," I say.

"I mean, not entirely. But I don't think he's going to get up there and deliver a manifesto in code. I think it's going to be pretty clear what he really means. What other people think he means is going to be the trouble. Fortunately, not our problem," Dean says.

"Well," Sam cuts in. "That depends on if he says anything about Emma."

"It's starting," I announce.

We watch as the footage of the message starts. Angus Pierson stands at a podium in a navy suit and yellow tie, his hands occasionally lifting a stack of notes, then settling them onto the stand again. He looks nervous and unsure for the first couple of seconds, but it's like a switch turns the instant he realizes he's being recorded.

He's suddenly confident and strong in his posture. He leaves the notes down and his eyes only barely flicker down to them as he speaks. He doesn't smile or try to joke. Every word is carefully measured and offered with solemnity and at least the appearance of earnestness.

As I'm listening to him refute everything being said about him and ask those watching to closely examine what they think and believe, I think I notice something behind him. At first, it's just a flash, but when he shifts his weight again, I can see it clearly. I reach out and grab Dean at the same second my husband says my name through the phone.

"Babe, I've got to go," I say. "Dean is with me. I love you."

Eric is already calling by the time I hang up. I lift the phone to my ear as I tie up my boots.

"I'm on my way."

CHAPTER TWENTY-NINE

T HE GARDEN WHERE PIERSON DID HIS SPEECH IS STILL BLOCKED off when we arrive, but flashing my badge to an officer who already recognizes me gets us past security quickly. Eric is already here, and I'm relieved to see him standing with Pierson.

"Where is it?" I ask, jogging up to him.

"Over there," Eric says, bouncing his head in the direction of the podium. "Nobody has gotten anywhere near it except for a guard I stationed there."

"Perfect," I say. "Thank you."

Dean follows me as I run to the podium. I know the officer's face and he steps out of the way to grant me access to the space diagonally behind where Pierson was standing not too long ago.

"Shit," Dean mutters under his breath when we see the low stone retaining wall.

A distinct spiral is sketched in what looks like chalk on the stone. It's not immediately visible and we likely only noticed it because our brains are now primed to see them, but it's there. What matters is that we did notice it.

"Who set this all up?" I ask, pointing at the podium and the sound and lighting equipment.

A producer comes over to me. "Hi, I'm Kyle. I handled putting all this together."

"Agent Griffin," I say. "When was this set up?"

"This morning," he says. "Usually I like to have a little more time, but Angus insisted on doing his speech outside from this particular location. It's always a challenge to shoot in a public location. We had a permit, so we were able to block off the area, but it wasn't like we could set up hours in advance."

I nod, wanting him to stop talking.

"Was this here?" I ask, gesturing to the wall.

"The wall?" he asks.

"The drawing on it," I clarify.

He shrugs, opening his mouth as if to say something, then closing it again and swinging his head slowly back and forth as if completely befuddled by the question.

"I have no idea," he admits. "I was supervising the setup of the equipment. What I paid attention to was that there weren't any people in the area, it was clean, and there was a good backdrop."

"Did you take any pictures of the space before you set it up?" Dean asks. "Any test footage?"

"Yes," Kyle nods, snapping his fingers and widening his eyes. "I can get that for you. Just one second."

He scurries off and Eric comes over to us with Angus Pierson right behind.

"He doesn't know if the spiral was there before he set up the equipment," I tell Eric. "But he's going to check the pictures and test footage to see if he can find it."

"Good," Eric nods. He gestures at Angus. "This is Angus Pierson. Angus, Agent Emma Griffin."

"Agent Griffin," he says, extending his hand and shaking mine with the kind of strength and force that might be described as sincerity. "I asked to be introduced to you so I could apologize personally. I didn't mention you directly in the recorded message to protect your privacy however much it can be. But I want you to know how deeply sorry I am for how all of this has turned out."

I'm not sure what he's apologizing for, and I look over at Eric for help.

"The rumors that Angus is in some sort of leadership role with these Seers are unfounded," he states. "But some of the discussion in the group is based on a blog he created. It seems a lot of what he put up, including some artwork he did, was misinterpreted and blown out of proportion."

"Eric is being very generous," Angus says. "The truth is, I was incredibly stupid. I intended to use my blog as an avenue for discussion and commentary. But what I ended up doing was sharing misinformation without context or proper disclaimers. I never intended the upheaval my posts caused. I was just trying to make a statement in my own way. It was meant to be satire, like a real-life political cartoon. But it didn't come across that way.

"I apologize so deeply for the way people took what I said. It's not what I believe, and it makes me sick that there are people who didn't understand what I was trying to do and have taken it to the extreme that they have. I didn't come up with any of it. I don't believe any of it. They are just things I heard some talk about, and I thought it would be interesting to put up for people to think about and discuss. It wasn't meant to be taken literally, and I certainly didn't intend on any harm coming to you."

I am decidedly not happy about what he's saying, but the most important thing right now is making sure he stays safe.

"He needs to be secured," I tell Eric. "He can't be alone. It would be best if he could be relocated temporarily."

"What's going on?" Angus asks.

"I'll explain it to you when you're in a safe location," Eric tells him. "Right now, I have to ask you to cooperate and trust us."

The extreme irony of the situation isn't lost on me, and I wait for Angus's reaction. I feel what he does in this moment will be the greatest reflection of what he actually thinks and feels. His nod is reassuring.

"Great," I say. "Thank you. Go with Eric. He'll make sure you're kept safe. I'll be in touch later."

Eric looks at me. "Are you alright?"

"I'm fine," I say. "Just get him somewhere. He's not to be out of sight at any time. Call me with the details when you have them."

He gestures for Angus to follow him and they hurry toward a black car parked nearby. I feel better as soon as he is ducked inside and the door closes. But that relief leaves more room inside my head for me to think about myself. I'm suddenly very aware of my own spiral and the question that lingers with it.

When is he going to come for me?

CHAPTER THIRTY

THE NEXT FEW DAYS TICK BY UNEVENTFULLY. BUT NOTHING HAPpening makes the time slower and every second more pronounced. My thoughts rattle around in my brain and as I stare out the living room window at a cold, steady rain, I can't help but think about Jay Bradley and Lori DeAngelis. Even as the images of their bodies, cast against the same kind of dark gray sky, swell in the front of my mind, I'm brought back to the same thoughts of the garden and the chalk spiral.

Sam's hand on my back is warm and reassuring. I press back into it, relishing his presence. He puts a cup of coffee in my palm and leans down to kiss my cheek.

"Are you alright?" he asks.

"I can't stop thinking about the garden," I say.

"Where Pierson did his speech?" Sam asks.

I nod. "It's fairly new. The city just finished a major multi-year project beautifying the city and adding green spaces and safe gathering spots. That park is one of the last pieces to be completed."

"It's really nice," he comments.

"It's also within three blocks of where I was attacked."

"Do you think Pierson knows that?"

"No," I say. "He doesn't know I'm the surviving victim. No one does. My name was kept out of the papers and never put on the news. One thing that was good about Creagan was when he wanted to get something done, he sure as hell got it done. And he didn't want anyone knowing one of his newest agents was nearly the victim of a serial killer. People keep asking if this could be a copycat. It's not, but if anyone had caught wind of my attack back then, there would have been more.

"He chose the garden because it looks nice. It shows his commitment to the city and to the mission of unification. It was good optics. But I can't get it out of my mind."

Sam stands behind me and I lean into him fully. "Angus called Eric today. He asked when he can leave the hotel and go home."

"What did Eric tell him?" Sam asks.

"He asked me to make a decision. I told him it makes me feel better to know he's in a secure location and being monitored, but I know he can't stay that way forever. It's been a few days and nothing has happened. Of course, that was the point of putting him into a secure location to begin with. Nothing should happen when somebody is under Bureau surveillance at a controlled hotel.

"But I understand his frustration. I know he doesn't want to just sit around and keep waiting. He wants to get back to his life, and I don't feel like I can stop him anymore. I'm going to tell Eric to let him know he can leave whenever he wants. I just hope nothing happens."

"And what about you?" Sam asks. "I hope nothing happens to you."

"So do I," I mutter.

"Somehow I don't think we are talking about the same thing," he comments.

I look up at him, already hating what I'm about to say. "I need to go back. I need to see it again."

"Why?" he asks. "Why would you want to go back there?"

"I haven't been in that parking garage since the day he attacked me. I wouldn't even go back during the investigation. Do you know how that makes me feel? When I look back on that whole time in my life, I have to know that I ran. Maybe not when he was walking behind me. And maybe not when he jumped on me. But after? After, I ran like a coward. I let a building terrify me and I couldn't even fully be a part of the investigation. An investigation into what happened to me."

"You were scared," Sam shrugs. "That's perfectly understandable. And it's nothing to be ashamed about."

"I know it's not," I say. "But I was the only one left."

"Exactly," Sam points out. "You were the only survivor. A man who had already killed two people tried to kill you as well, and you made it through. Of course, you were going to be afraid."

"But I was the only one left who could speak," I say. "The only one who still had a voice. I let the other two down. And I stayed away from that parking garage all this time, and for what? Because I think he's still there? Because he's hovering in one of the corners or under a car, waiting for me to come back so he can finish it off?"

"Why do you want to go back?" Sam asks.

"Because I can."

The rain has finally quieted down by the time I arrive at the parking garage that afternoon. All that's left is the wet chill in the air and a bleak gray sky. The garage isn't busy. I wonder if it has fallen out of favor over the years as other options have opened, or if I've just caught it at a quiet time. Either way, there are only a couple of other cars in place when I drive through the entrance.

Ahead of me, the arrow painted onto the pavement is worn and weathered. The edges are chipped and, in some places, the paint is gone altogether. I remember walking over the top of it that day. I wanted to walk in the direct middle of the path rather than near the edges. It made me more exposed, which in that instance was a good thing.

But even then, the thought flickered briefly through my mind how strange it was to pass right over the arrow. Almost like I was giving whomever was following me directions.

I drive over the arrow now and follow the same route I always took to my usual spot. This was something I did every day for months and even though it's been so many years, I still feel familiar and comfortable sliding into that painted rectangle.

Second floor. Fourth row. Eighth spot.

I don't know what it is about this spot that made it mine. Maybe it was just because it was the one that was available on my first day. Maybe there was some kind of specific draw to it when I was driving around. Maybe Bellamy read my horoscope that morning and gave me clear instructions of the numbers I should keep in mind and I used them to choose the spot. I don't remember. But whatever it was, that became my favorite place.

I parked there every day. Occasionally a morning would come when that specific spot wasn't available and I had to settle for another one nearby, but I stayed as close as I could to the spot. *My* spot. It felt like a good choice at the time. No matter how tired I was at the end of the day, at least I wouldn't have to struggle to remember where I parked my car.

Now I realize it was the first step in setting myself up for my attack.

I don't blame myself. I won't say I haven't gone through phases when I did. There have been plenty of dark days when I told myself every bit of it was my fault because of something I did wrong that day. Some decision I made, or something I didn't do, that would have kept him away from me.

Rationally, I know that's not the case. He would have been there no matter what. Barring not going to the parking garage at all, there's no decision I could have made that day that would have stopped him. That was the day he chose for me.

And this is the one I've chosen for myself.

"Do you want me to come with you?" Sam asks when I reach for the handle of my door.

I know he wants me to say yes. He wants to be right there beside me as I walk around. But I shake my head. I need to do this by myself. At least for a moment. I need to reconcile with the space and with myself.

I walk away from the car and follow the spiral of pavement back down to the entrance. Being out of his sight is going to make Sam crazy, but I want to retrace my own steps. This time, my gun is on my hip.

Every second of that walk is clear and sharp in my head as I recreate it. It's like I'm superimposed over myself, living that day and this one in the same moment. I can feel my younger self walking along with me, and if I hesitate, it's like she steps out in front and I can watch her.

I knew he was there.

But I wasn't going to look back at him. I wasn't going to give him the satisfaction of tossing even a momentary look in his direction. I didn't want to acknowledge him.

I follow along the same path, feeling the tingle of his eyes on me again. This time, I want to turn around. I want to face him, to confront him and force him to come at me with my eyes locked on his. If he wanted me, he was going to have to fight for me.

Sam is turned around in his seat watching for me as I get back onto the second level of the garage. He doesn't say anything, but I can see the relief in his expression.

Stopping in the spot where the attack happened, I closed my eyes and let the reminiscent sensations come over me. My memory echoes the sound of the woman who called out, distracting him and allowing me to get enough of an upper hand to get away. This time, I'm not on the ground. I know the direction he ran to escape and I go there now. Gripping my phone tight in my hand, I go into the enclosed stairwell and start up.

At the bottom of the first flight, the door opens, and Sam comes in.

"I'm not letting you do this alone," he says.

There's no argument. There's no question. It's a declaration and I'm glad for it.

He doesn't say anything else as we climb up the steps to the parking garage. I'm grateful for his presence. No one knows for sure what happened once my attacker got up here. We can only assume he ran down the ramp to escape. The police responded quickly and searched the garage, including the stairwells and elevators, and saw no trace of him. Going down the ramp was the only option.

I walk to the edge of the garage and look out over the city from this vantage point. It's dizzying, even though it's not extremely high. Standing there, I feel like I got everything I came for. I don't know if I can call it catharsis. But I do know that some part of my fear, buried deep down for so many years, no longer feels so heavy.

As I turn to tell Sam I'm ready to go, something catches my attention out of the corner of my eye. I walk to the top of the ramp and look down. At the bottom is what at first looks like a pile of blankets. Then I see the hand stretched out on the ramp as if the person is trying to climb back up.

CHAPTER THIRTY-ONE

"THE TAG SAID 'HERESY,'" I TELL DEAN LATER AFTER WE'RE finally able to leave the parking garage.

"Another that isn't one of the seven deadly sins," he offers.

"I noticed that, too," I nod. "He sustained burns over a good portion of his body and preliminary examination from the coroner shows extensive damage to his throat and airways."

"He inhaled fire," Dean says.

"That's what it looks like," I nod. "But his clothing wasn't burned, and neither were the blankets put over him. There was no fire damage anywhere on the ramp or the surrounding sidewalks. And the fire department didn't have any reports of fires in the area near the time of death."

"Do you know who he is?" Dean asks.

"Not yet," I admit. "There wasn't any identification on him, which is different from the other victims. That tells me either he was caught when he didn't have his wallet on him, or he doesn't have identification at all."

"What are the chances he doesn't have identification?" Dean asks. "Everybody has identification."

I shake my head. "Not everybody. But we are trying to find a way to track down his identity. The burn injuries to his face were pretty extensive, so identification of the body isn't going to be possible just by looking at him. We're going to need dental records or hope for a surgical implant with a serial number on it."

"Could this be who that spiral was intended for all along?" he wonders. "I know you said all the other spirals have been right there at the murder sites, or at least very close. But what if the killer intended on killing this victim there in the garden, not knowing the speech was happening? He could have put the spiral there ahead of time, but then had to change his plan at the last minute."

"I asked the same thing," Sam chimes in, coming into the room holding boxes of takeout that smell amazing but do nothing to stimulate my appetite. "That guy Kyle said he wasn't able to set anything up until just before Angus did his speech. And the pictures he took right before setting everything up are clear proof that the spiral was there. Maybe this victim frequents that park at that time of day."

"I did go back there and noticed a lot of people tend to have morning coffee out there or take their lunches and eat them out of the park. Even when it's cold. Maybe our victim is somebody who does that on a regular basis and the killer knows that, so the spiral was put there with every intention on that being where he committed the murder," Dean offers.

"In front of all those people?" I ask. "You just said there are a lot of people there almost all the time. But he's going to burn somebody to death right there? No. That spiral was for Angus. Remember, we found another one at the site of the burned victim."

"The killer had to change his plans," Sam says. "If you believe Angus was meant to be murdered there, then you have to believe it's possible for the killer to manage the feat even if people are around."

"Maybe another method of murder, but not forcing someone to eat fire," I say.

"Another method, then," Sam presses. "A shooting. A fast stabbing. The point is, he could have planned on killing the victim in the park, put the spiral in place, and then had to change everything when the speech was set up there. When he caught up with the guy a few days later, he killed him in a different way and left the spiral in the new location."

"This is all assuming he somehow didn't know about that speech. It was advertised. We knew it was coming. Why wouldn't he? And the spirals are different. Not just in different locations or made out of different materials. There is a different number of rotations in each of the spirals. Besides, these spirals mean something. They aren't just arbitrary. He'd already made one. I don't think he would make another for the same victim," I say.

"You got two," Sam points out.

The spiral painted on the wall in front of my usual parking spot is long gone now. It was scrubbed away years ago during a regular cleaning of the parking garage. But I still have a picture of it. I remember the nine swirling circles around the center point, the same as the ones on the storage unit door.

"Mine were years apart," I tell him. "And he did attack me after making the first. Maybe that was all that spiral could represent."

There's a knock on the door and Sam goes to answer it. He opens it and Eric walks in, his phone still in his hand as if he's just finished a conversation. His eyes meet mine.

"That was Angus," he says.

"Is everything okay? Is he all right?" I ask.

"He's fine," Eric says. "Maybe a little shaken up."

"Why?" I get to my feet, ready to react, but he turns his phone screen to me. "What is that?"

"He got that in the mail today," Eric says.

"What is it?" Dean asks.

I take the phone out of Eric's hand and examine the image more closely.

"It's a tag," I frown. "Like the ones found on the victims. It says 'fraud,' but it's been crossed out."

I turn the phone to show Dean and Sam the picture. The tag looks exactly like all the others, and the handwriting of the word 'fraud' is the same. But it has been crossed out with a gold permanent marker.

"What does that mean?" Dean asks.

"It's been crossed out," Sam says. "Canceled."

"I don't understand," Eric says. "Why would he get a tag with a canceled word written on it in the mail?"

"When did he get it?" I ask.

"It was waiting for him when he got back home today," Eric says.

"Can you find out the postmark? Find out when it was sent."

He sends a text, and a few seconds later, a response arrives. He reads it, then looks up at me.

"It was sent the day of his speech," he says.

"Does anybody have a copy of it? Is there a way we can access a full recording of his speech?"

"Sure," Eric says. "Why?"

"We didn't get to hear all of it," I explain. "Only the very beginning. We don't know exactly what he said. But I have a feeling it was significant. I want to listen to it."

A few minutes later, we sit down with a recording of the press conference queued up on my computer screen. I press play and we all listen as Pierson adamantly denies having anything to do with the Seers and apologizes for confusing or upsetting anyone. Much like he did when he was talking to me, he lays out his intentions for his blog posts and admits it didn't work out the way he meant it to.

When it's over, I scan back to the beginning and listen through again. It doesn't get all the way to the end before I stop it.

"He apologizes," I say. "That's what happened."

"He apologized?" Eric asks. "We know that. He specifically came to you to apologize."

"I know," I nod. "But that's the point. He apologized for misleading people and for causing trouble. He denounced the entire group and everything they were saying and planning. His sin wasn't canceled. It was forgiven."

"So he didn't die," Sam says.

I shake my head. "It still doesn't make sense. If he would have been killed, there would have been seven victims. But three of the tags have words written on them that aren't the seven deadly sins."

"Eight, Emma," Sam reminds me. "Eight victims. You can't forget yourself."

"There was no word written on my tag," I say.

"That doesn't mean there wasn't going to be," Eric says. "We've already established he writes the words after he's finished with the person. He didn't get a chance to with you."

I let the breath slide from my lungs. "Alright. Eight victims. But four of the deadly sins, one blank tag, and three other words that I guess you could consider sins. And they still don't fit. I can almost understand Angus's tag. Fraud. He did spread false information and people believed he was something he wasn't. It doesn't add up exactly, but it's something. The other ones, though? They just don't make sense. I've combed through the lives of the victims and I couldn't even come up with a creative way to link any of them to the words attached to them."

"We don't know about the burn victim," Eric points out. "Without even knowing who he is, we can't know anything about his life."

"Even if we did know about him, it seems like that's a pretty broad stroke to make. Heresy isn't all that specific anymore when you really think about it. Yes, centuries ago there were very clear rules on what you were allowed and not allowed to believe, but that doesn't exist here anymore. Not for mainstream society. And it certainly isn't going to get anybody burned at the stake. But the definition is a belief that contradicts orthodox belief systems. That can really be interpreted as any belief because it's going to go against some orthodox system some-where," Dean says.

"Burned at the stake," Sam mutters almost under his breath.

"What?" I ask.

"He said burned at the stake. Like how heretics were burned at the stake centuries ago."

"They were," I nod. "Joan of Arc. John Hooper. Hugh Latimer."

"I know," Sam says. "What I mean is the victim was burned. The punishment corresponded with the sin."

"But Lori was hit by a car and Paisley was hit in the back of the head. I'm fairly sure those aren't traditional punishments for any sin," I reply. "I hate this. I feel like we're going in circles."

"Or spirals," Sam jokes.

"You only get away with that one because we're married. Watch it next time, buster."

"Yes, ma'am."

We break into a much-needed laugh, but the weight of this case is really starting to get to all of us. It feels like every time we're getting closer, another random detail appears. It's like having a handful of tiny pebbles rather than a solid piece of stone.

ROBERT
PORTER

TEACHER, SON, FRIEND

CHAPTER THIRTY-TWO

A S SOON AS MY FATHER GETS HOME FROM WORK, HE JOINS IN OUR brainstorming session. While he was at the office, I sent him pictures of all the murder scenes and asked him to print out zoomed-in images of all the spirals. When he brings them to me, I spread them out on the coffee table and kneel beside it with a large black permanent marker. I go across the images, noting on each one when the spiral was first noticed, or if there was any evidence of it existing before the murder.

In some instances, I can't say for certain when it was made, but I know it was there when the body was found. But in every case when we know when the spiral was made, it was there before the murder.

"Making the spiral isn't part of the murder when it's happening," I say. " I think it's a warning. A sign that it's going to happen. Remember when we saw it behind Pierson. It instantly told us he was in danger. We didn't even know what was going to happen, but we saw it and it instantly acted as a signal. I think that's what it was in every one of these situations."

"But why a spiral?" Sam wonders.

"And why are they different?" Dean adds. "It isn't just that they are different because he used what was available in the area, or tried to make it fit in with the rest of the surroundings. If he went through that much effort to make them, he could make sure they were all the same design."

"Explain to me again what's different about them," Dad says.

I use the tip of the pen to show him the revolutions of the spiral.

"It's different on most of them," I point out. "Not just how big it was made, but how many of these circles are in them. Angus's had eight. The burn victim had six. The roses in the cemetery had seven. They didn't even go in order like he was adding victims as he went."

"You said most," Dad points out. "Which ones are the same?"

"Jay and Lori," I tell him. "The original two victims. Their spirals have the same number. Just two. And then mine. Both times there were nine."

"So when the same word was used—or in your case, a lack of word—here were the same number of rotations in the spiral," Dad muses.

I nod. "I figured the first two victims had the same because they were killed so close together. Maybe that was his original intended signature. But then why would he change it just two weeks later when he came after me?"

"Maybe the words correspond to the number of rotations?" Sam offers.

I touch the tip of the marker to the center of the spiral in the picture of the parking garage. As I swirl it around, following the curves, my mind counts the circles. My hand stops and I stare at the paper. Suddenly, I'm on my feet.

"Emma?" Dad asks.

I'm already darting down the hallway to his office. The enormous bookshelf lining one wall was the first thing I made sure got put back when he came home and took back over the house. Every one of the books he loved had been packed and stored while I tried to figure out what I was going to do with them. I still remember sitting on the floor surrounded by the towers of his books, tears streaming down my face as I thought about him reading them. The one I grab now feels so heavy when I pick it up and hold it in my lap. Heavy in size. Heavy in significance.

I carry it back into the living room with me, my heart pounding in my chest and my ears buzzing.

"What's that?" Sam asks.

"This isn't the seven deadly sins," I tell everyone. "And it's isn't eight, even though I would have been the eighth victim." I drop the book down onto the middle of the table, making it shake and the papers around it billow up. Some float down to the floor, falling like rain. "It's nine."

"Dante's Inferno," Dad whispers.

"This is one of three epic poems Dante wrote. The title of it is one of the most commonly known titles, but most people have never read it. They don't actually know what it's about. In it, Dante ventures down through hell, encountering people who are being eternally punished for a variety of transgressions during their earthly existence. He described nine distinct circles that gradually descend deeper down to the core, with each circle featuring progressively more severe sins and punishments."

"The spirals represent the circles?" Eric asks.

"Yes, but more importantly, they represent judgment." I flip open the book to an illustration at the beginning. "This is Minos, the judge of the dead in the underworld. It was his responsibility to determine the fate of all the souls that came before him. When he made the decision, he would wrap his tail around the soul a specific number of times. That would represent the circle of hell the soul was damned to."

"They aren't just warnings," Dean says, sinking down off the edge of the couch to kneel beside me so he can look more closely at the images of the spirals. "They're sentences. He's condemning them before he carries it out."

I flip through the book again to an elaborately decorated image in the back illustrating Dante's vision of the circles.

"Lust," I point out. "The second circle. Punished by being tossed back and forth in a storm. Both Jay and Lori were killed during severe storms. Gluttony. The third circle. Punished with putrid icy mud."

"Paisley had mud in her throat," Eric says.

"Greed. The fourth circle. Punished by pushing huge weights. That victim, Cole Burrows, had all of his ribs broken. It seemed like he was beaten to death, but I think he was crushed. Heresy. The sixth circle. Punished by being trapped in a flaming tomb. That victim was burned and forced to consume fire."

"What about the cemetery?" Dean asks. "His tag said 'Violence.'"

I nod, swallowing hard as I realize I was wrong about the tag in the cemetery. "The seventh circle. Punished by being submerged in a river of blood. He didn't get a chance to murder him, but he covered his grave with red rose petals. And Angus, fraud, the eighth circle."

"What about yours?" Sam asks. "What's the ninth circle?"

I run my finger down the page until it lands on the image of the centermost circle in the depiction, the deepest pit. "The worst circle. The one where Satan himself is trapped in a lake of ice to be tormented for eternity. Treachery."

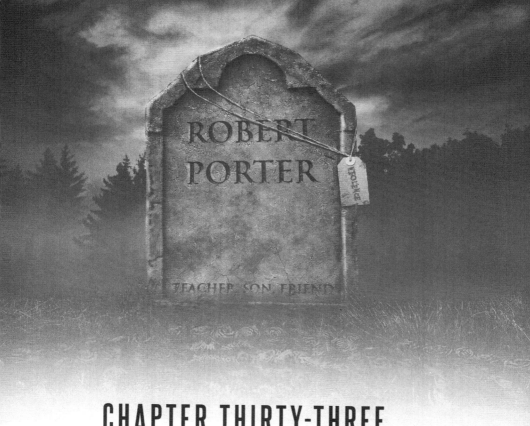

CHAPTER THIRTY-THREE

"**A**LRIGHT, SO WE KNOW THAT THESE SPIRALS WEREN'T RANDOM. They weren't just put there haphazardly. They had intention. They were being condemned for specific sins after being warned," Dean recaps. "But I still don't understand. Even with this explained, it doesn't link up. The sins don't correspond. For each of these people to be condemned for one of these sins, they would have had to have committed them. But they didn't."

As I filter these details through my mind, the picture becomes clearer. Realization starts to settle in and the pieces begin to tumble into place. The picture still isn't fully there, but I'm starting to see it differently.

I shake my head, reaching for the files of the victims.

"I don't think that's the point," I say. "Yes, these people were being condemned. But maybe not for sins they committed. Look at this. Angus Pierson was condemned for fraud, right? The eighth circle. We already admitted it seems like a bit of a stretch to describe him as a fraud.

Just because he represented information incorrectly and got people talking about things doesn't exactly constitute being a fraud. But look at the way that Dante described that circle. Those were condemned to the eighth circle included panderers, seducers, flatterers, sorcerers, imposters, hypocrites, and sowers of discord."

"Sowers of discord," Eric speaks up. "That's exactly what he did. The posts he made riled people up and created upheaval and conflict."

"It isn't what they did," Dad offers. "It's what they influenced others to do."

"Just one," I say. "I believe the killer is punishing the people who caused him to act in these ways. Every one of these victims influenced a single person to act in a way he perceives as a sin. And he condemned them for it. So, who did they influence?"

"Emma, who did you influence?" Sam asks.

"It's a poem," Xavier says later when we manage to get him on the phone. "Not a religious text. In its time, Inferno was part of the larger work: the Divine Comedy. It had a good ending. Dante didn't end up having to stay in hell. He slid down Satan and scrambled his way right on back onto Earth. Not exactly the type of playground equipment I'd be jumping to try out, but it worked out for him."

"So, you're saying you don't actually think these have anything to do with sins?" Dean asks.

"That's not what I'm saying," Xavier clarifies. "I'm saying it's important to remember the good ending. He's not intending on staying in hell. He isn't going to be punished. This is a man who wants to shimmy down Satan's back and pop back up on Earth in time for lunch. He's creating a better future for himself."

"By killing people?" I ask. "Maybe I'm not interpreting the text the same way that other people do, but wouldn't murder constitute violence? That seventh circle we've been talking about? And while we're at it, one of the Ten Commandments? I think we consider that an actual religious text and not a poem."

"Yes," Xavier acknowledges. "But you have to remember, the people who are condemned are the ones who were still guilty of those sins when their souls went for judgment. Murder is an isolated, one-time kind of sin. It can be forgiven. Others are ongoing. There's the need for continual purification. It's why there are volunteer ministers and prayer groups who come in here every week, and regular services in the chapel. Even the worst of the worst in here have the option for redemption. Maybe not in the eyes of society, but that's not what they're after."

My mind is reeling. "You're saying this is someone who's trying to better themselves."

"Self-improvement through murder," Xavier says. "I doubt that one's going to hit the New York Times bestseller list."

"Actually, it probably would," I say. I pinch the bridge of my nose between my finger and thumb, hoping to relieve some of the pressure behind my eyes. "Alright, so what we're saying is these victims aren't being punished for committing these sins. It's for something they did that caused the killer to do something. His motivation is to get rid of what caused him to go astray."

"And likely, in his mind at least, to prevent other people from following along in that same path. He's protecting them from the damage that was done to him," Xavier adds.

"So, we're no longer trying to figure out how these sins were expressed in the victims' lives. We're trying to figure out what they did that influenced someone to commit that sin."

"Which means it was someone they all could have interacted with," Dean says.

"Not necessarily," I counter. "Angus didn't directly interact with most of the people he frothed up. In his case, it could be as simple as someone who read his posts."

"Broadening the potential scope from people he knew and engaged with to anyone who might have come across his posts doesn't simplify the situation," Dean points out. "Dig deeper, Emma. Remember, people don't always realize how influential they actually are until the worst has happened. These people might not have known what they were doing when they were sealing their own fate. Because it doesn't matter what they did. It matters what someone else thought of them."

"Let's start from the beginning," I announce. "Lori and Jay. What about them might have influenced lust?"

My father's living room has become the war room for this investigation. The couch has now been pushed to the other side of the room, replaced by a roll of butcher paper stretched across the wall and pinned in place to create a surface where we can write notes and post images.

Sam, Dean, Eric, and my father perch around the rest of the furniture, each of them holding a notebook so they can write things down.

"Jay Bradley was a married man," Sam starts. "He was happy with his wife. They were very content and together. Even if they didn't exhibit a lot of public displays of affection, just seeing them together could inspire a single man to feel lustful."

"That's a possibility," I note. "Which means it would have to be somebody who knew them as a couple, or at least was able to watch them in their day-to-day life. Maybe a neighbor or a co-worker."

I jot down notes about that and I turn my attention to the picture of Lori DeAngelis up on the wall.

"I have a couple of guys going through everything she ever posted, wrote about, spoke about, everything to try it to find something that would inspire lust," Eric says. "I told them not to be too discriminatory. Pick anything that could bring any of those thoughts to mind."

"Well, she was a woman on the internet," I offer. "There are all sorts of sickos out there with zero boundaries who harass and pester women with even minimal online presence. That's still a pretty wide net. But how about Cole? Greed."

"According to the description in the poem, greed doesn't have to just be about money. Those who hoard goods and resources are also considered guilty of the sin of greed," Dean says. "I did some looking into his background. He's a survivalist. He made his money off of teaching people how to go out into the wild and get by on the absolute bare minimum, using what they find in nature."

"That doesn't sound much like a hoarder," I say. "Sounds like kind of the opposite."

"Well, up until recently," he says. "A couple of years ago he opened a small, secondary business focused on a very precise niche market for those wanting to survive a specific sort of hazard."

He sounds like he is being purposely careful with his wording, and I throw him a look.

"Like the zombie apocalypse?" I ask sarcastically.

He gives me a shrug and a small nod.

"You can't be serious," Eric says. "People pay to learn how to survive a zombie apocalypse?"

"Absolutely," Sam tells him. "And it's not as ridiculous as it sounds. Well, it can be as ridiculous as it sounds. But for most people, it's not actually about zombies."

"Just the apocalypse?" Dean asks.

"Or at least a catastrophic event rendering life as we know it obsolete," Sam shrugs. He looks over at me and catches my raised eyebrow. "There's a show about it."

"Is this what you do in the middle of the night when I'm away in the field?" I ask.

"I've learned the importance of water purification tablets. And how to craft a distillation setup for when those tablets inevitably run out without modern manufacturing," he says.

"I could have told you that," Dean says.

"I probably could have, too," Eric adds. "Maybe not the distillation part."

'Wait," I say, shaking my hands over my head. "Stop. This man charged people to learn how to survive a zombie apocalypse-slash-catastrophic event not involving the reanimated dead, do I have that right?"

"I mean, that's what it says here," Dean shrugs. "And I haven't done much digging into the company directly, but what I do know about this industry is that it rakes in the big bucks. Lots of well-heeled stockbrokers and hedge-fund managers pay a pretty penny to have a guy like him outfit them with the latest and greatest in tactical bunkers and custom gear."

"That sounds like straight-up greed to me," I say. "He was taking advantage of people so he could make money."

"Not necessarily," Dad says. "I know it sounds ridiculous when you talk about it that way, but the principles these experts teach are often just extreme versions of self-sustaining lifestyles. Think about people immediately after the Depression. They bought large amounts of canned foods and household materials and held onto them just in case they ever went through something like that again.

"During the Cold War, families built bomb shelters they filled up with food and supplies to make sure they would be able to get through something disastrous. It's the same thing, just a different name. Some people take it moderately, others go to the extreme."

"Preppers," I say. "You think the killer might have taken one of the survival courses and become an extreme prepper?"

"It's a possibility," Dad nods. "That would constitute greed because he would have accumulated a large number of goods he was keeping for himself, but it would also place the blame on Cole Burrows because he was the one who influenced the killer to do it in the first place."

"Can we get a list of everyone who ordered those courses?" I ask. "Then we can narrow down the demographics into men of the right age range and geographical area. It should give us a smaller pool to work with."

"I'm on it," Eric says. "I'll see if I can find a cross-reference with any of these other victims, too."

"Good thinking," I say. Eric turns to his laptop and begins typing away, his fingers moving so fast they're blurry. The man is a technical genius. I have no doubt he'll be able to find something useful.

"The same basic principle can be used for Angus's fanbase, but it's going to be more complicated," Dad says. "You're going to need a tremendous amount of cooperation from judges and from the internet companies to get that information. Doing that takes a long time, and even then, at best you'll end up with a bunch of anonymous usernames that we'll have to dig into."

"We should get it started," I say. "Every detail is going to help. But we'll just also keep it in mind if we find a suspect to talk to. Alright, the man in the cemetery."

"Robert Porter," Sam says. "I did some research into his death and confirmed he was killed during an incident with police. Apparently, he was driving erratically and suspected to be under the influence. When he was pulled over, he refused to get out of his vehicle, take the keys out of the ignition, or take his hands off the wheel. An officer reached in to take the keys and Porter stomped on the gas. The officer was dragged several yards, then fell off the car.

"The rest of the responding police chased Porter for quite a distance, deployed stop sticks, and eventually had to use a PIT maneuver to stop him. He tried to avoid the move and overcorrect, and ended up rolling several times and going into a ravine. It killed him instantly."

"That's horrific," I say. "But I wouldn't necessarily call it violent. His behavior wasn't violent to others. Almost self-destructive."

Sam nods. "I thought the same thing. Tox screen confirmed that he'd been drinking pretty heavily that night. My first thought was that he may have been in some sort of domestic dispute, but it seems that he'd just had a few too many after a heavy workout at the gym, affecting him more than he'd thought. He was a gym teacher and reportedly a total fitness nut."

"But still, violence?" I press. "Reckless and dangerous for sure, but that doesn't click with me. How was he inspiring violence in our killer?"

"When I investigated him further, I found out that while he was a gym teacher when he died, his previous career was actually as a military recruiter."

"War," I say, remembering the description in the book. "Violence against others."

"I'll see what I can do about finding a list of his recruits."

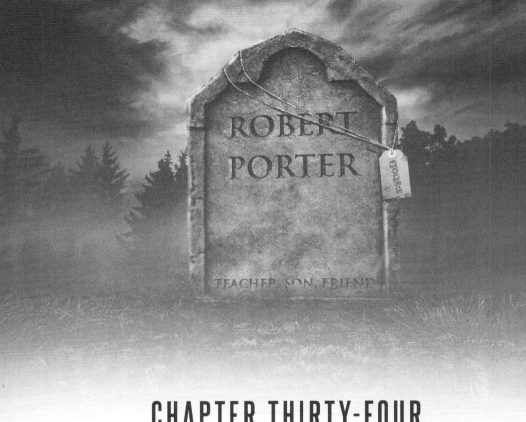

CHAPTER THIRTY-FOUR

WE STILL HAVEN'T BEEN ABLE TO IDENTIFY THE BURN VICTIM, which means we're at a standstill with him. Unless we can find out who he is, there's no way to understand how he might have influenced the killer. That leaves Paisley and me.

"I know there are plenty of people who would say I betrayed them," I say. "But I don't know who I might have influenced to be treacherous. Especially that long ago. I was just at the beginning of my career. I'd helped with a few cases, but I hadn't led any. It would be a few more months before I started out on my own."

I close my eyes and reminisce, trying to remember what cases I could possibly have been involved in back then. I've always considered Travis Burke my first case—a man who murdered his wife and buried her under concrete. That case came back only a few years ago, when his secret lover came after me for revenge.

"Maybe it doesn't have anything to do with your job," Dean says. "There are other ways to betray people other than sending them to prison."

"I just don't know," I say.

"How about relationships?" Dean offers. "Anyone that you dated years ago who might have had a girlfriend? Or been married?"

I shake my head.

"No. I was with Sam until right before I went into the Academy and then my next real relationship was with Greg. The only thing that might come close to fitting in with that is the Dragon, and that wasn't a real relationship; I was undercover. Considering he's dead, I don't think it's him. But even then, it doesn't really apply because I'm the one who betrayed him."

"We're going to have to think harder," he muses. "What about that cult you investigated? The Society for the… what was it?"

"Betterment of the Future," I inform him.

"That's right," Sam perks up. "Your spiral was drawn on the door of the storage unit where that group had me kidnapped. One of the women they had captive escaped and told you everything. That could be seen as a betrayal."

"That's true," I acknowledge. "But I don't think that's it. This happened before I ever had anything to do with them. I know the leader thought he was God, but he couldn't look into the future and know what was going to happen to his cult. And if he could, he did a really bad job of stopping it from happening."

"Damn," Sam says. "I didn't think about that."

"I just don't know who else it could be," I say.

"I can pull out your case files," Eric says. "Maybe you can sift through old cases and find people you don't remember. You have handled a lot of cases over the years. You may have forgotten someone."

"Thanks," I tell him. "That will help."

"That just leaves Paisley," Dean says.

I sigh.

"Yep. Gluttony."

"Did she write cookbooks on the side or anything?" Dean asks.

I laugh. "I wish it could be that simple. This one's hard. She didn't work in a restaurant or a bakery. She didn't decorate cakes or make everybody brownies all the time. She wasn't a bartender. The description of gluttony includes addictions, but while she went through a really rough time, her mother, her medical records, her friends, her police records, none of it gave any indication she ever had a problem with drugs or sold drugs."

"You're going to have to go talk to her mother again," Dean says. "Find out more about her."

"I know," I say, but there's no longer any laughter in my voice.

I'm not looking forward to going back to talk to Cassie Graham. She's a perfectly pleasant woman, but I don't want to see that pain in her eyes again. I know the conversation we must have is just going to hurt her more. It's hard enough having to come to terms with the reality of her daughter having been murdered. Now I'm asking her to help me find a reason for it.

It feels like I'm skirting dangerously close to blaming her for her own murder. The thought of that disgusts me. No matter what she may or may not have done, Paisley did not cause her death. And she didn't deserve her murder.

None of these victims did. The killer may have blamed them all for where his own life went astray, but none of them deserved to be murdered like this.

And though it pains me, the only path I have left is to skim that line. I have to delve into who she was and the life she led to find something this killer could blame for his actions.

The next day, I'm back sitting on the floral couch in Cassie's living room.

"I really appreciate you being willing to talk with me again," I start. "I know this isn't easy for you, and I'm going to make it as quick as I possibly can."

"I want to help you any way I can," she tells me. "I want to know who did this to my little girl. I just don't know what more help I can offer you."

"Paisley never had a problem with any type of drug, did she?"

"No," Cassie insists forcefully. "Never."

"I'm not trying to judge her," I say. "Please, believe me. I'm trying to understand the motivation behind the man who did this to her."

"I'm sorry," she says.

"You have no need to apologize," I tell her. "The store where she was found. When that business was open, she worked there, didn't she?"

"Yes," she nods. "I'm sorry I didn't mention it when we first spoke. I didn't even think about it. It's been a while since the store closed, and she had some negative memories of it."

This piques my attention.

"Negative memories?" I ask. "I was led to believe she enjoyed working there."

"She did," Cassie says. "There was just an accident and it caused some problems afterward. It didn't have anything to do with the business closing down, but she blamed herself for it. She felt like the accident was kind of the beginning of the end. I mean, given the advent of cell phone cameras over the last decade, I can't imagine how much longer a camera store would really stay open. I always tried to tell her that, but she never believed me."

"What kind of accident?" I ask.

"She was in the stockroom trying to find a particular item for a customer. They were adamant that they needed this very specific item that had to be kept in the back and Paisley always wanted to make customers happy. She wasn't overly enthralled with the position. But she always said she could dream about the career she was going to have in the future, but until that happened, she was going to make the most of what she had in the moment."

"That's a good way to look at things," I note.

"That's how she always looked at things when she was younger," Cassie says. "Before her divorce. When she started saying things like that again, I really hoped it meant she was on her way back up. That I was getting my daughter back. She really dedicated herself to anything that she was doing, and that included going above and beyond for anyone who came into the store."

"Why don't you tell me what happened that day?" I prompt her. I am normally content to just let grieving people express themselves in whatever way they feel comfortable doing—it can lead to information coming to light that they might not at first consider useful, but that can really turn the corner of an investigation. This time, though, I'm hoping to steer her in a particular direction. There are so many possibilities with this case that I'll need her to narrow it down as much as she can.

Cassie nods. "That day, she went into the stockroom to find that item for the customer. There was nobody there to help her, but she saw a box of what she was looking for up on the top of a shelving unit. Since it looked stable, she decided to climb up. Unfortunately, she lost her footing and grabbed onto the shelf. It wasn't as steady as she thought it would be and the entire unit came down. Two of her co-workers had heard the initial sound of the fall and came in. They were caught beneath the shelves as well.

"Paisley had a couple of bruises and a fairly decent cut down one leg, but her coworkers fared a bit worse. One broke her arm and collarbone, and the other broke both legs and his pelvis. On top of that, tens of thousands of dollars in inventory was broken. The store tried to place the blame on Paisley, saying she was being unsafe, which she was, but that didn't mean it was totally her fault and should be responsible for everything.

"It was a difficult battle, but eventually it was shown that she was partially responsible, but that the store was also responsible because of a lack of equipment like stepstools to get inventory off the shelves, and the shelving units should have been secured to the floor and to the wall to prevent accidents like that. Insurance paid the medical bills and the two more seriously injured coworkers had workers' comp."

"Wow," I say. "That does sound like a lot for her to go through. No wonder she had negative memories of it. Do you by chance remember the names of the coworkers?"

She shakes her head. "No. I tried to stay out of it as much as I could. Paisley wanted to handle it like an adult and I didn't want to step on her toes."

"Thank you," I say, standing up. "I think that's all I need for now. If I think of anything else, can I get in touch?"

"Of course."

ROBERT
PORTER

TEACHER, SON, FRIEND

CHAPTER THIRTY-FIVE

O N MY DRIVE BACK TO MY FATHER'S HOUSE, I DETOUR TO DRIVE
past the parking garage. I want to look at where I discovered the
burn victim again. Since there were no burn patterns or other damage to the area around him, it was obvious he wasn't murdered there but
brought there and dumped. It's still difficult to imagine how someone
would be able to bring a body that horrifically damaged to a public location like that and leave it.

I'm curious about different ways the killer could have accessed that
area of the parking garage. I plan on coming back later with Dean anyway, but I figured driving by would give me a quick head start. But as
I drive it down Barton Street, behind the parking garage, I see it isn't
empty. A handful of people are standing together on the spot where
the body was found. They appear to be holding hands, their heads
ducked down.

I park on the side of the road and walk over.

"Excuse me," I call out as I approach. One of the people's heads lifts and the face I see confuses me. Violet. "What are you doing here?"

"Oh, hello, Emma," she smiles. "We are just here saying a prayer. Our community parish is preparing for the funeral for this poor soul, but the chief informed me the body isn't being released yet."

"No," I say. "This is a murder. And that person still hasn't been identified. The body can't be released for burial yet."

She nods.

"I understand. I only wanted to offer our respects. We don't mean to be in the way."

The group leaves, walking without urgency around the ramp and into the parking garage. I watch them curiously. Something about the interaction strikes me as strange. I take a second to look around. The area has been cleaned up, but there are still traces of the horror found here. Black streaks across the sidewalk and dark liquid soaked into the seams between the squares mark where he was lying. They will likely be there for months, if not years, and people will all too soon forget what they were.

It's one of the surprising and often disheartening things about death. It's shocking and horrifying in the moment, but people quickly move on. As soon as the idea becomes familiar in their minds and they can cover up the thoughts with other ones until it creates a buffer, the intensity of the reaction is no longer there.

Marks on the ground from where a tortured human body lay should cause revulsion and deep sadness for as long as they are visible. But the memory will fade. People will start to think they came from an oil leak or an engine fire. They'll forget about the man who lay there dead. And then the rain and the sun will wash and bleach them away until it's nothing anymore.

I step back from the bottom of the ramp and look up and down the back road to see how many angles someone could use to approach this spot. It's a one-way street, so they couldn't have come up from the back portion of the parking deck. There's an alley across the street, however. It's narrow, pressed between two buildings, and likely not even wide enough for some people to walk through. But it could be used by the right person.

There are also the stairwells and elevators inside the parking garage. He could have driven into the garage, parked, and transferred the body using those access points to get to the roof, then carried it down. But it's hard to conceive of someone being able to do that without leaving any trace of the body on any other surface in the garage. I step out into the street, craning my neck left and right, to see as much of the building as I can.

And then I hear a squeal and sudden roar like an engine. It's so loud it's disorienting.

It takes a second to process that the sound is coming from above me. I look up to see what it is and find myself staring directly into the headlights of a car careening through the concrete barrier.

Straight towards me.

My mind doesn't process the situation. I can't fully understand what I'm seeing until it's almost too late. At the last second, I throw myself out of the way and curl up to protect my head and face.

The car smashes into the ground with a massive, sickening crash; bits of metal and glass scrape my back and arms as I run away. I high-tail it away from there, pushing myself to the brink, hoping it won't explode. Fortunately, there's no heat coming from behind me, and once I've made it to the corner, I whip out my phone and dial for emergency assistance.

"9-1-1, what is your—"

"Emma Griffin, FBI. I'm at the garage at 14th and Barton. I need emergency backup immediately. A car just fell out of one of the levels and crashed on the street. I'm going to check for survivors."

"Get away from the car," the dispatcher tells me. "Don't get any closer to it."

"I don't know if anyone is inside," I say.

"Backup is already en route. You need to keep yourself safe. Get away from the car in case the gas tank explodes."

I want to try to help, but I know she's right. I get to the end of the street as fast as I can, suddenly realizing that pain is racing up my leg and stinging in my back. In fact, I'm having a hard time walking. My left leg doesn't want to cooperate for some reason.

Just as I turn the corner to get out onto the main street, the ground beneath my feet shakes with the force of an explosion. Someone screams near me and I realize it's me.

What could be a second or an hour later, I don't know, a pair of hands take hold of me and help me onto a stretcher. The first responder talks to me as they load me into an ambulance, but I'm not really registering what he's saying. At first, it seems like he's being far too chipper for the horror that just happened. Then I realize he's trying to keep me focused and awake. I can't go to sleep. They need to keep me awake and out of shock.

I can't get them to tell me anything, and almost as soon as we arrive at the hospital, a mask covers my face and I sink into bright white oblivion.

The next thing I know, I wake up to the feeling of Sam gently stroking the back of my hand with his thumb. My throat is dry and my skin stings.

"Hey," I croak softly.

He smiles at me and the same place in my heart that always melts a little when he does that goes soft. I'll never get enough of my husband's smile, equal parts sexy and little boy sweet. It sinks in that I'm lucky to have this moment to see it again.

"Hey yourself, beautiful," he says. "I've been waiting for you to wake up."

"How long have I been here?" I ask.

It feels like my throat is going to crack with every word.

"About twenty-four hours," he says. "Let me get the doctor in here to check you out and see if you can get something to drink."

He pages the doctor, then comes back to my side.

"This is just perfect," I groan. "Here I am trying to save the world and they take a whole day away from me."

Sam tries to laugh but I see a tear forming in his eye. "Hey. None of that. I'm fine."

"I was so worried about you," he says. "When I heard what happened, I was terrified he had done it. He'd come for you and I wasn't there to protect you. I knew I shouldn't have let you go by yourself."

"You don't have to let me or not let me do anything," I reply. "It's not your responsibility, Sam. I love you and I am so happy that you love me. But I never want you to feel like anything that happens to me is your fault. I made the decision to go to the parking garage. I don't know what happened after that."

"A car drove through the barrier and off the side of the garage. It crashed just a few yards from you. You had a lot of glass and some metal shards lodged in your back and upper arms. Something hit your left leg and caused a deep puncture, but no broken bones. The 911 dispatcher said you tried to go to the car to see if anyone was inside, but she made you leave. Just in time, apparently. The gas tank ignited and the car exploded. You were far enough away to avoid serious injury, but you have a few minor burns."

"Was there anyone inside?" I ask.

"They don't know yet," Sam shakes his head. "The explosion was intense and the flames burned so hot, everything inside was incinerated before it could be put out. Right now, they don't have any confirmation of human remains, but they're still examining the car."

The doctor comes in and Sam goes out to call everybody while she's checking me over. By the time he comes back, I know I'm going to have to stay for at least another night.

"I thought you might," he says when I tell him. "Fortunately, I have reading materials for you."

"Oh?" I ask.

He nods and holds out what looks like a stack of papers printed off the computer. "Courtesy of Xavier and the Breyer Correctional Facility."

I laugh when I see the title of the newsletter, cringing at the pain the laughter causes.

"I'm sure this will be very enlightening. Are there pictures of his creations?"

"Oh, you know there are," Sam grins. "I also brought your computer in case you just can't stand the thrill of the newsletter anymore and need to read something else."

"Like case files?" I ask.

"Or fluff pieces about baby animals," he offers. "You never know."

I level him with a look. "You think I'm going to sit and read about baby animals at a time like this?"

"It's theoretically possible."

"Sam, when someone tries to kill me once, I'm offended. When they try to kill me twice, that's when I get pissed off. I'm not about to let him go for the hat trick."

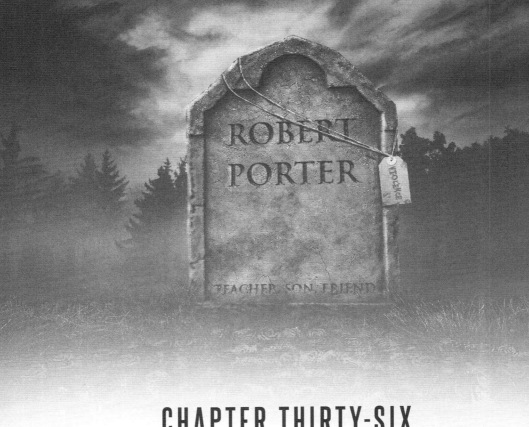

CHAPTER THIRTY-SIX

S AM STAYS WITH ME UNTIL I SHOO HIM AWAY, CONVINCING HIM the people back home need him to be a sheriff right now. All I can do is lie in a hospital bed, and besides, I have doctors and nurses to take care of me, not to mention Dean and the FBI agents Eric sent to keep watch over the door. I'm only going to stay here as long as they absolutely make me, so he just needs to go home and do what he needs to do.

Despite all my big talk, I miss him as soon as he leaves. But I can't stand the thought of him just sitting around in the room with me, taking more time away from the work he loves and the people who depend on him.

I read through the prison newsletters Dean printed out for me, and I'm actually surprised at some of the features. My favorite part, of course, is Xavier's Crochet Club Corner. I don't know how he managed to both establish a crochet club and get his own column in the newsletter so quickly, but I guess I should know by now not to ever underestimate him. He had two goals walking into that prison. And he has more than accomplished one of them.

The Crochet Club Corner is featured in two of the newsletters I was given. Both describe the projects the men are working on and the types of yarn they've received from donations. One mentions the special guests who came recently and took time to sit with the guys and stitch together as they talked. I know from many people, there's something comical about imagining prisoners sitting around making blankets and doilies, but I see past the humor to a deeper benefit.

The activity allows them to feel like they are achieving something. Like they are creating something real and tangible. And they are, even if it is just a scarf or a pair of gloves. But beyond that, it's a chance to sit and talk. The volunteers who come through listen to them and show validation they might not get at other times.

Looking at pictures of some of the projects, I'm almost certain I can pick out the ones Xavier made. I don't know for certain, of course, but there are a couple of the pieces that just have that quality about them that feel like Xavier. Perfectly precise edges. Even stitches of exactly the same size. A hat far too large for a normal person's head because he got distracted and lost track of the increase rounds. A black scarf with one inexplicable hot pink stitch directly in the middle.

There are other completed pieces, too, and evidence of people just learning or giving up partway through. Bits and pieces litter the table behind the display of finished projects. Remnants of long rows. Partially finished circles. Something that looks like a Christmas ornament.

When I'm finished reading the newsletters, Dean comes in with lunch for me.

"I didn't want to stick you with the hospital food," he says. "How's your appetite?"

"Not great," I tell him. I run my fingers along the line coming out of the IV bag overhead and coming down into my arm. "I'm guessing whatever they have in here is cutting that down for me."

"Those would be your pain meds," he says.

"Pain meds?"

"Yep. Did you think you would almost get crushed and exploded by the same car in a span of a few seconds and not have them hook you up to something to take the edge off?" he asks.

"And here I was just thinking I was healing up stunningly well," I mutter.

He laughs and reaches into the brown paper bag he's holding to produce a massive burger.

"Best veggie burger in the city," he announces. "Extra cheese. And onion rings."

"It's a good thing I have you around to make sure I get a well-balanced, healthy diet while I'm in here," I crack.

Usually, it's Dean seeking out the healthiest menu item he can and doing things like bouncing around on a yoga ball while he's working. But every now and then he splurges, and I'm fortunate enough to usually be the one to do it alongside him.

We eat for a few moments with nothing but our happy food sounds around us, then Dean wipes his mouth and looks at me seriously.

"I'm really glad you're okay," he says.

"Thank you. I am, too."

"I know they're still trying to figure out if there was anyone in the car, but do you think..."

I shake my head, not needing him to finish the sentence.

"He wasn't in there," I say. "He's going to this extent to purify himself by removing the obstacles in his life to get some sort of redemption. He's not going to get that by killing himself. If there was anyone in that car, it wasn't him."

He tilts his head slightly to look at me. "Do you know who it might have been?"

I tell him about the strange interaction with Violet outside the parking garage right before the crash.

"When the police came earlier to take my statement, they didn't mention her or any of the group being around or giving them any information. They didn't say there was anyone in the parking garage when they went inside, either. A big part of it was destroyed, but they didn't see anyone else running from it or standing outside."

"Why would she try to crush you with a car?" he asks.

"I don't know," I reply. "But they didn't find a man anywhere, either, so at this point, I was nearly killed by a phantom." I take a final bite of my burger and put the rest of it aside for later. I reach for my computer. "Speaking of nearly killed, I need to look something up."

"That was an odd segue," he comments, settling the computer into my lap.

"Meh," I say, shrugging the one shoulder that isn't completely bandaged. "Is it, though?"

"For you? No. What are you looking up?"

"When I talked to Cassie Graham the other day, she told me about an accident Paisley had at work. Remember her body was found outside the building that used to be where she worked?"

"Right," Dean says.

"Well, as it turns out—as always—there was a lot more to the story. One day at that camera store, she was in a pretty serious accident that sent two of her coworkers to the hospital with broken bones. One broke both legs and his pelvis."

"Ouch," Dean interjects with a whistle.

"Yeah. She was the one who accidentally tipped over the shelf that fell on him. It would have taken many months of medical care and rehabilitation to get better."

"Wow," Dean says. "We definitely didn't get that story from the beginning."

"No. And I don't think there's anything nefarious behind that. I just think that her mother didn't think it mattered. Or it didn't come to mind while she was trying to cope with the loss and trying to figure out what to do next."

"I can understand that," he nods. "But what are you looking up about it?"

"I'm trying to see if I can find the names of the people who were involved in the accident. Cassie didn't remember them, and they might be protected, but there could be an article about it. If there's not, Cassie mentioned there was a pretty contentious battle over who was responsible for the accident. The courts ruled that both Paisley and the business were partially to blame, but that means there was a court case and that would be public record."

It takes me a few minutes of searching, but finally, I find what I was looking for. "Here it is. The other two are identified only as A.B. Browning, female, and C.J. Easton, male. Cassie told me the guy was the one whose pelvis was broken, so that means C.J. Easton."

"Alright," Dean nods. "What does that tell us?"

I reach up and run my fingers down the tube of my IV again. "Someone who breaks that many bones and spends that long in the hospital sure is going to need a lot of pain medication to deal with their recovery. Gluttony. Over-indulgence in food or drink, as well as other addictions."

"See? Now aren't you glad I got you a veggie burger?"

"Just for that, you owe me an entire tub of ice cream when I'm out of here."

CHAPTER THIRTY-SEVEN

W ITHIN TWO HOURS, MY ROOM IS FULL OF PEOPLE AND VOICES and the rustling of papers.

Dean, Eric, and my father sit on a chair and couch off of the side of the bed while Sam looks at the screen of a tablet propped on the bed table. Each of us has files, records, or a device open and we are searching through almost frantically.

"Here it is," Dean says. "Caleb Joshua Easton. He used to live across the street from the Bradleys. He's listed as living with his parents and two siblings."

"There are comments from a 'CJE' on Lori's podcast," Dad adds. "It's not conclusive, but it's something."

"I'm still searching recruitment records," Sam chimes in. "We should be able to run through the military databases to see if there was ever anyone by that name enlisted."

"Perfect," I say. "Get that done. We need to trace this guy to the victims in every way we possibly can, then track him down. The more information we can find on him, the easier it's going to be to find him."

"But how about you?" Eric asks. "This is working for the other victims, but not you. You've never had a case with a Caleb Easton."

"I know," I say. "I'm trying to figure that out. Right now, we have enough from the other victims. Let's just keep going."

The guys stay with me for another couple of hours before they need to disperse with the promise of continuing their research. I'm left with my case files from that time, hoping something will trigger a memory for me. Though the name Caleb Joshua Easton hasn't shown up in the cases, I'm looking for anything that might be a link.

I feel like I've gone over the same files twenty times when something I hadn't even considered before catches my attention. I pick up the notes Dean made for me to check the listing of Caleb Easton living near Jay and Seema Bradley. It confirms what I thought it would and I turn back to my files.

A case has bubbled back up to the surface of my mind, one that I'd managed to shove down and forget about. It wasn't that it was a particularly big or sensational case. I wasn't even at the lead of it. But I remember it being extremely difficult for me. And the hardest part was watching a teenage boy give a statement revealing his father's extensive criminal activities.

He did it because I'd spoken with him about it. Because I'd told him how important it would be for him to make that break from his father so he would have a chance at his own life. He didn't want to. He loved his father, and it hurt him to think of being the reason he would end up in prison.

I'd convinced him he wouldn't be the reason. His father was the one who committed the crimes, so he would be the one responsible for putting himself in prison.

The boy believed me long enough to give the statement, but that was destroyed at the moment of his father's conviction when he shouted out that his son had betrayed him.

I cover my mouth with my hand, shaking slightly as I read through the statement. The words draw out the sound of the boy's voice, and for the first time in years, I remember what he looked like. His parents referred to him as Junior. His father had a different last name. Because he was a minor at the time, his name was redacted out of the records. I'm sure I heard it then, but it didn't stick with me. All I could remember was Junior.

Maybe if he had spoken a year later, I would have recognized him as he wrapped his hands around my throat and tried to strangle me to death.

Before I can reach for my phone or get my computer, the door to my room opens.

"Emma?"

I'm stunned and relieved to see Violet's head pop into the room. She smiles at me; I brush the tears off my cheeks and try to shake the trembling out of my hands while gesturing for her to come in.

"Come on in," I tell her.

"I'm sorry to just show up like this. I heard you were here and I wanted to come by and make sure you were alright."

"I'm glad you did," I say. "I've been really worried about you."

"About me?" she asks. "Why?"

I look at her quizzically.

"The crash. It happened right after you and the others went inside the parking deck. Within just a couple of minutes. Weren't you inside when it happened?"

She shakes her head.

"No. I didn't even know what happened until just a few hours ago. The details of it haven't been on the news. Just that there was a crash back near the parking garage."

"I don't understand. I saw you walk into the garage. You and the others walked around the ramp and into the parking garage. I had long enough to look around and see if there was another way to access that area of the garage, then the car came over the edge and smashed into the ground. I don't understand how you could have had time to get into the garage, find your car, and drive away."

She lets out a slight laugh that is at once reassuring and inappropriate.

"We didn't drive," she says. "Our car wasn't in the parking garage."

"What?" I asked. "But you walked into it."

"We walked through it," she clarifies. "I have never been to that garage before, so I didn't realize that Barton is a one-way street. We got turned around just ended up parking down the block. After we saw you, we went back through and caught our ride. It only took a few seconds and we were already several blocks away before we heard the crash. We had no idea what it was. I'm so sorry to have worried you."

I feel like things are blurring together and I'm having to peel them apart like spiderwebs to make sense of any of it. I remember Violet's church group isn't from here. They're from Parson. Paisley's murder and Robert's grave are there, but all the others were focused here. That means she traveled here to pay her respects to the unknown murder victim.

"When I spoke to you outside of the garage, you said you expected that your group would be handling the burial for the victim. But why would you assume that here in D.C.?" I ask.

"The Brother told us he was going to make arrangements for it since no one had been able to identify the body," she says.

"His brother? How do you know it was his brother if we haven't identified him?"

"Not *his* brother," she corrects me. "The Brother. He's training for the ministry through our leadership program. He's the one who brought us here. He had business further on, so we traveled with him and stopped here. We decided to stay here for a few days and he's headed on his way. He'll pick us up on his way back through."

"Business further on?" I raise an eyebrow. "What do you mean?"

"Part of his ministry. He volunteers at prisons. One in particular is about an hour from here."

"Breyer Correctional Facility," I say.

"Yes," she says, seeming surprised at first, then smiling. "Of course, you would know the name. You're an agent. Well, he has a pull in his heart to help those who have strayed far from the path and want to return."

"This Brother sounds like a swell guy," I note.

"He's just wonderful. He's not a pastor yet, but one day he'll make a fine one. We all look forward to his leadership when he finishes the program."

"Did he ever interact with Paisley?"

"Oh, absolutely. As soon as they met, it was like they'd known each other for years. I can tell you there were plenty of us who thought the two of them would make a lovely couple if Paisley could open her heart again. But she never had the chance."

My stomach is twisting. Heat that has nothing to do with my burns is stinging along my cheeks.

"Violet, can I show you a picture?" I ask.

She nods. "Sure."

She helps me get my files into my lap and I pull out a still from the video footage of Caleb Easton being ushered out of the precinct. I show it to her.

"Does he look familiar?" I ask.

Her mouth falls open in a gasp. "How did you get a picture of Brother Easton when he was so young?"

I feel like I'm going to burst before Violet leaves. I snatch up the prison newsletters and look at the images of the crochet projects again.

"Shit," I mutter. "Shit, shit, shit."

I dial my phone as fast as I can.

"Emma, how are you feeling?"

"Eric, we need to get Xavier out. Now."

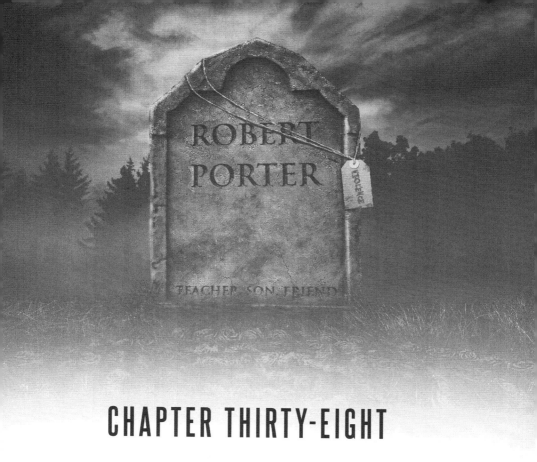

CHAPTER THIRTY-EIGHT

Caleb

CALEB EXPECTED TO FIND HIM IN THE CORNER OF THE RECREATION room where he always was during the ministry volunteer visits. But when he walked in, he didn't see him. A twinge of anxiety twisted in his chest. This wasn't the way it was supposed to be. Xavier was supposed to be sitting right there. In the same chair he always did. The one next to the table holding all the finished projects.

The sight of the yarn sent a shiver down Caleb's spine, but he didn't show it. He was willing to touch it, to wind around his fingers and follow the instructions. If it brought him close. Gained trust. Put him in the right position to make absolution easy.

A new prisoner sat alone at the table. He had the sullen, angry look of someone just coming to the realization that he'd destroyed the life he knew, and the new one he would have to face from now on would be unimaginably difficult.

Caleb could help him. He could sit with this man and talk through everything holding him back. He could give the man a chance to unlock the darkest corners of his soul and empty them out, knowing he could recognize whatever demon came out of him.

This man would be one he would save.

But first, he needed to finish his purification. It should have only been one more. Just Emma Griffin. But now there were two. He would be done soon.

Xavier today. Emma as soon as possible.

He walked up to the table and looked into the man's intense blue eyes.

"Good evening, brother," he said. "I'm wondering if you could help me. I'm looking for a guy who's usually around here at this time. Name is Xavier."

The cold-eyed man nodded. "Chapel."

Tiny droplets of a smile formed on Caleb's lips. Perfect.

"Thank you."

He walked out of the room and made his way quickly to the chapel. He knew he couldn't do it there. He would have to get him away from the sacred space. But it was a perfect moment. Just the two of them before he drew him away.

Caleb nodded greetings at a couple of the guards as they passed his way. He knew at any second, they could stop him. Technically, he wasn't allowed to just be wandering the prison unescorted. He was supposed to stay only in the recreation room or the small annex off to the side if there was a small group meeting. But the guards rarely interfered with him. They liked him. They liked what he did for the prisoners.

He reached the chapel and stepped inside. This room was always just a touch warmer than the rest of the building. He took a moment to breathe in the feeling of it before looking around. The feeling of divinity. Of purpose.

It didn't take long for him to find Xavier. He easily recognized the back of his head where he sat alone at the edge of the center row of seats.

This was risky. Caleb knew it. But as soon as it was done, he would be nearly complete. It would be just one more step until he was fulfilled and whole again.

He walked down the aisle and stopped next to Xavier. The man didn't look up from the stitching he held in his lap.

"Evening, Xavier," Caleb started.

"Hello," Xavier replied.

"What finds you here in the chapel tonight?"

"I just wanted to be here."

"I understand that," Caleb said. "You felt your soul calling you here. Your heart's heavy, isn't it? There's something bothering you and you don't know how to deal with it. I can help you with that. You can tell me what's upsetting you. Anything at all. It'll give you the chance to unburden yourself before the end."

Xavier's hands moved at a steady pace, turning out perfect stitches at an almost hypnotic rhythm.

"There are so many things that bother me," he said.

"I'm sure there are. Tell me about them."

Caleb was torn between wanting to receive anything Xavier needed to say and knowing they needed to get out of the chapel before someone else came in. He needed to get Xavier somewhere else and be finished. But the pull kept him there.

"The sound of someone taking the pop-top off of a can of soda when they haven't lifted it up enough. It scrapes and makes my teeth feel cold. When the fitted sheet pops off the side of the mattress and then the corner is just off completely in the middle of the night and I'm sleeping on the plain mattress. I guess that's two pops. Pop goes the weasel. Both the song and the game. Green Pop Rocks. The sound of a latex balloon popping, especially if it is in the process of being inflated. Popcorn in my teeth."

"Xavier…"

"That song in that play where the girl goes POP-ular, like it's two different words or there is a particular significance to the 'pop' element of it. That's all the pop-related ones I can think of right now."

"Xavier, I'm glad you could share…"

"Carpet in dining rooms. Carpet in bathrooms. Rugs on top of carpets. Muzak. The fact that it's called Muzak. The derogatory attack on elevator music. The fact that elevator operators don't exist anymore. The fact that I cannot be an elevator operator. The fact that if I was an elevator operator, I would have to allow other people to ride my elevator and wouldn't get to choose which floor they went to for them. Tilted picture frames. Broken picture frames. Cluttered picture frames. Stock photos of women laughing while they are eating salad. Salads that are made of iceberg lettuce and nothing else but are not a wedge. Sugar alternatives. Especially the pink one. Digital menus at restaurants."

He continued to ramble on, his hands never stopping, his eyes never moving from the long chain of stitches that fell from the end of his hook. Caleb listened to him, trying to let him get everything out. But soon he couldn't take any more of it.

"Xavier, let's go somewhere else," he said. "Somewhere more comfortable where we can sit and really talk."

"I'm comfortable."

"But it would be better if we could sit across from each other and really talk. Come on, let's go find an office to talk in."

"Can't," Xavier shrugged. "It's against the rules."

"Well," Caleb said, feeling like he'd gotten a hold on him. "You are crocheting out of the recreation room. That's against the rules, too."

"I don't like when rules are broken," Xavier said. "When people do things they aren't supposed to do."

"I know how that feels. It's frustrating to see people around you failing to live up to what they can be. But that's the beauty of absolution. It can be forgiven," Caleb said.

"Have you ever needed to be forgiven?"

The question made Caleb pause. He watched Xavier's fingers start to twist and wind the yarn he had just stitched. The fact that he wasn't looking at him was putting him on edge. He wanted to be able to look into Xavier's eyes and see the person beyond them.

"Of course, I have," Caleb said. "Everyone has."

"Why did you need to be forgiven?" Xavier asked.

"For things that I did. For things that I didn't do. Come with me. We'll talk about it."

His chest was starting to flutter. His eyes moved up to the front of the chapel, to the plain wooden cross on the front of the podium. He looked down at Xavier again.

"Have you ever coveted someone?" Xavier asked. "Longed to have what her husband had with her?"

Caleb swallowed. "Yes."

"Have you ever kept more than was your fair share?"

"Yes."

"Have you ever been addicted to something, needed it even though you knew you shouldn't have it?"

"Yes."

He was speaking through gritted teeth now, the twisting of the yarn in Xavier's fingers feeling like it was the pipes of his throat and the veins drawing blood into his heart.

"But you were forgiven," Xavier said.

"Yes."

"How? Who are you to come here and talk to us like you're better than us? You think you're pure. That the world hasn't touched you. But you're just like us."

"It has," Caleb snapped. "But I stopped it. I was willing to do what needed to be done to excise myself from a life that doomed me and make myself something more. It was taught that if your eye offends you, cut it out and cast it aside so it can't offend again. That's what I did. I cut them out. I cast them aside. I rid myself and the world of what ruined me so I could be whole and they could never hurt anyone again. But I'm not done."

"No, you're not," came a different voice.

Caleb's head snapped up at the sound to see none other than Emma Griffin walking down the aisle toward him, her face a steely mask of determination. He turned to look over his shoulder and saw the blue-eyed prisoner standing in the doorway.

Xavier's hands kept moving.

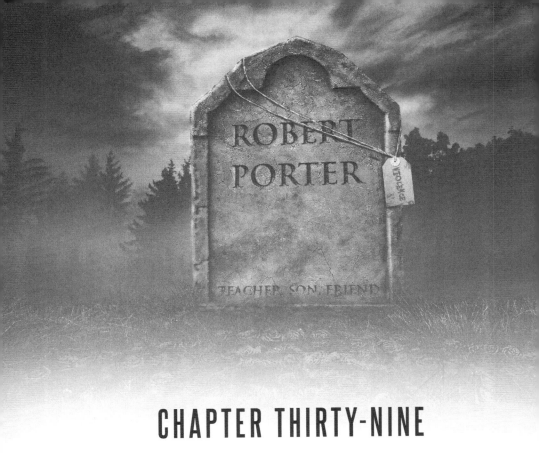

ROBERT
PORTER

TEACHER, SON, FRIEND

CHAPTER THIRTY-NINE

I CAN STILL SEE THE TEENAGE BOY WHO CRIED WHEN HE TALKED about the crimes his father committed and the pain it caused his family. When he told the investigating officer how much he worried about his mother because he didn't want one of his father's criminal associates to come and hurt her.

He's older now. Without the hood and mask concealing his face, I can see the years. Of course, there are even more now than there would have been behind all of that. He looks at me like he doesn't see any of them. I'm the same person.

"You aren't done, are you?" I ask. "Because you haven't gotten me. You killed seven people and celebrated the death of another because you thought spilling their blood would bring you absolution. But it started with me, didn't it? All of this started with me. You betrayed your father when you gave the statement that got him convicted, and you never let that go. So you hunted me. You killed two people before you could build up the courage to come for me. But you couldn't do it."

"I wanted to change my life," Caleb replies. "I felt guilty for what I did and all the damage I'd caused. I wanted to fix it all."

"And you can't because you haven't been able to take me out of your life. You've tried twice. I don't know who was in that car when it went over the edge, but we'll find out. And we'll find out who you burned and shoved fire down their throats. And we'll make sure their names are placed on your head. But for now, here."

I step toward him and stand still, opening my arms out to my sides. Caleb doesn't react.

"Go ahead," I dare him. "Finish what you started. I'm not afraid." He still doesn't move and I reach in my pocket to take out the tag he left beside me on the ground years ago. I hold it out to him. "Here. I brought my own."

He reaches for the tag, and the moment his fingertips touch it, he drops to his knees.

"I can't."

"Tell me what happened."

"When you got away, it woke me up. I realized I needed to focus on other things, to stay above everything. It was a gift to me that I got away, and I didn't want to squander it. So I joined the military. When that was over, I tried to rejoin life. I got a job, but that didn't last."

"Because Paisley Graham fell and injured you," I say. "And you got addicted to your pain medications."

"I couldn't think of anything else and then when I tried to get off them, I started remembering everything that happened to me while I was in the service. I couldn't believe some of the things I'd done. That I let someone lead me into that. My life was collapsing. Then I found my path again. I wanted to change. To be better."

He looks up at me with a mix of fear and contrition in his eyes, but I don't buy it.

"When I realized who Xavier was and that he knew you, it was like I was being spoken to. This was what I was being called to do. I needed to complete the journey. It was making me stronger. I was going to help people."

"No, Caleb. You killed them. That isn't how it works. Now you'll never get the chance again."

A guard comes from around Dean and scoops Caleb off the floor. Fury flashes in his eyes, mixing with the sincerity that had just been there to create something sick and milky in the stare that wouldn't leave me as he backs away.

I don't know if we're ever going to get the full story behind the seven murders. It might not matter. As of now, they don't belong to Caleb anymore.

I walk the rest of the way up to Xavier and look down at his hands.

"What did you do, Xavier?" I ask.

He holds up the tiny noose he crafted. "I gave him just enough yarn to hang himself."

I pull him into a hug. "Perfect."

Dean comes down and the two embrace. When they step back, Dean looks at me.

"How did you know he was going to go after Xavier?"

"The pictures of the crochet projects from the newsletters. Up at the top of the table were a bunch of little things that looked like someone just hadn't finished them. But when I looked at them again, I realized what I thought was the beginning of a Christmas decoration was actually one of the spirals. It had five circles. Wrath."

"Do I have to leave now?" Xavier asks.

I nod. "Yeah. I think your cover is pretty well blown."

"Just as well. I'm pretty sure I know how Jonah got out."

EPILOGUE

"WE FINALLY GOT INTO MARIE'S CLOUD STORAGE," SAM TELLS ME.

"What did you find?"

"It's hard to tell. So much of it was encrypted and a lot has been lost. All we can really find are fragments of information. But what we could find is that she was apparently doing extensive research on a company called Alfa-Corps."

"What is that?" I ask.

"I don't know yet. I need to do some research into it. From what I've heard, it's a pretty big umbrella corporation that covers a lot of different things."

"I wonder what she was researching about them," I say. "That sounds different than the other stuff she'd been doing."

My phone rings and I reach for it expecting it to be Dean. He and Xavier are meeting Sam and me here and we're going on a little getaway to celebrate Xavier's homecoming. But it isn't Dean's number on the screen.

"Hi, Louise," I say, carrying the phone with me into the bedroom so I can finish packing.

"It isn't Louise, Agent Griffin. It's Angelo."

"Oh, hi, Angelo. What can I do for you?" I ask.

"I need to talk to you about the picture you showed us the day you came over to Louise's house. I know that woman. Her name is Miley Stanford."

AUTHOR'S NOTE

Dear Reader,

Thank you for reading *The Girl and 7 Deadly Sins*. I hope this book entertained you and took your mind off of the craziness going on in the world. I appreciate your continued support with the Emma Griffin series!

If you can please continue to leave your reviews for these books, I would appreciate that enormously. Your reviews allow me to get the validation I need to keep going as an indie author. Just a moment of your time is all that is needed.

My promise to you is to always do my best to bring you thrilling adventures. I can't wait for you to read the Emma & Ava books I have in store for you!

Yours,

A.J. Rivers

P.S. If for some reason you didn't like this book or found typos or other errors, please let me know personally. I do my best to read and respond to every email at mailto:aj@riversthrillers.com

ALSO BY
A.J. RIVERS

Emma Griffin FBI Mysteries by AJ Rivers

Season One

Book One—The Girl in Cabin 13*
Book Two—The Girl Who Vanished*
Book Three—The Girl in the Manor*
Book Four—The Girl Next Door*
Book Five—The Girl and the Deadly Express*
Book Six—The Girl and the Hunt*
Book Seven—The Girl and the Deadly End*

Season Two

Book Eight—The Girl in Dangerous Waters*
Book Nine—The Girl and Secret Society*
Book Ten—The Girl and the Field of Bones*
Book Eleven—The Girl and the Black Christmas*
Book Twelve—The Girl and the Cursed Lake*
Book Thirteen—The Girl and The Unlucky 13*
Book Fourteen—The Girl and the Dragon's Island*

Season Three

Book Fifteen—The Girl in the Woods
Book Sixteen —The Girl and the Midnight Murder
Book Seventeen— The Girl and the Silent Night
Book Eighteen — The Girl and the Last Sleepover
Book Nineteen — The Girl and the 7 Deadly Sins

Other Standalone Novels

Gone Woman
* Also available in audio

Made in the USA
Middletown, DE
21 July 2022

69840451R00128